THE SLIP SWING

J. MICHAEL MCGEE

SUGAR
GROVE
PRESS

SUGAR
GROVE
PRESS

Published in the United States by Sugar Grove Press
an imprint of Sugar Grove Media LLC
Pompano Beach, Florida 33062
http://www.sugargrovepress.com
Copyright © 2021 by J. Michael McGee

This is a work of fiction. Names, places, characters and incidents are either the product of the author's imagination or are used fictitiously, and any resemblance to any actual persons, living or dead, businesses, organizations, events or locales is entirely coincidental. All trademarks mentioned in the text are the property of their respective owners.

The Slip Swing / J. Michael McGee
Cover Design by Andrii Dankovych

ISBN 978-1-7347034-5-0
Library of Congress Control Number: 9781734703450

ACKNOWLEDGMENTS

The author wishes to acknowledge his wife, Cindy, for her patience in the reading process, Write By Night for their expertise in editing and Cecilia Ward of Sugar Grove Press for her unique eye in all that goes into story layout. Also, much appreciation goes to Andrii Dankovych for the cover design.

This book is dedicated to Elizabeth Ann. Her mirthful laugh forever lives.

Cometh a stranger in the mist.

PART I

1

He hummed some country song, unaffected by what he'd just done. In the passenger seat next to him, leashed to a seat belt, a young golden retriever whined. Its head drooped toward the floorboard.

He put on his blinker and accelerated around a semi, being careful to keep to the speed limit. He reached back and adjusted the blanket over the body.

She came to, first smelling his aftershave, then hearing the whine from the front seat. She bit the duct tape around her wrists. She played back what had happened. He'd been at the Trail and the grocery store stalking her. And he'd probably set up the whole fender-bender incident. He'd asked to come in the condo to do a follow-up. But that didn't seem right. He didn't seem right. He knocked her out. Now she was here. She bit down again, this time on her emerald ring. Where was he taking her? Why did he take Norris?

Why hadn't she remembered what the self-defense trainer said? "If your gut says something is amiss, then it probably is."

The radio station he was humming a song to interrupted its

program for a news blast that former First Lady Barbara Bush had died. After 15 seconds it segued back to the song, "This Ol Boy Only Wants Some Lovin." He sang along believing he could carry a tune. Whatever it was he wanted, she wasn't going to let him have anything of her. She would die first.

2

I t was April, late afternoon, the sun an orange ball slowly falling.

I parked under the ol' hickory and headed toward the feeder path into the refuge. In the past weeks, since winter had blown out, I'd begun my walking routine again. Doing so was a fitting way to conclude the day and to ward off the urge for a shot of Jameson.

By most standards my gait was a stroll. But a long stroll, and one which took me down to the city center and back, four and three-quarter miles to be exact. The more adventurous jogged the route and its tributaries.

The refuge, commonly called "the Trail" by the locals, got its name from the now-defunct railroad line, the MK, that ran through the city in the 1950s, when the town was sleepy and persons from points east and west hadn't moved in to take advantage of the property values. When the railroad went bust, the track was dormant for twenty years. But then, after the country's track-to-trail reclamation project began, the rail ties were pulled and the thick vegetation, which had canopied the track, was trimmed and a trail system was created, some two hundred-plus miles across the state.

I made a mental note that my journey should take an hour and verified the ETA on my return with my cell phone. I was as mindful about carrying the device as I was purposeful in forgetting it. A news app I had pinged media hysterics about Trump's latest tweet. An orphan cumulus drifted in and checked the sun. Taking my shades off, I hooked them to my jersey and pulled down my walking cap. The temperature dropped. A gust of wind blew some paper cups against a trash bin.

At the Dulcimer Bridge Underpass a solitary jogger ran in place as if she were waiting for someone. She sported black spandex jogging shorts and an ocher-colored tank top. She looked in my direction, then disappeared into the tunnel, auburn ponytail flapping.

Had I seen her before? Possibly. Like most of the women who donned the latest sportswear, she seemed compulsive about a routine: *I'm late! I'm late! For a very important date.*

Inside the tunnel I dodged a mother sparrow nose-diving to keep me away from the nest she'd built in a crack in the concrete roof. Since I had been a regular trail patron, last year and this year, I had seen her build the mud home, and now she was raising two little ones in it. Yesterday she had been sitting proudly in the nest, young birds chirping. Today, strangely, she was back rebuilding her nest. Had robber birds visited? I looked for feathers lying about. Nothing.

Beyond the tunnel the woman had stopped and was looking at her watch. As I exited, she turned slightly toward me with a perplexed look. I kept my focus forward, careful not to be too taken by her.

She looked back almost through me into the tunnel, then nervously to the trail ahead. Two joggers passed, oblivious to us. When I was within earshot she looked up, her eyes not quite meeting mine.

"Excuse me, sir. Uh, I know this sounds stupid, but..." She looked back again at the tunnel, then around to the trail ahead. "Uh, would you mind walking with me for a bit?"

My heart jumped. "Sure," I said without hesitating. I half expected my buddies, Malone or Peterman, to holler from the bushes, "You're dreaming. Pinch yourself, old man."

"Oh, thank you," she said exasperatedly. "I was coming up this way, and...oh." She glanced again at her watch, which looked pricey, while slightly twisting an emerald ring on her finger. "Uh, a half hour ago or so, some men jumped out onto the trail and started following me. I don't know what happened to them, but I really don't want to go back that way without someone with me."

Two more joggers hustled by. "Did you get a look at them?" I asked.

She drew a little closer to me, folding her arms, seemingly to shake off some shivers, but kept her eyes glued to the trail. "Uh, no. But...well. He...they smelled. There was a kind of, uh, smell like dirty clothes. I don't know. Musty. But I really didn't get a look at them."

I was brought back to my past life out West when I worked as an investigator dealing with jailed incorrigibles and their bail requests.

The sorriest cases were the transients who were booked for vagrancy, no home. They stank like wet dogs from the sweat and days without bathing. For those men, county lockup was a blessing.

"Like a wet dog?" I asked.

"Yes. That's how they smelled."

"Well," I said, "there have been some reports of homeless men camping out over by Flat Bed Creek." I had my beliefs and the most pressing was that women shouldn't run, walk, or do much of anything alone, especially jogging the trails in wooded areas.

She nodded. "You say homeless men camp out by Flat Bed?"

"That's what I heard. But I haven't seen any on the trail."

Three men raced by toward the underpass; the one closest almost ran into her. She didn't budge, but scouted the trail from side to side. Her perfume reminded me of petals of some kind.

"It's not too far now," she said. "I guess I should have thought about doing this a little earlier in the day." She looked up at me, waiting for any counsel I might give her.

"Well, it is probably a good thing to walk, jog, or whatever with someone else. If you are a woman," I said, my tone paternal.

Just before Bridge 10, where a tributary trail went one way and a narrow road cut down from the hillside, she stopped. "I think it was somewhere near here. It seems like they came from in there." She moved behind a small pine as if to hide while I investigated.

I edged down the small escarpment to a Norway spruce, which offered a dry haven for whatever wildlife—or human—needed its shelter. A small man could have gotten a few nights of dry sleep under it, if he was creative. The ground was soft and cool, no signs of boxes, food wrappers, or other evidence of human activity.

"Well, if they were in here," I hollered, "I don't see any trace of them now." She didn't answer.

I checked a bit further down the hillside then stepped back up to the trail, slapping off the dirt. "He or they could have been in there," I said, peeking around the pine. "But..." She was gone. Two more cyclists sped by as I took off my cap and scratched my head, just as the sun reappeared.

I looked back for an ocher-colored top and checked the thickly vegetated tributary path, guessing she'd taken off through there with some other joggers. I should have warned her more about the dangers of jogging alone, but then again, women today want to exude independence and self-sufficiency. Implying they are anything less can spark rabid reactions.

The down and back journey went quickly, mostly because I was invigorated. It had done me good to have a woman ask me for help, something that for all too long had been missing in my life.

3

_____

STRANDS

I n my bedroom, I let the ceiling fan blow over me. Nestled next to me, purring, was my housemate of three years, Pig, a feline tabby. I tried to remember any distinctive features of my friend. Thirtyish, pretty, a bit distracted.

The AC kicked on with a clang from the bowels of the apartment basement. I did a google search on my Android for any reports of assaults on the Trail. Nothing.

My building, the Allegro, was a seventy-plus-year-old, five-story, red brick located on the college campus, and mostly housed graduate students. Except for two long-retired schoolteachers, Ms. Spragg and Ms. Cooler, I was the oldest. The owner of the building had recently constructed verandahs on the upper floors that faced campus and had dug out the parking lot in the back of the building and made a small swimming pool to compete with student housing being built in the nearby downtown area. I was waiting for my rent to go up.

I did three sets of curls with my dumbbells and gave my strands a one hundred-time brush over. I flossed. I wasn't done for. Last year I had worn my hair in a ponytail, then shaved my head; now the hair had grown back, but at a slower pace than I'd hoped. I tuned in an

ESPN rugby tournament from Ireland and watched young bucks getting their jollies off and testosterone out.

The end of my fourth year of teaching was nearing. The first three years with the district had been spent at Wolfcreek, an alternative school for problematic boys, located in an abandoned residential facility that once housed a school for the severely developmentally disabled. An evangelical church group owned the property and had been anxious to sell it.

Last year, though, district officials had put a stop to the school and were about to return all the kids to their home schools. They planned to buy the property and to use the primo property for gifted students. An associate of mine, some would say more than that, stepped in at the last minute and bought the building and the property. She and I, and the school's administrator, Doug Donovan, a former priest, had big plans to make a charter school on the property. And give those kids who needed an alternative brand of education just that.

But the district filed an injunction preventing us from doing so and also halted the sale of the property, claiming some first right of refusal to purchase it. So for the time being the buildings were closed and the grounds unattended.

My part in this perceived conspiracy had not endeared me to the district's higher-ups. If some of the schooly types had their way, I wouldn't have gotten a contract for this year, but the kindly retired lawyer and seasoned board member Jimmy McCauley had made a plea for me to be put somewhere.

Now I was teaching social studies at one of the four high schools in the area to kids who weren't too social. Three of my students from last year were placed in classes with me, Every Stout, Terrance Sanders, and Bobby Malloy. While they took other classes with other teachers, I was charged with keeping them in line.

Teaching wasn't a calling for me, just a job. And so far I hadn't been extended a contract for my fifth year, which was no surprise since I was less than my principal's favorite. Summertime, despite it all, would bring a renewal to my thinking.

4

T he week raced by. April was closing out. Each day I took to the Trail at precisely the time I'd met my disappearing stranger. Friday, Peterman called me before my sixth-hour class to see if I could play nine holes before sundown. "Looks like rain," I said. "Let's do it Sunday."

"You're a nimbus," he said, laughing at our inside joke about the dark cloud that follows one around. "Call me later," he said.

Peterman was my mate from the old days. He lived alone in a shoebox apartment that doubled as an artist loft. His vocation was mural painting, along with sketching renderings of local persons, as well as playing poker and handball, and now and then teaching art at the town's women's college. While we didn't have sit-down coffee daily, he was a trusted friend and would be there through the thick and thin of it all.

After the last bell rang, I exited the classroom without tidying up for the weekend, opting for an after-work food trip, usually left for the early a.m. hours on Saturdays.

~

WHEN I PULLED IN THE GROCERY STORE LOT IT WAS FULL OF LATE-MODEL SUV's and new compacts, along with a Mercedes XL 500 parked catty-corner in two spaces. It wasn't the ambiance of the store, named Schvester's, that gave me the shakes; it was all very upscale. But it was the basic process of shopping that gave me great angst and engendered the feeling of biting loneliness, which I'd come to call the "gut crawls" since my years of being a divorced man. I locked up and headed in. Rain.

Inside, the aisle signs gave me directions. Chris Cross played on the PA. *Was he still alive?* After asking a clerk where the Wheat Thins were located and retrieving two boxes, I decided I'd return for more supplies when the store had fewer patrons. I made my way to the express lane. A woman ahead of me with her infant in a front pack was laying out cans, milk, and other groceries on the conveyer. She checked her cell against each item she took out of the cart, seemingly to coordinate some record of her purchases. A middle-aged clerk reminded her the express lane is for those who have ten items or less. "Just remember next time," she said with a forced smile.

I grabbed for a Mr. Goodbar, but quickly reshelved it. I noticed that the date on the cover of the nearby *People* magazine was off a year. *Even publishers make mistakes. Did* People *have to be recalled? What year is it?*

The wheel of a cart in line behind me slightly edged against my ankle. I moved up without looking back, setting my purchases down on the conveyer. The woman with the baby paid and the clerk called out, "You two enjoy the beautiful day."

Was she being sarcastic? When I came in, rain clouds were looming.

Petals. I glanced backward.

A woman with shades and a blue sundress over spandex shorts stood staring ahead mannequin-like. *Was it my disappearing stranger from the Trail? A lot of lookalikes.* I moved forward as the woman ahead of me pushed her cart out.

"How do you want to pay for this, sir?" the clerk asked, interrupting me from myself.

"Uh. Cash," I said.

"Five eighty-three," she said.

I paid and stepped over several yards to another checkout area to buy a Powerball for the Saturday drawing.

"Johnny Football will be a first-round pick for sure," a radio broad-caster said.

"He is already in the NFL; or no, he's been let go!" I said out loud to the clerk, who just smiled vacantly. "He was drafted, uh..." The clerk handed me my lucky numbers with puzzlement. My eyes caught an auburn ponytail flapping, disappearing into the outside hallway. I followed.

Another clerk pushing a train of twenty carts into the store kept me at bay. The woman exited the store. Traffic bottlenecked. I hustled to catch up. My insides churned. The clouds, ominous when I entered, had cleared. The sun was out.

An off-white Ram pickup stopped, cutting me off from my pursuit. The driver eased his truck onward. Friday-night shopping.

An electronic car locator sounded out like an injured goose. As I neared my car, I saw "my girl" standing between a black Focus and the passenger side of my Jeep. Sunglasses were now cast upon her fore-head. She was holding the car lock contraption. No trace of her cart or groceries. *Had her car been there when I parked?* Other patrons walking to and from their cars seemed oblivious to her or the sound. She pushed her shades over her hair, shaking her head at the electronic key gizmo. "Dammit."

"Trouble?" I said.

"This thing," she said coyly, seeming to recognize me. "It won't shut up." She handed me the device.

I calmly pushed the red icon. "New technology." *Odd she didn't know the red icon on the accessory would stop the alarm.*

"Oh, thanks," she said.

I wondered if the car alarm was a decoy to draw me in. "You were on the Trail, what was it, a week or two ago? You asked me to..."

"Oh, yes," she said. She leaned back against her car and stared at me, trance-like.

"Pat," I said.

"Penny."

I offered my hand, but she didn't oblige. A petal fragrance overtook me.

Then she said, "Did you ever find those men?" The question was asked like a plea to not give up.

"Men...no. All of a sudden, you were gone."

She didn't respond with an "I am sorry about that," but pulled her shades down and slid into the car.

"Take care," I said. She backed out without checking for oncoming traffic, or saying goodbye.

A rusted beige Ford van followed her out of the lot. And just like at the Trail, she was gone. The storm clouds returned. Rain soon. I sat in my Jeep for several minutes trying to sort out the dissociative feeling I had just had. I should have snapped a picture of the Ford for reassurance that I wasn't dreaming.

5

Potbellied Behemoth

The week started up with the kids, juniors, having their first case of spring fever. It was the time of year when the girls tested their parents and teased the boys with navel-peekaboo jeans and then some. Dress codes had changed drastically over the decades. If I had a daughter, I was certain I wouldn't let her out of the house with such a butt-naked outfit.

The days skipped by. The year was winding down. Everyone was nervous about contracts for the next year. The dutiful teachers, those with tenure and those teaching the hard sciences, all had gotten theirs. If I got a contract, great. If I didn't...well, no one was depending on me for bacon on the table, so to speak.

Before I could turn around, it was Friday again and I took the long way home: expressway to Bearden Boulevard, to postpone an evening of yakety-yak shows. I'd skip a walk in the woods today.

At Bearden I swung in the Staples lot for a shortcut to my street. A mist from the Old Town Cemetery blew down from the hilltop, interrupting the balmy day. In front of me a rusted-out beige Ford van bumped into a black Focus, seemingly on purpose.

My alarm went off—Penny!

I pulled over and stayed put, within earshot of the two vehicles. There was no movement in the van or the car at first, then a big-bellied behemoth with a keychain dangling from his side dropped out of the van. He walked to the front of his vehicle and with his boot kicked his bumper, checking for any damage. He then turned to the small compact and its driver. A woman got out.

It was her! She had on her spandex jogging shorts below a short blue sundress. *Too much of a coincidence.* She timidly approached the cowboy. When she saw the back bumper of her car was off its hinge, she just said, "Oh, my goodness."

Whether those innocent words were enough to provoke the man or whether he was working on intimidation regardless of what she said, he moved within inches of her and lashed out. "If you wasn't such a ditz-head little girl and hadn't stopped, this wouldn't have happened."

I opened my car door. Quick temperature drop? The mist lifted.

I sprang out. Within seconds, I took the steps over and grabbed the collar of the wannabe cowboy's Wrangler shirt, too wound up to get a good look at him, but with a backward jerk and forward thrust, threw him to the ground with an ease curious to me. He thumped onto the concrete, face down, just as a black-and-white pulled up out of nowhere.

I was standing over the cowboy when I heard, "Freeze!" The cowboy groaned. In my peripheral, an older plainclothes cop and a younger uniformed officer approached. The younger one grabbed my right arm, twisted it behind my back, and quickly walked me to my Jeep. I remember thinking, as my nose cracked against the metal of my hood: *I hope the girl isn't just a Penny lookalike.*

I jerked up. "Stay put, understand?" the young cop said. His fingernail clawed into my neck. He threw me down again in a cuff-'em position. From the area of the fender-bender, I heard the familiar voice say, "He was just helping me, Officer."

My head was cranked toward my windshield, squished onto my hood. I heard the plain-clothed officer converse with the cowboy. I couldn't make out what they were saying. My young cop was now talking to Penny.

Blood dripped out of my right nostril. I used my shirtsleeve. I had momentarily forgotten about how strange it was that I had again been on the scene when this damsel was in distress. I surprised myself how quickly I reacted to the cowboy's move. Did he really do anything, or had I just overreacted? Did he purposely bump into my friend's car? I couldn't honestly say. He hadn't hit her, or even made a threatening move; or maybe he did. I heard names of insurance providers being given, then a door closing and the van driving off. *The van? Was it the same make and color of the van I saw at the grocery store the previous week?*

Finally, the boy cop returned to me. He let me stand. The plain-clothes cop had gotten in the black-and-white, back turned toward me.

Arms folded, Penny looked at her car, then at me. I gave my name and address to the boy cop. Penny came over and handed me a Kleenex from her jogging-pants pocket.

The cops waited until the wrecker arrived. The boy cop offered to give Penny a lift home, to which she replied, pointing to me, "He'll do it." He gave me the once-over and got in the squad car. He and the plainclothes man, his head still turned away from me, conversed and drove off. The police vehicle didn't have the insignia of the city, but was from somewhere else. Not normal; possibly a sheriff vehicle. But I didn't feel like trying to piece together any more strangeness today, and besides, I was happy about this fluke.

"Are you sure you can drive?" Penny asked, getting into the passenger side of my Jeep. I pressed the Kleenex against my nose. I noticed she wasn't carrying a purse or cell phone.

"I'm okay." *Again, the scent of petals.*

We drove off, following her Focus to Clyde's Auto Body, the cop's recommendation. "Your tags expired last year," I said as an icebreaker.

"I am so sorry that this happened," she said, ignoring my observation.

I nursed my nose with the Kleenex in one hand, the other hand on the wheel. I wanted to say something like, "Honestly I haven't been following you, even though it might look like it." But she didn't bring up the coincidence. I detected an ever-so-slight Southern drawl, not a Deep South, molasses-oozing accent, but more specific to certain words that were vowel-heavy like "nice." "You have been so niiice," she said.

While this incident and the two prior episodes with her all seemed a bit dreamy, I asked myself, what else do I have to do? So take the ride.

At the auto body shop, an attendant, who had a pasty color to him, came out of the office. The tow-truck driver unhooked Penny's car, then tooted a goodbye, as if this process was routine for him. The attendant walked over and leered in.

I asked if he was Clyde. He said Clyde was dead. He asked for Penny's keys. She produced the keychain from a pocket of her sundress. He stuffed them in his pocket and swaggered back to the office. I checked the area for any other mysterious characters.

6

NICE PLACE

As Penny directed me to her home in the hoity-toity neighborhood called the Bluffs, I had a lot of questions I could ask; like why it was that all three times I'd been in her vicinity she'd always worn jogging shorts, two of the times covered in a sundress. Where was her purse and cell phone? But I decided to play along with matters as they came my way.

At her condo subdivision, she told me to pull over by a security gate. A camera was fixed atop a pole, which gave a wide-angle view of anything sinister. I punched in the six-digit code she gave me and the gate was raised. I slowed over three speed bumps and then at a Trevi Fountain-like wishing well, she said, "Turn here."

Down three condos on the right, I pulled in front of a white-brick residence with a Mexican-tile roof with two Doric columns on the front porch. Small pines sat on each side of a short brick walkway leading up to the front door. Her unit was separated from the one next door by her garage and the neighbor's garage. *Should I turn off the engine?*

"Nice place," I said.

"Oh," she said, her accent less evident. "It's my aunt's. I'm taking care of it for the sale."

I nodded. She didn't explain and I didn't pursue what she meant by "the sale."

"Will you come in? And let me get some iiice for your nose?"

At the doorway she said, "Oh my goodness, I gave the whole keychain to the mechanic."

My blunder. I had let the mechanic take the whole set, without reminding her to just give the guy the car key. "We can go back and get them. It will just take a couple of minutes," I said.

"No, no. Your nose. I think…" She reached into a planter box sitting on the steps and pulled out an extra key hidden under some bark chips. "There." She quickly turned and looked across the street. A curtain in a window quickly closed.

Had the accident bonded us? I didn't know. While she seemed at ease with me, she had an urgent quality to her. Almost like she needed to take care of undone business, possibly matters pertaining to the sale. Regardless, I felt a momentary surge of strength from the ordeal, bloody nose aside.

She opened the thick walnut door. Inside, an atrium let in the afternoon sunlight. She picked up the mail, which had dropped through the door slot. She quickly sorted. "Junk," she said, discarding most of the paper into a small gold trashcan. She tucked a Nordstrom and an Appleseed's catalog under her arm, placing the name of the van driver's insurance agency in a drawer of an oak French secretary, looking at me as she did. "For safekeeping. My special hiding place."

"Good idea," I said, agreeing, but not understanding why she'd want to hide an insurance agency name from herself.

To the left of the entranceway was a sunken living room, with a circular couch and an ottoman arranged around a fireplace. Standing beyond the ottoman was a baby grand, which looked more for decoration than playing. On the other side of the entryway was a small half bath, then a spacious hallway leading to what I guessed were bedrooms. I followed her toward the kitchen. The place had a sterile quality, but then again, she had said something about a sale.

"Let me get you some iiice. I guess that is the best thing for this kind of injury."

She took a small washcloth out of a drawer beneath a marble

countertop and wrapped it around some ice cubes, then handed it to me. Our fingers didn't touch. I put the ice pack on the bridge of my nose. "Now. That should make it better," she said.

I sat at the breakfast bar, while she checked her answering machine. She studied it as if she were waiting for something. The first two messages had someone on the line, but quickly ended with a dial tone. The third, almost inaudible, like from a roadside stop, said, the best I could detect, "Ms. Theira...something, we will need to stop by sometime to get your statement," then some muffled words and a dial tone.

She turned back toward me, as if looking for my reaction to the calls. I tried not to be the busybody. I didn't know if she was scared, perturbed, or what. Could have been related to the accident.

"Get the message you wanted?" I said.

She didn't answer, but dismissed herself to the front hallway and the bathroom. I put the washcloth down in the sink and as I did, a red trickle dripped from my nose.

I studied the kitchen for markers of anything personal. None. The Nordstrom catalog on the countertop was addressed to a Margaret Johannsen. The date on the catalog was one year old. Not unusual to keep old catalogs around, but if it just came in the mail, then somewhat strange.

There had been a reason that I had spent nearly twenty years working in the criminal justice system before my teaching gig. I always had a nose for a mystery. My primary responsibility had been investigating the accused's requests for bail, but as years went by it morphed into something more. And I became more a special sleuth, as I liked to think of myself, for the judges.

There were times when he or she would come to me and just say in a clandestine way, "I am needing some information about so-and-so. Know how I might find that out?" And I'd oblige with what it was I could uncover without the judge having to wait for that information coming through the proper channels of the county attorney or public defender investigators. I got pretty good at finding information that, although it couldn't be introduced into court, was useful when making any number of rulings from the bench. And such a skill endeared me to the judiciary, at least those that summoned my services.

I pulled out my cell from its pocket holster to sate the urge to photograph my surroundings, but Penny returned, still in her jogging shorts and blue sundress. She had kept herself in shape, calves well developed, but not overly so. But something about her fit into the shorts unnaturally.

I tried my best to start a conversation, but she just came up to me, *petals*, quickly sized up my injury, and said, "I think your bleeding has stopped." She turned and walked toward the door. I rinsed off the washcloth, left it in the sink, and taking the hint, followed. On the way out, I laid my card on the French secretary.

At the door she stopped. "Will you look into this?" I said I would, not really knowing for sure what she meant.

She waited on the steps while I backed out, looking across the street. I took a last look to wave a goodbye, but she was gone.

7

I'M HERE TO SEE A FRIEND

On Saturday mornings KAMO had three hours of Sinatra. By the time I got to Clyde's to pick up Penny's keys, I'd sung along with "Summer Wind" and three other hits from the Chairman's London concert for the queen. I pulled into the lot. The business wasn't open.

The stained garage window prevented me from seeing whether there was any action on the inside. I examined my options. It was after opening hours even for a weekend, but no trace of workmen. The cinderblock wall which cordoned off the backyard from the world invited me over.

I hopped up and sat for a moment searching out across the roofs of a half dozen cars. No sign of a Focus. Hoses were strewn about; several large oil drums were positioned here and there. A rook cawed from the hood of an old Econoline van. Except for the color, it looked like the van from the accident with the potbellied cowboy type. I jumped down to take a closer look. Navy blue had been spray-painted over the van's exterior, albeit badly done. And the paint job was not new. It was hard to tell the vehicle's original color. The van that Penny hit was beige, if my recollection served me. I looked for any trace of black paint left from Penny's car on the front grill of the van, just as sirens blared past the yard, going somewhere. *No trace of paint.* I snapped several photos of the van with my cell's camera, not knowing why, other than to document the creepiness of the place.

Was this when the Doberman was let out? I walked, crept actually, through the yard, realizing I was trespassing. Hell, this technically could be burglary. The rook flew off. The rusted automobiles dated back to the sixties, Impalas, a Dodge Dart, two Corvairs, but no trace of a Focus, or any sign of any new make.

I scooted past the back windows of the garage, through the yard and over the wall to my Jeep, waiting for someone to arrive. No one did. I headed over to Penny's to report the garage was still not open for business and that her car was nowhere to be found.

The streets were mostly empty this time of day, given it was still early and it was Saturday. Something about the mornings gave the day hope. I examined myself in the mirror. I didn't look too bad, considering that I hadn't shaved.

I wanted to impress this young thing, but the notion that it would ever really happen was a fantasy. At the gate to the Bluffs, a retiree in a security uniform palmed me to a halt. He waited for me to say something. No one had been at the gate the preceding day, when Penny had given me the code.

"I am here to see, uh, a friend," I said.

The man stepped back in the gatehouse and came back out with a clipboard. He stood by my car. "Your name," he said.

"Pat Riordan."

"You are here to see?"

"Penny." He waited for more. I looked in the seat for any trace of paper, or a receipt from the body shop. "Uh, I am afraid her last name escapes me." *The name on the magazine?* "Her aunt is Margaret Johannsen," I blurted out.

He stepped back in the gatehouse then came out and went to the rear of my Jeep and copied down my license number. He peered down at me, clipboard in hand. "You want to visit a friend, but you don't know your friend's name. Is that right?"

"Yes, that's right. And it is a Margaret Johannsen who lives here. But I don't know her niece Penny's last name," I said. *What name did the voice ask for from the answering machine?* "It's the niece I am here to see."

I explained that I was just an errand person and that this Penny might need her vehicle, but that the garage where she left it is closed. And that the previous day I took her home and that the security camera should show that I was in fact with her.

"Write a note and I'll give it to this Penny woman should she come a-looking."

"If you'd call her, I am sure she'll say it is all right for me to visit. She gave me the code, last night. I punched it in. The camera should show that," I again said. I tried to remember the number, eight-three-something-something-nine-two or two-nine.

The geezer looked at me blankly, as if trying to assess whether it was he or me who had the story and events confused. "All tapes go to the security office. And there is no Margaret Johannsen here, to my knowledge." He motioned for me to wait with his index finger. He stepped again into to the guard station, then returned. "Dead," he said. "Died last year, according to a note in the resident book. Place been locked up since then."

"Dead. Uh. That explains it," I said. "Her niece is here for that. She is here for the sale. She said that. Just call the number you have."

"Like I said, mister. That place has been locked up. And no one has been there. No phone." Goosebumps ran up my spine.

"But I was here yesterday, with Penny, the niece. And the phone rang!"

"Mister. You are right about there being a security code," he said, pointing to the small box affixed atop a concrete entrance stand. "I'd take off if I was you."

I left my number with the old guy. No one had been on duty the previous day when I was with Penny. Odd. I sat for a moment just like at the grocery store, trying to sort out this puzzle.

8

———————

SPEED BAG

At home I watched Saturday-morning *Tarzan* reruns, figuring out my next move. Three encounters with this Penny, and now her car seemingly evaporated into space, and what else? I escorted the woman home after her accident. It wasn't my fault the garage was closed and the gate guard wouldn't let me in the compound. Why spend a Saturday worrying about it? I stuffed my Everlasts into my sweatshirt pouch and headed to Sensei's dojo for a work out. The world was always clearer after a sweat.

~

I'D MET SENSEI WHEN HE OPENED THE SMALL MARTIAL ARTS DOJO FOUR years earlier. His given name was Tom San and he'd been in the States from Japan for ten years. Since moving to town he'd refurbished an old abandoned warehouse. Now it was known as San's Dojo. We had bonded. He had a sage-like quality. While he'd pushed me to work with him, moving up the ladders of aikido belts, I pooped out on that for the time being for a more primitive workout on the speed bag.

Pounding the bag was a kind of high, listening to it reverberate against the wood it hung from; not to mention the fanciful stares from occasional onlookers who seemed mystified someone could keep up a cadence with the bag for more than just a few seconds. It was one of the macho exercises I had trained myself to do, just simply because it was macho.

I entered the dojo with some patrons already huffing about in the workout rooms, but to no one at the front counter. Each of the two large exercise rooms, separated by the small office and Sensei's living quarters, had free weights, three punching bags, and the newest-edition Nautilus walking machines.

The patrons who frequented the gym could eyeball their progress in the long mirrors, which ran the length of the north wall of both workout rooms. "I not in favor always looking in mirror at self for this and that," Sensei had said. "But customers like to know how this and that look." I went to my customary station, the room with the speed bag. After twenty minutes I felt relaxed and headed up to the front to just sit.

Tom San was now doing his usual hobnobbing with the regulars at the small entrance counter. "You get good sweat going today, Mr. Pat," Tom said, ringing up a customer as I sat in a new leather chair. He threw over a towel.

"Yes. You did a good thing when you put up the speed bag." I draped the towel over me like a sheik.

"You only one I know who use little bag," he said. "Most only interested in kick bag. And even that not too much."

"We see you in two days," he hollered out to a flushed-faced middle-ager.

"What you up to on this fine day?" Tom said, this time tossing over a bottle of water.

I unscrewed the cap and took a swig. "Well, Sensei, I am on the trail of a missing car and a mysterious woman."

He nodded enthusiastically, not fully comprehending, but moved around the counter and sat down in the plastic chair next to me, studying me for clues. "Sound like movie."

"Movie. I guess it does have the making of some B script."

I told him about Penny. He nodded as I replayed how I met her. He asked if this Penny was pretty and that wasn't it about time for me to meet me some nice Japanese girl who wouldn't be such a sphinx. "You say she appear three times same place as you?"

"I know it sounds strange, but coincidences do happen."

"Especially if one party wants them to," Tom said. We sat in shared silence for a minute, until another patron arrived for Tom's attention.

I sat for a moment longer then stood and groaned, even though all I'd done was twenty minutes on the bag. I threw the towel in the large utility barrel, waved a goodbye, and followed two coeds out, both chatting on their cell phones. If this mystery persisted, Tom would be there to listen.

9

I'm No Stalker

It was noon.

I made another run by Penny's condo, pulling up to the entry-way. The same retiree was on duty. He gave me an acerbic glare from his post.

"Get a chance to drop the note by?" I asked.

He searched a clipboard. "I been busy. But I'll get to it." He looked again for a name. "Margaret Johannsen?"

"No," I spewed. "That is the dead woman who owned the condo. But it is this woman's niece who I need to get the message to."

I wasn't sure he understood; dementia, possibly. "I'll tell you what. If you let me take the note to the condo, I'll be right back and you won't have to worry about it."

He pondered my offer, but as quickly said, "I can't let no one in without a special number or unless they is accompanied by a resident. You said when you was by earlier that you punched in the number last night. How come you don't just do that now?"

"Look," I said, pleadingly. "I don't remember the number. I am not some stalker. I am a local teacher. All I want to do is to clear up this thing and tell the lady I couldn't get her car."

The man shook his head and walked back inside the station, mumbling something about rules. I turned around and drove back out to the street and pulled over half a block down from the entry gate under an elm and got out.

"Fuck this shit." I looked back to the entrance area to make sure the old guy hadn't gandered at me, then without a thought scaled the six-foot wall.

Second trespassing today. *Ridiculous to think a block wall would keep anyone out.* But I guessed, just like the gate, more for show.

I waited on the other side for sirens, then walked as if I belonged. Each yard was the product of a professional lawn service. A woman carrying a poop bag followed her rat terrier to the middle of the median. Did she see me land on this side? As I remembered, there was the Trevi-like fountain, water gushing out, which was just up from Penny's condo. I walked past the woman and her pooch.

"Nice day," I said to her. She smiled back. I knew I looked out of place in my sweats, but then again it was Saturday. Most residents were older. But with my gray cropping, at least I might be pegged as belonging.

I looked back, paranoid-like, as the woman turned back toward me momentarily, then to her bag and dog. All these high-dollar condos looked alike. And I didn't remember the address. At the fountain, which provided a scenic amenity and a roundabout for traffic, I remembered Penny had directed me to take a left. Sprinklers were at work already. At the third condo on the right I stopped. Same Doric columns and pine shrubbery, as I remembered. Was it too bold to just knock?

At the door, I listened for music or something inside, then knocked. I stood back from the small peephole, so she could get a good look at me and knocked again, then found the doorbell. No answer. Check the backyard, away from the garage and the adjoining condo. The backyard wall jutted out beyond the front of the home. I hopped up onto the ledge. Did anyone see me? I dropped down. If Penny were in, this fence hopping wouldn't exactly brighten her opinion of me. The backyard was neatly manicured like the front.

Behind me in the street the hum of a high-dollar auto moved down the small roadway. I froze until it passed. A swing on the small back porch was the only item lending a human touch to the surroundings. I tried to peek inside the sliding glass door, but the windows were tinted. I took a last look around, realizing that I might be pushing the envelope with my criminal behavior, scaled back up and over the wall and returned to the front door. *Common sense said ask the neighbor next door.*

The key! Penny had retrieved a spare key from the planter! I dug around. *Nothing.* I took a quick look behind me. Across the street I thought I saw the neighbor's curtain budge. *No mind.* One last ring. I stepped back then walked to the street, and over the fence to the outside.

10

One thing I had become aware of while living alone was that, especially on weekends, to keep from imbibing it was important to keep moving. If exhausted from physical work, at least during the day, the nights were easier to take. I swung by Briar Crest Bagels.

Inside, Shayna, an overly welcoming clerk, asked, "Late lunch, Pat?"

From behind the shelves where the bagel baskets hung, Lynn, the baker, announced that a new batch of cinnamon raisins had arrived. "Fresh bagels, hot from the oven." Two baby boomers hung over the counter and scrutinized the new products.

On Saturday, the breakfast crowd stretched into lunch and late afternoons. With artist ease, Shayna neatly sliced and placed the tuna sandwich in front me, alongside a dill pickle, a bag of chips, and a paper cup. I grabbed one of the chocolate chip cookies wrapped in cellophane, made through her prowess as a bagelmeister, paid, and sat down.

Fox News spieled out a broadcast from the wall-mounted TV. I picked up an edition of the big-city paper published 125 miles away. A below-the-fold front-page headline read, "Missing Persons Cases on Rise in U.S." The AP story related how in recent years state registries of missing persons had risen. And unless someone is located within forty-eight hours of disappearance, the chances of them being found are lessened greatly. I googled the story on my cell for any more information and to learn whether there was any report of local disappearances.

The story gave breakdowns of age, race, and genders. Quotes were given from police about the growing number of human trafficking crimes worldwide, and also mentioned the transient nature of Americana in which families were no longer staying together, thus more missing persons. The short of it all was that no one had answers to any of it. I let the story go and got distracted with the TV world of political chatter.

"We are still in a war. Freedom is messy and costly," a surly-mouthed bureaucrat told a gathering of reporters. "They will attack again," he said. "They hate us for our way of life!"

One of the retirees sitting next to me said something about "towelheads" and how we'd all be better off to just bomb the whole place.

I wanted to interject my thoughts into the discourse, but then again, I didn't need the agitation. I chomped down my sandwich, let the meal settle, reading the small news trailers on the TV, then waved a goodbye to Shayna.

From my cell, I called Malone. His wife, Sheila, answered.

"Just a minute," she said with the curtness of a city clerk.

There was chatter, which sounded like scolding. "Hello," Malone said, sheepishly.

I knew it was futile to even inquire whether he could come out and play. "I take it this is a bad time."

He sounded perturbed, but I guessed that was more due to something on the home front than with me. "Yeah, let me call you back."

I hung up, knowing the call wouldn't come until Monday when we were both at work. Malone was on his second decade of marriage. I guessed I was a threat to the peace and harmony of his wedded bliss.

∽

I'D COME TO CARRYING MY GOLF CLUBS WITH ME FOR THESE JUST-IN-CASE times and drove to the course, E.L. Barkley Municipal. I joined up with a young lad who slammed the ball off the first tee three hundred yards. I poked mine down the middle, 225, and was grateful I did. At the end of nine, I thanked the kid for his patience and letting me look for my balls in the woods.

The clubhouse was full of duffers watching Golf TV, drinking beer, and settling up bets. Several looked familiar from my school days, but I didn't feel like how-you-been talk, and knew they likely didn't either. I paid for a beer, took the cup outside to my Jeep, and sat, contemplating whether another drive-by of Penny's was in order or if I should just call it an early day.

At home Pig scolded me for my absence. We fell asleep to Van Morrison's *Avalon Sunset* CD and me counting the number of strokes I took over par.

11

WHY DO YOU ASK?

T he doorbell rang, then a knock, and the bell again. I checked the clock. It was ten pm. For a fleeting moment I hoped Penny had somehow found her way to my place. I shuffled to the door. Anything was possible. Through the peephole I saw two serious types with ties. One rang the bell again. "Yes," I called out. "Just a minute."

There was silence, then an official-sounding, "Patrick Riordan?"

I zipped up my shorts and opened the door.

"Are you Patrick Riordan?"

The older flipped out an ID, which read Detective Sgt. Donald Cromwell. Had I seen him before? The other did the same, his name Stephens-Christian. "Are you Patrick Riordan?" the older one asked again.

I tried not to act nervous. To my knowledge I hadn't broken any laws, unless...

"I am. What can I do for you?"

The two studied me quickly. The younger one pulled out a pad and wrote down my apartment number. Cromwell asked if they could have a seat inside. I looked down my building hallway to check for any curious observers.

No one was about.

"Be my guest. Humble abode." I threw some laundry off a small couch I had recently acquired and motioned for them to sit, nonchalantly placing my cell phone on the kitchen counter. I leaned against the counter for what was going to be bad news, I guessed.

"You rent or own?" the one with the pad asked.

"Oh. These are all apartments. I rent."

They had accusatory looks. "Do you have an idea why we are here, Mr. Riordan?" the lead cop asked, looking at the pictures I'd recently hung, one of a saguaro, the other of a bridge in County Donegal, Ireland.

"I really don't." I had the inclination to get up, move around, do dishes, or straighten the pictures, just like the suspects on *Law and Order* do when they are being interrogated, but stayed leaning against the counter top.

"None whatsoever?" Cromwell asked, with the beginnings of a scowl. "You sure?"

"No. Uh. I suppose you are here to tell me though." My years as an investigator had inoculated me to a cop's ruffling. I knew if they were here they likely already knew more than I wanted them to know about my life.

"Does the name Margaret Johannsen ring any bells?" the young one said, looking up from his notepad.

"I know the name, but not the person."

"Is that right?" Both waited, checking to see if I flinched.

"Why do you ask?"

The note-taker closed his pad. "Well, Mr. Riordan, last year Margaret Johannsen died. And we have witnesses who confirm you were seen at her condo last evening, entering the condo that has been vacant for some time. We found this on an entry table and a blood-soaked washcloth in the kitchen sink."

I nodded and felt my stomach churn. I looked at my now-crumpled business card. "You she say died last year?" *The codger at the condo gatehouse had told me as much.*

"Last year, March 7th," Cromwell said.

"Were you at this condo yesterday evening?"

"I was. And I was with her niece, Penny, uh...I know her as Penny," I said, about as firm as I could be. "And the washcloth has my blood on it."

Both waited for me to explain. I told them how I came to be in the condo. And that if they were accusing me of some dastardly deed, all they had to do was to ask my new friend Penny.

Both men leaned back on the futon, looked at one another, sizing up what I'd said, then in unison they leaned toward me. "You say you were with this Penny last night?" the young cop asked, scribbling down something.

"That's right," I said. "Did you ask her? I have been trying to reach her all day." I took a seat on the wicker rocker and stared back at the two.

The two waited for me to squirm. "Well, Mr. Riordan," Cromwell said, staring at my card, which just read "Teacher" followed by the name of the district. "You sure you were with the niece of this Margaret Johannsen?" I nodded. "Because this niece was reported missing over one year ago."

I felt a thump from my insides.

Cromwell continued. "We got an ID on her, don't we?" he asked the younger cop, who nodded. "The best we know, she came here last year to take care of the condo when her aunt died. Seems the old lady had a stroke, according to our records. That place you were in has been in probate since last year. Vacant. Aunt dies. Niece disappears. And now you're telling us you were there last night."

I tried to keep calm for what was clearly going to be finger-pointing. "That's right. I was just with her last night."

Cromwell gave a perfunctory nod, the kind I guessed he gave to all suspects whom he didn't believe.

If I had been lying, now was the time to stop talking. Guilty men have sealed their fate by talking too much. The more they talked, the more the lie grew and it was harder to replay the story the next time. The truth was easy to retell, backward and forward.

"And the thing of it is, Mr. Riordan, twice today you were seen in the vicinity of the decedent's house, a gated community," Cromwell added. "What have you to say about that?"

I walked around the counter into the kitchen and pulled out a Mendota from the refrigerator, more to collect myself than because of thirst. I took a swig and returned to the interrogators. Cromwell traded glances between me and my overflowing waste can.

"So why don't you tell the story of how you met this Penny from the beginning. Do we have a picture of this Penny from any missing persons file?" he asked his partner.

His partner fingered his phone to find a photo on some registry. "No, but I am sure we have one somewhere."

"Who reported her missing?" Cromwell asked the younger cop.

"I'll have to check," Stephens-Christian said. "It seems she came up missing due to her not being seen around the condo. When her car wasn't in the driveway, the neighbor lady reported the woman hadn't returned home. The same neighbor who saw you enter the premises last night and again today, Riordan."

Now it was just "Riordan."

"Seems the neighbor had gotten friendly with this Penny because she was helping with the aunt's estate," Stephens-Christian said. "They were going to have a high-end estate sale the weekend before this Penny woman disappeared."

"Oh. I remember. Never found her car though," Cromwell said, shuffling around some. "According to what the neighbor said, it was a late-model compact. But no trace, anywhere. And no property ever recovered, driver's license, nothing. Vanished. Forensics did find blood spattered on the hallway wall and hair in the bathroom. But this was last year. And without the niece around we don't know if they were hers. Didn't pursue any DMV match with the girl. The blood didn't match the aunt's though. What do you know about that?"

"I don't know anything about that! You say last year?"

Cromwell leaned forward. "Where were you last year, Riordan?"

"Teaching here. In the district's at-risk school. Different one than I'm at this year."

"Were you at this condo last year?" his tone accusatory, eyes penetrating.

"No!" I said. "The first time was last night."

Both men continued their deep stares, then Cromwell said, "Go on, Riordan. Continue with how you met this Penny."

I related some of the story, which started with me meeting her after the accident and ended with me being the good Samaritan giving her a ride home after dropping off her car at the garage. I opted to leave out the earlier encounters, certain that would peg me as a stalker.

When I ended my story, each man continued their accusatory glares, clearly thinking I was connected to the whole thing, dead aunt and missing niece. They waited for more. I knew where this would lead. They planned to tie me to the woman, recently missing, neat and tidy-like. I again reminded myself, *Say as little as possible. Let them do the talking.* Most cops I'd been around were talkers. The good ones were listeners. Cromwell was a talker.

12

QUESTION, RIORDAN

"Q uestion, Riordan," the older cop asked. "How did you get the security code to get into this gated community last night? Security camera just shows you and no one else going through. Of course the camera doesn't show all of your old...what is that you drive?"

"It's a Jeep," I told Cromwell. "And look! Like I said, the woman, Penny, was with me last night. I don't know why the camera doesn't show that. But she gave me the code. How else would I get in?"

Cromwell fidgeted and adjusted his white shirt, as if tucking in his girth. "That's what we are trying to figure out..." He straightened a *National Geographic* and *Golf Digest* on my coffee table, sighed, looked at me, head tilted, and said, "Well, Mr. Riordan." (Now "mister.") "The thing of it is, Clyde's Garage, if that's the body shop you are talking about, closed down months ago."

"Over a year ago," the young cop said.

There was silence. The AC kicked on. The older cop continued, "We searched the condo today and found a blood-covered washcloth and your card. What are we supposed to think? You say this Penny had an accident in a parking lot. And you happened to be there to come to her rescue. You claim the police came. No one was cited since there were no injuries and it occurred on a private lot. The real puzzle, Mr. Riordan, is that this Penny has been missing for over a year. And you expect us to believe you were with her last night and witnessed an accident she was in. The agency that answered the call, you say, was not local."

"I don't think the police car was local," I said. Now was the time to call a lawyer. The only one I knew, other than retired lawyer and school board member Jimmy McCauley, was Steinhaus, and the last I heard he was in rehab.

"Didn't you get the name of either of the officers?"

"No," I said, wishing now that I had.

"That aside," Cromwell continued calmly, "I am thinking that you went back to the condo today because you remembered you'd left some evidence, your card and the washcloth last night, or sometime. But you couldn't get in. Now I don't know what went on there last night, or for that matter last year. Hell, you might have been with a woman last night at this condo. For all I know, whoever you were with last night might be connected to this missing niece of the Johannsen woman." He stopped to see if I'd protest or admit to any wrongdoing. "Anything you want to tell us?" He waited. I stared back.

I wanted to counter, saying, "Who commits a crime and leaves their business card behind?" But I kept silent. Cop tactic. Get the suspect on the defensive. Even if the person isn't guilty, rapid-fire accusations can make a person act like they are. But these two were jumping the gun accusing me of a crime.

I repeated my story, until Cromwell realized he wasn't going to get a confession from me. "Okay, Riordan," he said. "We could bring you in for breaking and entering. But we will wait on that. That will be the least of your worries, if this thing turns south on you. Don't leave town."

And with that, both men left.

An eerie feeling jolted me momentarily, remembering the recent news story I'd just read about the number of missing persons being on the rise. I nursed my Mendota, but needed something stronger; a shot of Jameson would do. Today was not the time to play investigator myself, although my instincts told me to.

Why hadn't I told them about the note with the van driver's insurance company information that Penny had hidden in the French secretary? They could verify that an accident had happened yesterday by getting the information from that note. I'd need to retrieve it. The investigator in me wanted to ask whether Penny's credit card transactions or VIN of her car had been checked on, given that Cromwell was claiming Penny had been missing over a year. But that could come later.

I let Pig nestle into me on the futon.

13

_____

ALICE

S unday left me with a kind of emptiness. I wasn't guilty of anything, but somehow felt like things were closing in on me. Cromwell said there had been an indication of an assault in the condo last year, but no follow-up investigation, other than this Penny being put on a missing persons list. He didn't elaborate and I didn't ask for details. Any missing person must be placed on a national missing persons registry. That was state law. It seemed that simple police work would trace cell phone activity, if Penny had a cell phone. Cromwell didn't say whether that had been done. My Penny hadn't mentioned or produced a cell phone. In fact, she hadn't offered much of anything about herself. But there had been a landline in her aunt's condo, which had rung while I was there.

The cops implied I was less than an honest bloke, even though I'd been straight with them, or at least as straight as I needed to be. No wonder poor slobs confessed to anything. What I needed was a picture of Penny. And I needed to talk to the neighbor lady, which might mean another hop over the gated community fence.

But instead of another break-in, I opted for a drive to Aunt Alice's.

~

IT WAS SPRING AND THE COUNTRY WAS RIPE WITH SMELLS. THE TRIP TO Alice's home in Brookdale meandered through the Brunner Pass, which was the most scenic drive in the state. If I ever owned a home again, I promised myself, I'd plant a pine, birch, or spruce tree like those which lined the highway on the way over. There was something about the trees that took me away from what it was that was causing me consternation.

I hadn't called Aunt Alice recently. The times I did, she'd talked of Uncle Fred's passing. He had been gone for two years. "I want you to have his Thunderbird, Patrick. It would make him happy," she'd told me. I'd said I'd oblige, but would have to find a place to park it first.

Alice never got too weepy about Fred. But I knew she was lonely. Her two daughters, my cousins, didn't really keep in touch with her like she wanted them to. Maureen flew for Southwest and had done so since she'd dropped out of college twenty years earlier. Deidre was in nearby Chapwell Falls, teaching school and married to a character who, according to Aunt Alice, was socially beneath her.

The drive was therapeutic. As I got older I knew the missing key to my life was that I didn't have a family of my own. But then again, most days I was just keeping one step ahead of myself. Notions of supporting a family teemed me up with worries. And on a school-teacher's salary no less. But then again, there wasn't anybody in my life right now. Last year I'd had two romances; the first with a twentysomething, now long gone, and the other a thirtysomething, Colleen, also gone, but still in communication with me due to her connection with the property that housed Wolfcreek, the school where I'd taught last year.

~

AT ALICE'S I TURNED OFF THE JEEP AND GOT OUT TO THE OPENING OF the screen door and Alice stepping out, dishrag in hand. She beamed out a smile.

"Patrick," she called out. "I was just thinking about you. I can't believe you are here!"

"I bear no gifts; just an empty stomach."

She scurried down the porch steps and reached up and pecked me on the cheek. Her perfume emanated out. It wasn't old aunt perfume, but more like the scent of some high-priced toilet water. Her home was an old Victorian, without the amenities of the well-to-do.

Almost as quickly as she led me into the kitchen, she began telling me that she been "beside herself." She first laid out what seemed to be ready-made sandwiches and said, "Eat. You are too skinny." I knew she'd get to what it was that was bothering her soon enough. And I was someone to vent to, who she knew cared.

The roast beef sandwich was neatly sliced with a thin layer of honey mustard, my favorite, next to a dill pickle and barbecue chips, with a big glass of milk as a chaser. While I was trying to move my diet toward vegetarianism, beef lathered in any kind of mustard was hard to turn down. As I dug in she sat down with her cup. The grandfather clock, which was a fixture and an heirloom of sorts, chimed twelve counts from the large living room. She let me dig in before venting.

"I am so worried about Deidre, Patrick. I think that man of hers is abusing her." She stared into her coffee mug, waiting for me to interject something.

"What makes you think so?" I asked.

She lightly tugged on a strand of gray hair that had found its way down the nape of her neck.

"It is nothing specific. Although the Lord knows she doesn't really call me anymore. But when I call her, her voice is kind of distant."

I chomped down on the sandwich, then the pickle. Alice quickly cleaned up my crumbs from the flowered tablecloth, then got up to refill my empty milk glass.

From Deidre, she went to talking about Maureen and how with all the terrorist problems she hoped that she'd be all right. She showed me a picture of Maureen standing in front of the Eiffel Tower. "You were once there, weren't you, Patrick?"

After lunch we sat out in the two rockers on the porch. Passersby threw outs waves to Alice on their way home from one of the seven churches located in the town center. I rocked and listened to Alice talk about how the local VA chapter had been great to her since Fred's passing.

I was stressed more than I knew. Little sleep from the night before. No teaching contract yet for the next year, a missing woman, and the police acting like I might have some connection. I dozed off in the rocker. When I awoke, the well-worn WWII Navy blanket Fred had kept since his days as a submariner was draped over me.

It was midafternoon. Alice asked if I had the time to drive over to Chapwell Falls for a look-and-see about Deidre. I said I'd try. I left with more sandwiches and a couple of apples. I'd tell her some other time about my predicament.

14

CHAPWELL FALLS

I could hit Deidre's for an early dinner. She'd always been happy to see me, even though we hadn't communicated recently. The trip to Chapwell Falls was a simple one through a glen, which at one time carried a railway line. The same railroad line that had been torn up and was responsible for the MK trail and the elaborate park system where I had first met Penny.

Penny. I had met her in three different environments and I had to believe that was more than just a coincidence. In an eerie way it seemed she was always trying to tell me something. The Trail, the grocery store, and the accident with the rusted van.

In all the times I'd spent putting together reports for the court out West, some thousands of narratives I'd written about the social history of a criminal defendant, I really hadn't been concerned about the rhyme or reason why cops did what they did, or for that matter why an alleged crime occurred.

And when a judge asked me to look into something, all very clandestine-like, I never wrote anything down, I just gave him a verbal report on what I had found. Now, several years out of the system, I wondered what was being done back there at my old job without my terseness in report writing. I knew that had I stayed in the desert someone would have likely been writing an analysis of my own crime: "Prominent Cardiologist Slain by Ex-Husband of Doctor's Lover."

At the Aaron Burr Fork, I took the single lane toward Chapwell Falls. It was still a mystery why the fork was named after the infamous American. The only thing I could figure was that Burr headed west after his duel with Hamilton and somehow wound up this far out. Might be an interesting research project for my students.

I purposefully left my cell phone at home so I couldn't be accused of not answering calls by anyone wanting to contact me, namely the police. And thus, I didn't have it at Alice's, so I couldn't call ahead to let Deidre know I was coming by to visit, and I didn't have her number anyway. But then again, by dropping in unexpectedly, I'd get an idea about what, if anything, was actually going on and get to take a better look at this guy who Deidre married.

Women: Alice, Deidre, Penny.

It was five p.m. when I rolled into the little town, named by and for the Chapwell family who started the lumber mill on the Little Watchahoo River. In its day the town teemed with people, stores, and log barges. But after the lumber business died, so did most of the town's inhabitants. There were still oaks, hickory, and walnuts shading the two main streets, like in Brookdale, but the place had a loneliness to it.

I slowed at Deidre's street and edged over to the curb at a small, two-story Cape Cod. Nice, but not kept up. It was an unfortunate aspect of dying small towns. I'd explain, if Deidre was in, that I decided to take the long way home from her mom's and thought it was high time to see my cousin, all very happenstance-like.

A young golden retriever greeted me at the driveway, sniffed, and then said *Follow me*. I did, past the red pickup and to the porch steps. Since I hadn't seen Deidre for a while, I didn't know what she drove. I doubted whether it was a Chevy truck though. It was likely the husband's. I rang the bell, which chimed three times. The dog sniffed and waited. Despite the gentle coolness of the evening, which would have called for just the screen door, the whole home seemed uncharacteristically locked up. I rang again. Was it only yesterday that I was doing this at the condo, looking for Penny?

No answer.

I really hadn't traveled out of my way much, but I wanted credit, or something to show for the kind gesture, other than a lick from an affectionate pup.

I made my way around to the back of the house and the fence which cordoned off the yard. I unlatched the gate and gave three raps at the back door. I had no concern that Deidre was in peril, although Alice feared something was amiss. But that was likely just motherly worries. The pup stayed with me, seemingly wanting something. There were no signs of activity inside. The dog followed me across the backyard to the neighboring home, a Tudor, and climbed up the steps with me.

I rapped the doorknocker a couple of times. Many of the old homes in this neighborhood weren't built with garages, or if they had them, they were pint-sized, so nearly everyone parked in the driveway. Two late-model Buicks told me that some seniors probably resided inside. A white-haired head appeared from behind the door curtain.

"Hello," I said, with a smile.

The woman stammered, "Who are you?"

"I'm looking for the couple next door," I shouted. "The couple next door. Deidre and, uh…"

The woman shook her head, scared-like, and uttered, "No," then let the curtain fall back. Frightened and old.

The pup followed me back to my Jeep. I looked for any signs of life up and down the block. Red pickup in the drive, but no one answering at Deidre's. Of course, it was Sunday night. Maybe they'd gone out for dinner.

I scribbled a note to Deidre saying that I had been by, and stuck it in her front door. As I opened the door to my Jeep, the pup tried to hop in. I grabbed for a collar, but found none. I picked him up with a grunt and pointed him in the direction of Deidre's.

"Stay," I said. He did an about-face and again tried to jump in, this time whining. Again, I pulled him out and carried him over to the house steps, at least fifty pounds of him. I hurried back to my car and rolled up the window. He chased after me and jumped up, paws on the side mirror, whining as I backed out. I gave a last look at Deidre's house. The pup barked, with a *Don't leave me* plea, from the driveway.

From the Tudor house I saw the living room curtain move. I drove up the old cobblestone street. In the rearview mirror I could see the pup running after me. At the stop sign, the dog jumped at my window, whining, barking, whining. Strange combination, I thought. He was hardly of the Cujo variety. I got out. He planted his paws on my torso. I examined the street, neighborhood; still no one. Not birds, squirrels, or other canines; nothing. Just me, the dog, and some apparently scared old woman. The dog whimpered, still hugging onto my torso. He hopped in the Jeep and cuddled up next to me.

15

LOOKING FOR A SUSPECT

On the way out of town, the pup found Alice's sandwiches in the sack. For a canine who'd just met this stranger, he seemed amazingly comfortable with me. If he could talk, what would he tell me? Alice hadn't said anything about Deidre having a dog. He was not collared, a responsibility I thought Deidre would have attended to if he were hers.

～

BY THE TIME I PULLED INTO MY COMPLEX THE SUN HAD GONE DOWN. I promised myself I'd check on doggie day care for my new friend bright and early the next day, then I'd check the Humane Society in Chapwell Falls for any lost dogs. But he was the least of my worries.

When I opened my door, a card from the big-bellied cop fell down. It was eight pm. My new roommate met my old mate Pig and nonchalantly found a place on my bed and proceeded to clean his extremities.

I called the number on the card. "Detective Cromwell," the voice said.

Cop works late and on a Sunday. "Yes, Detective, this is Pat Riordan. I found your card."

"Been out of town, Riordan?"

"Just a short visit to see a relative down the road."

"We asked you to stick around town, didn't we?"

"Did you?"

I was beginning to get the idea that Detective Cromwell was looking for a suspect and I was it. He was using the drop-by surprise tactic to rattle me.

"You teaching tomorrow?"

I said that I was. He told me to drop by the station after I got off. I drained a Mendota from the fridge and contemplated what was going on. I checked my phone for messages. Nothing new, except for emails from travel and fitness outfits I'd somehow subscribed to.

16

My new friend slept on the other pillow. He had been conditioned by a kindly soul it seemed and was well fed. Other than being a nervous sort, he was in good shape. At dawn I took him out for a constitutional. The day would be sunny.

When we returned, I obliged my new roommate with two chunks of cheese and some cold roast beef. I googled local vets and got the number of one just down the road.

"Harmen's Animal Hospital. How may we help you?" the young voice asked. I was given the go-ahead to board my guest for the day. And after the morning news and a search for something clean to wear, just so my students wouldn't accuse me of needing a keeper, we said goodbye to Pig and headed out.

~

"DOES HE HAVE A NAME?" THE GIRL AT THE FRONT COUNTER OF THE VET'S office asked.

"Well...let's call him Laddie, for today anyway."

She scanned for an ID chip, but found none. And with that the dog gave me a look of thanks and followed the young assistant to the kennels. I dropped by for a coffee to go at the bagel shop then made my way to school. One thing that my good principal couldn't hold against me was that I was an early bird. He might have problems with my disregard for paperwork, but I was definitely a show-up-on-time guy.

I parked under an oak and grabbed my briefcase with my weekly outlines, which substituted for any formal lesson plans.

"Mr. Riordan, Mr. Riordan!" a cry came across the lot. It was Christina Morales. I waited as she made her way toward me. She stood no more than five feet tall, and today wore one of those hip-hugging below-the-navel jeans. I suspected that she was trying to fit in with the Anglo crowd, given that she was one of only two Hispanics in the senior high.

"Hey, Christina. What are you doing here so early?" I knew the answer. She had been dropped off by her brother and cousin, who were day laborers. She had confided to me they'd just arrived from Mexico. I suspected illegally.

"Oh, my brother and cousin drop me off. They go to labor pool early so they can be first for work."

We walked into the building. A bold sign read, *Please turn off cell phones.* In an hour it would be teeming with high-hormonal teens. Christina had her hair pulled back with a blue barrette, which kept her shoulder-length locks off her back.

"You seem tired, Mr. Riordan," she said almost automatically, clueing in on the circles under my eyes. "Your lady friend keeping you too busy?"

"Nothing like that," I said. "I found a dog over the weekend and had to drop it off at the kennel early this morning. Guess he kept me up."

"Pets are nice," she said. "What will we be doing today in history class?"

"Just studying for the MAP test." The MAP was a state assessment given to most grades and had been used to quantify a school's teaching qualities. Rumor was that it would be done away with. But for now it was required. Good MAP results supposedly meant you were a good educator. Low-scoring schools and teachers were reprimanded. And since the test was given at the end of the year, teachers, fearing bad marks, crammed their students full of facts that would be on the exam. It was all useless. And the kids knew it.

Christina had latched onto me for most of the year. I didn't think it was anything other than a young girl in need of an older male figure.

She followed me to the copy room. As we were going in, Principal Rivy was making his way out. He gave me a formal good morning, looking at Christina with a worrisome eye.

Christina took charge, putting the test booklets in sequence for the respective classes. I dismissed myself from her side and headed for the cafeteria for another coffee.

"I'll get you a donut," I called back. By the time I returned, the papers for all my classes were neatly stacked and Christina sat reading a *Redbook* magazine. I hoped one day she'd find a Prince Charming who could buy her those things the magazine advertised.

17

I had a lot of restless energy. The MAP test was easy to administer, but it made the day go by slowly. Once, earlier in the year, I did a lecture on westward expansion standing on my head, because some of my junior class students were snoozing. It woke them up and established me as a cool guy who doesn't go by the books. Of course, as timing would have it, Rivy walked in on me that day. Since then, I knew he'd love to see me gone.

Christina had left me at the copy room, but showed in my classroom before the first bell rang. She looked bewildered and said she found a note with her name on it saying that she needed special attention for the MAP. She almost broke down.

"Why does this say I need a fa-ci..." She tried to pronounce the word.

"It says 'facilitator.' And that isn't a bad thing. It only means because Spanish is your first language you might need some help with the words. Okay?"

She looked hurt.

"And that special facilitator is me," I said.

She smiled. "Okay. I see you fourth hour." The first-hour bell sounded and she was off. I waited for my tenth graders. Two classes before lunchtime.

~

DURING THE LUNCH HOUR IN MY CLASSROOM, WHILE I WAS MAKING SURE each color code was coordinated with each test taker and getting crankier by the second, Principal Rivy walked in with my two antagonists from the city, Detective Cromwell and his partner, Detective Stephens-Christian. Rivy had a scornful mien and the two cops had we-got-you expressions. Rivy pulled up a chair next to my desk. The cops stood.

"Mr. Riordan, I am guessing you know these gentlemen," he said.

I said I did.

"Detectives Cromwell and Stephens-Christian tell me you are to report to their office this afternoon about a missing woman."

I waited to see if Rivy had more. He was clearly enjoying his role.

"That's right." I looked up at the clock. "This afternoon, not at noon," I answered, about as sarcastically as I could. "What seems to be the problem?"

Rivy looked over at the two cops. Both looked back, waiting for Rivy to puke out what it was he wanted to say. "Why didn't you inform me about this?" he said indignantly. "It is standard policy to inform personnel, as well as your direct building supervisor, if you are part of a criminal investigation. I am sure you know that."

I felt my neck hairs stand up. "The fact of the matter was that I wasn't aware of such protocol. And I didn't know I was part of a criminal investigation," I said, waiting for Cromwell to explain.

The younger detective, Stephens-Christian, looked on, as if he were learning a much-needed interrogation tactic.

"Well, Mr. Riordan, we asked you not to leave town and we don't ask people to do that who aren't persons of interest in a criminal matter," Cromwell retorted.

Rivy almost smiled.

"A person of interest," I said. New cop lingo for "suspect," since Laci Peterson was murdered several years ago in California by her good-looking husband. Or did it go back to the Chandra Levy disappearance, the one-time assistant to some US House member in the late 1990s? The girl's remains were later found.

Cromwell pulled up a chair for himself and another for the young cop. Cromwell let Stephens-Christian go at it. "Mr. Riordan, I realize that you seem comfortable with coming and going, being a single man. And having young girls as students who see you in a good light."

Where did that come from? I wondered. *No doubt from Rivy.*

"But a crime has been committed. And—"

Things were going too far. I had to say something. Insinuations about my character and implying I was in the teaching field because I was a pedophile. What did this cop know about me? "Hold it right there, Detective. What are you suggesting? You might get away with your brand of intimidation with Joe Schmoe off the street. But I have been in on investigations myself and—"

Cromwell quickly slung out a gibe, slightly edging toward me, and said, "We've checked you out, Riordan."

Principal Rivy leaned back in his chair and folded his arms as if to say *I knew you were no good.*

"You lost your job out West because you were a drunk. Even came to work once that way." He looked at Rivy. "And when your wife ran off with some doctor, you drove your van into his garage one Sunday morning, which resulted in you being arrested. The good doctor didn't press charges and neither did the prosecutors, who just happened to be your pals from the courts. But your boss made it mandatory for you to go to AA, which you refused to do. And so you were fired."

I wanted to correct his story, but unfortunately, he got most of it right. Cromwell turned to Rivy and said, "Great role model for our kids. And according to the good people out West, before you lost your job, you also had an inappropriate relationship with a college intern while you were on your drinking spree, which resulted in your department losing its intern program."

I didn't flinch at the story. I had replayed it thousands of times. Cromwell had nailed me to the wall; only thing was that none of it had anything to do with Penny or Margaret Johannsen or whomever these dimwits were claiming I'd kidnapped or done in. None of it.

My door opened for a peek-through from Christina. She stood there, unsure whether to stay or go, just as the bell sounded and a new herd stumbled in still digesting their lunches. The cops got up. "Three thirty, Riordan," Cromwell said.

I nodded. Rivy then told me to report to his office right after school, just loud enough so some of the kids could hear. He left with his new friends.

Christina took her seat near my desk. My two hooligan students, Every Stout and Terrance Sanders, who had been with me the previous year at Wolfcreek and had been placed under my governance, smiled up at me from their seats. "Cops, right, Mr. R.?" Every Stout said.

I reluctantly nodded. "What did you forget to do, pay a parking ticket?" Terrance asked. "They tow your car for that."

"No they don't, dawg," Every bit back. "They just stick another ticket on your windshield."

Christina just looked up at me with her puppy-dog eyes.

Every, whose front-row seat allowed him to sometimes blurt out expletives without being heard by all of his classmates, said, "I seen that old fat cop before, Mr. R."

Terrance scooted his desk closer to his brother-in-arms to listen.

I just said, "Really?" I actually wanted to hear what the boy had to say, even though I realized that it would likely be some tale. What I should have been doing was getting the classroom all on the same page with the MAP.

"Yeah. My Uncle Fran had me go downtown with him to pick up my ol' man. My ol' man had twelve-twelved his parole."

"Twelve-twelved" is prison slang for being discharged from parole.

"He was celebrating at the men's club, and I saw him walk out of the club with that fat cop. And when my ol' man got to the car, he said that cop was crooked. Uncle Fran told my dad he'd better be careful because that cop would press him to do stuff."

"Man, your ol' fat daddy—" Terrance began.

"Okay, gentlemen," I said, letting the last bell signal the start of class. "You two can pass these out."

18

LYING ON MY APPLICATION

At day's end I stacked the MAP tests in the proper files in the guidance office and walked into Rivy's office. Ms. Downey, the secretary and a lifer in the system, gave me a you're-in-trouble look. She quickly buzzed Rivy before I could ask her to. In a mortician's tone, she said, "He will see you now."

Inside Rivy's palatial surroundings, at least palatial by public school standards, he motioned for me to sit in front of him. He rolled his swivel chair up to the desk and breathed out a long sigh, which I knew was a tactic to let me know he had some bad news. My heart thumped.

"Mr. Riordan, we have a very serious problem here."

I guessed the man rehearsed what he was about to say since leaving my classroom at noon. He nervously played with some papers. "It appears there are discrepancies in your job application of several years ago." He perused the papers before him, which I barely remembered filling out. "In your application you neglected to indicate that you had been fired from a job."

I waited. *I hadn't been fired. That was a fact. If he was talking about my job out West, I was given the option to go to counseling, but didn't, and instead chose to leave. Technically, I was given an out. That's how I remembered it.*

"It is all very disturbing to the district, Mr. Riordan, given your position as a teacher." The door opened and a deputy superintendent walked in.

"You know Dr. Hoppings-Smite, don't you, Mr. Riordan?" Rivy said, as if we were old friends. I smiled the best I could. The good doctor had been instrumental in a covert operation a year ago to take over the alternative school, Wolfcreek, where I was teaching. She was also the plaintiff in a lawsuit against my friend Colleen Killingan, who had tried to buy the property the school was housed on with the plan to set up a charter school there.

I surmised Hoppings-Smite was present as a backup for Rivy for liability reasons in case I screamed, or in kid-speak, whacked him. She'd also likely brought over my application from administration for his perusal. Hoppings-Smite hated me, mostly, I guessed, because of my part in the plan the previous year that spoiled hers. She took one of the leather chairs and joined the conversation.

She listened as Rivy threw out what it was that was so disturbing about me. Misleading statements on my application was the first accusation. Not apprising the district office and the building principal about being part of a current criminal investigation, a second wrongdoing. And fraternizing with female students before school hours, which could be construed the wrong way. The last wrongdoing put the cap on the bottle.

"Let me get this straight," I said, spitting back. "You are claiming that I fraternize with female students. And whom would that be with?"

Rivy responded, "Uh...one in particular, Mr. Riordan. A Latinio girl. I see you each morning with this student. She obviously feels very strongly about you."

"Mr. Riordan," Hoppings-Smite interrupted. "This is your fourth year with the district. And image is everything. As a male teacher you have to be very careful. Quite frankly, we shouldn't even have to be having this conversation."

I tried to defend myself. But my words fell upon deaf ears. It was all very brief. I was fired. The criminal case, as they called what Cromwell had begun against me, had nothing to do with their decision, they said. I was to be let go due to lying on my application.

"We will have a substitute take over your classes," Rivy said. "Clear out your materials before you leave today." Both got up, signaling me to do the same.

I walked out, tail between my legs, letting shock set in. Ms. Downey gave me a disapproving glare. Ms. Jones and Ms. Wall, art and English, normally friendly, gave shameful looks as I made my way to my classroom for the last time.

19

DNA

T he First Precinct was downtown and was called the Law Enforcement Center.

I pulled in the visitor space in front of the building and took some deep breaths, still in a daze from what had transpired minutes before. I'd left my cell under my car seat during school hours and now pulled it out, scrolling down my contact list for someone to vent to. But I realized I had no one to talk to, other than Sensei and Peterman, neither of whom were phone talkers.

I was being set up for something that I just happened onto. Cromwell was all too impatient at wanting a suspect. I chomped down on two pieces of Big Red and walked into the station. Every Stout's comment about Cromwell being crooked ran through my mind. I should have asked the kid to elaborate.

~

MY LONG TENURE IN THE COURT SYSTEM OUT WEST HADN'T BEEN SPENT in police stations, but I'd frequented enough of them to know the protocols. Sitting in the lobby was an assortment of destitute types, likely waiting for their turn at being interrogated. And just as seen on TV, a uniform sat behind the glass at a desk. He asked me my business. I told him. He curtly said, "Take a seat."

Cromwell and his understudy appeared shortly thereafter and just as sharply said, "Step inside." The door buzzed open to a large room with desks and partitions flanked by small offices. The two directed me to one of the offices. I took a seat with my back to a one-way window. Both men drank Diet Cokes. Neither offered me one.

This was bullshit. Rivy at school and these two dimwits were cut from the same cloth.

"So, Mr. Riordan, I take it you have concluded your business at school for the day," Cromwell began. He knew damn well I had been fired. I lost it.

"Listen, chief. You fucking know I lost my job! So let's just cut to the chase and ask me what it is you want to ask me!"

Detective Stephens-Christian gave a quick look at Cromwell, which said, *You aren't going to let this civilian get away with that?*

"Mr. Riordan, if you want to get out of here today, I suggest you settle down," Cromwell admonished.

"What do you and your sidekick here think I have done? Let's start with that!"

Detective Stephens-Christian broke in at my description of him. "Listen, teacher, or should I say former teacher!"

Cromwell put up his palm. "Let's all relax."

Stephens-Christian gulped his Coke then almost as quickly left the small room, I guessed to take a peek from behind the glass at my back. Cromwell downed his Diet Coke and asked me if was I thirsty, as if hoping a soda would quell my anger. I didn't respond. From a small fridge, he pulled out two Diet Cokes, another one for him and one for me. "I suppose maybe I've jumped the gun, Mr. Riordan. Can I call you Pat?"

Here it goes, I told myself. Bad cop leaves, good cop befriends suspect. "If you want."

Cromwell popped open his second Coke and began. "The thing of it is, we are still puzzled about this disappearance. You say you took this Penny home. But she has been missing for over a year.

"And, Pat, you said yesterday that you had a bloody nose and that the stains on the towel we found at this condo might be yours."

"That's right. Except it was a washcloth, not a towel."

I popped the tab on my Coke and took a sip. I tried to give Cromwell eye contact, which I knew he was grading me on. Stephens-Christian stepped back in the room holding two paper sacks. He pulled out a cellophane bag from the sack and set it in front of Cromwell.

"This look like the washcloth?" Cromwell asked, holding up the bag.

"Could be," I said.

From the sack Cromwell pulled out another bag, with a large face towel stuffed inside. "Or this?"

"Uh, that is a little bigger than I remember."

"Come on, teacher. This wasn't last year. It was only Friday," Stephens-Christian said.

Cromwell broke in before I could rip into the boy cop. "Pat here knows about DNA testing. Right?" I nodded a yes.

Cromwell got up, went over to cupboard and returned with what appeared like a disinfectant jar and a swab. "Can we get a DNA sample for the record?"

I had nothing to lose that I knew of. "Go ahead," I said. I wasn't up on my rights as DNA sampling was concerned. I knew inmates processed into prison have a DNA swab done. But I wasn't in prison and had not been formally accused of anything. In fact, although I'd been fired and Cromwell had told principal Rivy I was a person of interest in an apparent crime, thus far there were no crimes reported, only a supposed missing woman, niece of a dead condo owner. I opened my mouth. The young cop swabbed.

After the two got what they wanted, and I was again asked to "come clean," I was given the okay to leave. I left with Stephens-Christian hovering over my swab stick like some curious freshman in a zoology lab.

20

I checked the answering machine as soon as I walked through my front door. There was a message awaiting me from Malone and another from a young girl that sounded like Christina. No name was left on her message, only, "I am sorry to hear about what they did to you."

News travels fast.

Laddie pondered the outside on the small balcony of his new home. Pig called for cat chow. I dialed Malone. His wife, Sheila, answered in her characteristically bothered tone. I said, "Hi."

She said, "Just a minute."

Malone was always more open to boy conversation when he wasn't in the company of his guardian. But when he told me that my good friend Cromwell and his sidekick had been by his place of employment asking questions about me, I took a fast seat in my rocker.

In a muffled voice he began his own interrogation, which ended with, "What the fuck is going on, Pat?"

I told him that I didn't know what Cromwell was trying to infer from my contact with Penny or how Cromwell found out I knew him. Malone listened to my story, about the accident and how I met Penny. I could sense his puzzlement. He was either offended that I hadn't told him about this young woman earlier or suspicious of my meetings.

"I'll get back with you later, man," he said, hanging up without letting me say "Later" too.

Laddie scratched at the screen. I had to admit I was glad he was with me, despite the fact that he was somebody else's dog. When I'd picked him up after the ordeal at the police station, the young vet told me he'd make me a good partner. She said so with some pity in her tone, I thought. Pig hopped up on my lap with consolation purrs.

IN THE MORNING, I OPENED MY DOOR TO A ROLLED-UP MORNING EDITION of *The Echo Times*. A below-the-fold headline read *Teacher Questioned in Woman's Disappearance.*

There was my name with my age in the lead, which said I had been dismissed from my teaching post as a result of the investigation of a missing woman and due to other improprieties. A quick-turnaround news story, less than twenty-four hours since I'd been canned. And no one had called me to get my version. Not exactly fair and balanced. The reporter, a Cynthia Crystal, hardly had time to write anything other than what appeared to be a press release from the district or the police department. A press release that was an all-too-quick turn-around, too.

I sank into the wicker rocker. The story was short. Was there a libel suit here? *Suspect.* I read on. It turns out that Penny's name, according to the story, was Theriault. *That was the name I now remembered I heard the caller give on the answering machine when I was with her at her aunt's.* Her aunt, Margaret Johannsen, a resident of the well-to-do Bluffs subdivision, had died the preceding year, and her niece Penny was caring for her, the story said. Shortly after Ms. Johannsen's death, Ms.Theriault came up missing. No photographs of me were included, for which I was thankful.

The story continued, saying local law enforcement had questioned me about my blood being found in Ms. Johannsen's condo. A rage came over me as I read the last two paragraphs. Crystal related that the police were investigating the Theriault disappearance, along with the disappearance of two other women, Tara Simon and Carrie Ann Lindsey, who were last seen jogging the MK trail.

I could hide out, a victim of a scathing news story, or attack. I pulled on my sweats and walked out into the morning.

Laddie took his morning constitutional, while I planned. I needed to drive back to Chapwell Falls. But I also needed to revisit the condo and talk to the neighbor lady who had identified me as the burglar. And I definitely needed to get my hands on the paper with the insurance company's name on in, which Penny had placed in a drawer of the French secretary. That should prove there was an accident and that Penny existed.

The highway had always been there when times were tough.

21

JOBLESS

I t was eight a.m. Tuesday when I drove up Alice's driveway. She was already busily pruning something in the flower garden that bumped against the porch. She set the clippers down, gave a big smile and an even bigger one when Laddie plopped out.

"Oh, Patrick, you have a new addition, I see." Laddie licked her ankles. Alice reached up and gave me a peck on the cheek. "No school today?"

I didn't want to rush into this whole thing and blurt out, "No, Aunt Alice, I am a serial-something suspect and I got fired from my job."

"You are just in time for muffins and coffee."

For the first time in the past several days I got that rare restful feeling, but within minutes I was almost teary-eyed as I told Alice about my predicament, working backward from the morning news story, to Cromwell, to Penny. When I finished, Alice took my hand and stroked it.

"Patrick, how in the world could this police officer think you could be involved in the disappearance of a woman? That is beyond belief. As a little boy you picked up worms off the sidewalk just so they wouldn't get hurt. And you love dogs and cats and you are supposed to have done, what? Kidnapped her?"

I guess Hitler liked dogs, too, I almost interjected.

"Well," I said, "I drove over to tell you about all this. Just in case you hear about it from some busybodies, you can tell them that I already alerted you to the news."

For the next few minutes we sat in silence. Alice wanted to do something. But what does a loved one do for a family member who has been accused of a crime? What does the suspect do? You surround yourself with people who believe in you. Alice was it for me. Malone was taking a quick exit out of our friendship. I knew after he read the *Echo* and his lovely wife, Sheila, got hold of him, our friendship would be terminated. I guess she was just protecting the family interest. There was always Peterman and Sensei. I'd talk to them when I got back. Both men were alone and we each needed one another. Neither were newspaper readers, or shackled to their cell phones, so communication from them about me wasn't expected.

"Do you need some money, Patrick? You know Fred left me with a little nest egg and if you are..." She didn't want to say the word "unemployed." She had lived through the Depression, World War II, and more of the trials of life than most.

Her dad, my grandfather, James Thomas Riordan, was a whale of a man. A housepainter and the kind of guy who thought nothing of helping out the downtrodden. But when he lost his contracting business, he never really got back on his feet. His amiable disposition waned over the years, helped along with alcoholism. I knew Alice worried that the males in the family might resort to the bottle should bad times happen. And she knew I was so inclined. I quickly shifted my thinking gears, so as not to wallow in the mud of a family curse.

"Thanks, Aunt Alice, but I'll be all right," I said, trying to convince myself as much as her.

We sat in silence for a while longer and finally Alice asked what my take was on Deidre and had I been by her place. I'd forgotten to tell the story about how Laddie arrived on the scene; even though that was one of the first questions she'd asked when I arrived.

"That man she is with is no good," Alice said.

∽

AT THE GRANDFATHER CLOCK'S STRIKE OF ELEVEN, LADDIE AND I TOOK some muffins for the road and made our way out to the Jeep, leaving a forlorn-looking Aunt Alice standing on the porch waving as her nephew drove off.

The Watchahoo was low for this time of year and looked like a creek when I drove into Chapwell Falls. I'd told Alice I'd do another check at Deidre's. The spring rains hadn't come. When they did, the river could run up to the rock wall, which diked Main Street from the rest of the village. I parked in front of Barner Drugs, telling Laddie I'd be right back. The front door chimed as I entered. A cherub-faced, white-haired lady gave a half smile from behind the counter.

"How do you do," I said as pleasantly as I could. The woman waited for me to continue. Her counterpart, another elderly sort, bald, with bushy white sideburns, appeared from behind a back curtain.

"I was hoping to visit the animal shelter, if there is one," I said, pointing outside at Laddie sitting up, ready for action.

The man walked up to the front of the store and looked outside. "No such place here. Town don't have enough money to fill in a pothole much less pay for a pound," he said.

I took a Snickers off the counter and asked the man if he'd ever seen Laddie before. The woman rang me up while he took another look outside. "No. But that don't mean much. We got a stray dog problem here, or used to, what with the mill closing and families leaving. Only thing that keeps us going is the Midnighter picking up salvage for down south."

"Midnighter?"

"That's the train. City fathers, if you want to call them that, made some deal with an off-track company that joins up down south somewhere with a bigger main line. Junk and salvage dealers bring in their hauls to the depot here and it gets hauled away. Some kind of waste hauling-train line. It connects with the KC line somewhere," he said.

The woman piped up, "The truth of it is that whether we had a mill or not, no one wanted to stay in town with a train whistle blowing at all hours of the night."

"So we went from a mill town to just a salvage yard stop-off. I ain't never seen a dog like that here, though. Most were old mangy types, stayed around the tracks for scraps. But we ain't got them no longer, somebody done away with them." The man exited though the curtain without an answer when I asked why the train came at midnight. The woman said, "You have a nice day, sir." I didn't want to know the details about the hounds.

Outside, Laddie wagged as I let him lick the Snickers wrapper. I drove through the village past the boarded-up businesses toward Deidre's.

22

SHE HAD TO LEAVE

At Deidre's, I edged my Jeep up behind the same red Chevy pickup that had been parked in the driveway Sunday. The house said "gone for the week," like the last time. I rang the bell, determined to get some answers. After the third ring and some raps, a groggy Kelvin, my cousin-in-law, cracked open the door.

"Yeah," he said, sounding like a blunt guitar string.

"It's Pat, Kelvin, Deidre's cousin."

He opened the door a crack more, enough to see my Jeep, scratched himself without concern, then just said, without looking at me, "Oh, yeah. She ain't here, though." He blushed slightly.

He looked at Laddie like he'd seen the dog somewhere. Laddie gave two low barks from the front seat. I half expected the guy, who I'd really only met once, possibly two times, to invite me in. But he just leaned against the doorjamb, boxer shorts and all. He had a stubble of beard and seemed to be proud of his gut, which he scratched again.

He had a tattoo on his left thumb joint of a skull and another tattoo with the Greek letters ZEX, which ran up his left wrist. I knew that Kelvin had no history of attending college. Furthermore, what my cousin, a schoolteacher, could have possibly seen in this schmo, I didn't have a clue. He quickly tucked his left hand behind his back when I gave the markings a look over. I guessed his age older than Deidre's, somewhere in the mid- to late forties.

He blurted out, "Oh, I guess she's at school, if you is looking for her." But as quickly, he changed his story. "She said she was leaving for good, so I called the school making up an excuse, said she couldn't make it in because she needed to attend to some sick kin. I ain't called today though." His blush returned.

Deidre didn't come from blue-blood stock, or even close to it, but she was educated and attractive in a demure sort of way. The question was, what did she find in this creature that possessed her to say "I do"?

"Leaving for good?" I waited for him to elaborate, but he just stared at me. "Can I use your restroom, Kelvin?"

He let the door swing and said, "Pardon the mess, I ain't much of a housekeeper."

The downstairs toilet was just off the living room next to a pantry. Kelvin's response suggested he'd been keeping house longer than a short while. I searched for any trace of her things in the medicine cabinet. It was unusually empty, but then again it was the downstairs bathroom. I glanced in the mirror. I didn't exactly look the part of an upstanding citizen myself, hair disheveled.

Kelvin had dressed when I finished my business and was standing by the door, inviting me outside. I looked for any sign of Deidre in the living room. There was a picture on the mantel of the two of them with a lake as a backdrop. She was wearing a monogramed blouse. A child-less marriage so far, even though I guessed Deidre likely wanted a family.

I wanted to challenge Kelvin about the legitimacy of his story about my cousin, but I walked outside instead.

Kelvin followed onto the porch. "How long you had the dog?" he called out, peering down.

"Actually..." I started to tell the story of my first visit to his house, over the weekend, but just called back, "Only a couple of days." If Laddie were his, he'd have said something. But what was Laddie doing here in the first place?

Kelvin crossed his arms, as if to say *Make yourself a stranger around here*. Laddie and I waved a quick goodbye. Kelvin didn't reciprocate. Our next stop would be the school. If I remembered correctly, Deidre taught fifth grade at the rural K-8 school. It was Tuesday, so school should be in full swing. I checked my cell for messages, hoping someone, somewhere, would have texted or called asking if I needed help. Nothing. The reality was, I lived a fairly solitary existence, which lent itself only to feelings of helplessness in times of trouble.

～

I DROVE BACK THROUGH TOWN AND STOPPED AT THE ONE SERVICE station, which looked like a 1950 model of an old Sinclair station. I looked for the identifier of the green dinosaur, but didn't see it.

Inside the office two seniors were sitting as if they were waiting for me. Probably just my imagination. One slowly got up. I said a hello and asked for directions to the school. The standing one gestured out the route to me and the other asked if I was the new fifth grade teacher. I played along. "Just here for an interview," I said.

One said there'd never been a man teacher over at the school. I quickly asked, before they had time to think, what happened to the other teacher.

"She had to take a leave or something for a sick relative," the sitting one said. *In a small town, news travels fast. Good and bad. Curious that Kelvin had already let his story out about Deidre to these seemingly innocuous old codgers.*

I left with a kind of numb feeling. Both men watched me suspiciously through the station's window.

23

Poor Dear Had a Miscarriage

T he school was on the other side of town, and I guessed not only serviced Chapwell Falls, but the country-kid population in the northern part of the county. Despite the fate of Chapwell Falls, this part of the world was seen as good cropland. And still had an outlying population surrounding the town to support a school.

I left Laddie and walked into the small building to the smell of lunch. The office was shoebox-sized. The secretary looked up. I introduced myself as Deidre's cousin.

The woman seemed almost apologetic as she related the story about how Deidre's husband had called saying she needed to be off the remainder of the year, which was only weeks away, due to a sick aunt. "We thought it all very strange. The poor thing has always been so dutiful in her work here. He didn't tell us much more."

I tried not to overreact. I almost forgot I had intended to drive to Brookdale and Chapwell Falls to forget my troubles, not to get mixed up in my cousin's mess.

"We have to hire a substitute to finish out the semester. That's if we can find one. Someone is filling in now. Poor thing, Deidre has had so much stress and now this. You are her cousin? Is it your mother who is sick?" the woman asked.

I thought quickly. "No, the other side of the family. I was just in the neighborhood and thought I'd say hi." I put out a feeler about Kelvin. "Don't suppose her husband, Kelvin, knows any more about her whereabouts?"

The woman let a bell discharging classes go through its cycle, then continued, speaking up a decibel, "Well, he never seemed any too attentive to her, what with the miscarriage and all."

"I didn't know."

"Oh, that is why the poor dear has been so, well, not quite herself. She wanted that baby so bad. And well, I guess it just wasn't meant to be."

I nodded and let the woman whale on Kelvin, which amounted to her saying that he was no more than a toad due to the way he reacted to her tragedy. And that no one understands what she saw in him anyway. "All those salvage men who work down there," she said, pointing evidently toward the old rail yard, "are a cut beneath the crawl. That's my opinion anyway."

Something wasn't jelling about Deidre, no more than with Penny. I left the building to a crowded hallway of twelve-year-olds on their way from and to lunch. Laddie barked at my return.

Alice would want to know about my findings. But what could I tell her? I wondered if she knew about the miscarriage. It seemed like Deidre didn't keep the matter too private at school, anyway. Chapwell Falls wasn't the size of town that you just drove around while you contemplated what to do about whatever it was that was bothering you. I called Alice from my cell phone.

She answered with her characteristic sunshine hello and fell silent when I related the part of Kelvin's story about Deidre needing some time away, minus the miscarriage. She asked where I thought Deidre had gone. I lied and told her I heard she was with a friend. "I am sure she doesn't want to worry you, Alice," I said, also reassuring her not to worry, which seemed to calm her. I told her I'd check back. She gave me a "I do hope you will be careful, Patrick." Laddie and I pulled over near the old mill bridge to do some thinking.

24

JEB'S

A car horn brought me out of a catnap, summoning me to figure out whether Kelvin's story was true.

Usually with marital situations, which I was all too familiar with, one party storms out. The other doesn't scurry to make arrangements, covering for work, when they aren't sure if the other half will be returning. But Kelvin had done just that. I decided to take another drive by Deidre's.

❧

KELVIN'S TRUCK WAS GONE WHEN I ARRIVED. I PARKED AND TOOK A gander at the Tudor next door where the old woman lived. I rapped on her door three times.

Just like last week, a gray head poked up to the window and waited.

"Hello," I hollered. "I was here last week." The woman gazed out. "I picked up a golden retriever here. My cousin lives next door. And I am trying—" With the word "cousin," or was it "next door," the curtain closed. I stood fixed for a moment at the door in what seemed to be a scene out of a Stephen King novel. Scared old woman, missing young woman, derelict husband of missing woman, and jobless man who is a suspect in another missing woman case. It was just past noon.

∾

I WASN'T A BIG LUNCH GUY, BUT JEB'S, WHICH I'D PASSED ON THE WAY IN, looked like a place I could get a quick bite. There were a half dozen pickups parked outside and a red one, like Kelvin's, with a Confederate flag decal in the lower-right corner of the cab window. I hadn't inspected Kelvin's truck closely enough at Deidre's to remember if the "Stars and Bars" were part of his insignia.

No-smoking ordinances hadn't caught on in the town yet. I took a seat at the end of the counter, as far away from the cigarette fumes as I could get. The chatter of the patrons quieted as I sat and flipped open a menu. Sitting several stools down was a thick-girthed, thirty-year-old woman wearing a tight black "Achy Breaky Heart Tour" T-shirt. She was shoveling in her lunch, as her offspring sucked on a soda. She gave me a *you're a stranger* look. I studied the menu some more.

I felt a breath behind me. "I thought you was leaving."

It was Kelvin. *Who was following whom?* He took a seat next to me. I hadn't scanned the area when I walked in. But I guessed he was sitting smoking in the corner with his cronies. I put the menu in the metal holder and gave him an inquisitive stare. I scratched my head in a Columbo fashion and said, "I was. But the thing of it is, I got concerned that I really didn't have anything to tell Aunt Alice."

Kelvin fidgeted. Had I told Kelvin that Alice was worried? "What do you need to say anything for?" he asked. "Ain't none of that ol' bat's business."

Another potbellied, scruffy-bearded type plopped down on the stool next to him, listening, but in a discreet way, keeping his head pointed straight ahead. The man had a wet-dog smell. With a quick look, I thought I'd seen him somewhere before. I was getting increasingly tired of the Cromwells and Kelvins of this world who worked their lives from an intimidation angle. My memory harkened to what Penny had said about the men who followed her on the trail: "They stank like wet dogs."

"What do you suggest I tell the ol' bat, Kelvin? That Deidre has been upset because she had a miscarriage and you weren't the most understanding husband about the whole thing? Or should I tell her that she left in the night to take care of a sick relative?"

Kelvin flushed. His buddy began playing with the menu holder. I couldn't see his face without bending around Kelvin. But I did see a ZEX tattoo on his forearm, the same kind Kelvin had. The waitress gave Kelvin some time to think by asking if she could take my order.

"Fries and a Diet Coke."

She poured a cup of coffee for Kelvin's friend. "That should do you, Leon," she said.

"Sounds like you been over at that school and been listening to those hens talk," Kelvin said, head half cocked back.

My blood pressure notched up. "What is it you want, Kelvin?"

He stood and picked up his cup. "I would just be careful, Teacher Man." He and his partner slogged back to a faraway booth.

25

SPANDEX AND A FOCUS

K elvin's words, *I would just be careful,* rang over and over as I passed through town, checking in my rearview mirror that I wasn't being followed.

The few persons shopping were either at the only department store, Reynolds Fine Wares, or at Mom and Pop's where I had made my inquiries about Laddie. Catty-corner at the intersection to the right of me, a small black sedan was stopped at the four-way. *Goosebumps.* Two white-hairs began to jaywalk in front of me. They stopped and waited to see my move. I stuck my hand outside and motioned them across. Each helped the other.

Beyond, the black sedan crossed the intersection. *Ford Focus.* Its windows were rolled up. The driver, a woman, looked in my direction almost as if beckoning me, then drove down the street between two dilapidated brick warehouses.

Laddie shot up from his supine position and barked. I crossed the intersection and pulled over, deciding to stop to get my bearings. A sign in the window of a nearby antique shop read, *"We buy your furniture. Estate sale auctioneers."* The store looked out of place in this neighborhood.

I let my car idle while I analyzed what had just happened. Things were getting eerie. I could succumb to these happenings, and if I did, I might just fold up. Or, I could keep plodding on, using these episodes as guideposts. Really I had no choice.

I continued down the narrow street, past the warehouses and toward two bridges, which led across the Watchahoo. One was a railroad bridge, the other for car traffic. I crossed over. On the other side the road meandered upward into a thicket of pines. Laddie seemed to know this place. No trace of the sedan. The road climbed through the trees, paralleling the rail line. At the top of the hill I saw a boarded-up depot. As I neared, Laddie began barking bullets.

"What is the story here, boy?" I pulled over into some foliage past the sign that read Chapwell Falls High Station. It was two thirty p.m. and quiet. I got out and looked back across the bridge down at the village for signs of a Focus. Church spires poked up in the city center. Once a quaint village.

Laddie shot out toward the depot, sniffing, and then barking like a beagle on the hunt. A loading ramp ran up to the building. Laddie sniffed his way up it and to the bolted door. He scratched at the door then sniffed his way down the other side of the dock and disappeared around the corner.

Up the wooded hillside behind the depot, another bark. If this dock was where salvage was dropped off, as Mom and Pop had said, the station house didn't look open for business. I guessed if trucks got up the hillside road like I'd just done, they'd likely drop off salvage at the loading dock. But I saw no trace of any metal, oil, or, for that matter, any dock lights, which it seemed would be needed for loading at midnight. I followed the barking.

"Laddie! Here boy!" He'd shot down a narrow trail into the woods. The trail got dark quickly. There was a dank smell. In a clearing, a rook cawed then flapped away.

"What is it, boy?"

He whined louder, dug some by the brush pile, and snorted as he pulled out, with his teeth and paws, weathered undergarments. He dug another hole and tugged out jogging spandex, a blue sundress, and sneakers, all of which had been in the ground for some time. *Goosebumps.* I didn't know whether to pick up the clothes or leave them. I could see an image of Cromwell, standing cross-armed, smiling, saying, "So this is where you buried your victim."

Laddie took off to another nearby site, pawing at the shrubbery. I stared at the garments. Although they were weathered from being in the ground for a time, each garment was identifiable. I picked up the dress. A flashback of Penny at the grocery store ran across my radar. *Too much of a coincidence.* On the inside of the dress a tag read Mayland's, a specialty store I knew of. I held onto the dress and stepped over to Laddie's new dig.

"What are you finding here, boy?"

Laddie dropped a frayed white dog collar at my feet. Written in its inseam were the letters NOR.

26

A RUSTED PICKUP

A fallen hickory offered repose. Was there a body nearby? Why else would a dress be buried? *Just make a call and let the authorities know what you found. But how would I explain why I was there to begin with?*

Laddie raced down the trail toward the boarded-up stationhouse, sniffing the ground. He barked, summoning me. I dropped the collar in the ditch where the spandex shorts and other clothes were buried, kicked dirt across the items, and followed Laddie's barks. I took the dress with me.

At the back of the depot, Laddie sniffed at the door. The windows, like the doors, were boarded. I peeked through a crack in one, but only met darkness.

"Hold on, boy." I dropped the dress next to the building, and took a fast walk back to my car, keeping an eye on the road, then returned to Laddie, who was pressing his head against the depot door, clawing.

"Let's see if this will do the job." I tried to pry open a window board with my crowbar. It cooperated with a crack. I yanked off the board, blackened with stain and years of wear. There was no illumination inside.

"Get back, boy." I used the crowbar to shatter the glass, when I saw that the latch above the window was undone. With two heaves upward it opened. I pressed myself up and inside. I really needed a flashlight, but opted to explore anyway.

Except for wooden benches running the length of the room and a TV, the inside was empty. Odd, I thought, that there was a television in a railroad station. The vertical bars at the ticket counter were surprisingly free of cobwebs, as were the corners of the room. Laddie barked. "Hold on, boy," I yelled back through the window. There was the distant sound of a truck muffler. I listened to see if it was going or coming.

It was coming.

I crawled back out, shut the window and jammed the covering board back the best I could, broken glass and all.

"Laddie!" He wouldn't budge from the door, clawing. The truck was somewhere midway up the road heading toward the depot. "Laddie, let's go!"

I started to hightail it around the building edge, stopped, swirled around, crowbar in hand, and picked up the dog like a sack of groceries. A heavy sack! The blue dress dangled from his mouth. The truck was nearing the top of the ridge. *Why was I running?*

I shoved Laddie inside my car, scooted the dog over with a fanny swat, and started it up. I let the car ease deeper into the brush, and shut off the engine. I stuffed the dress under my seat. Behind me, a rusted pickup sputtered to the top of the hillside.

The truck stopped. I slowly opened my door and dropped out to the ground, peeking through the brush back at the figure.

Kelvin!

He stood, examining the building, in a caretaker way, lit up a smoke, and walked up the ramp. He shook out some keys, opened the door, and disappeared inside.

Laddie barked. I hoisted myself in my vehicle and let the car coast through some weeds and around a couple of trees down the hillside to the bridge, where I started it up. Did Kelvin hear Laddie? I drove into town to the small parking lot of St. John's Catholic Church. My heart said step inside. My head said go back to Deidre's school.

27

CLASSROOM

There was no bus parked in the circle drive of Remway
County RR II School. It was three p.m. *Odd*. Just several
hours ago the hallways were bustling with activity. Early
out, possibly. The town seemed to be to running scared from
something.

"Wait here, boy." Laddie jumped from the front seat to the back as I
got out and checked the school's front door. Locked. I peeked into the
window. No one.

I took a look-and-see around the back of the building. It was
spring, and by all logical conclusions kids should be playing somewhere; but no one. I found a door. A broom was propped next to the
jamb, wedging it open. I stepped through. The hallways were quiet. At
first glance, the ambiance was classic grade school.

Drawings in the hallway depicted covered wagons, cowboys,
mountains, and Indians. I walked up a stairway where the upper
grades are typically housed, and to the classroom with "Mrs. Simpson"
written on the door. I reminded myself to somehow do a criminal
check (NCIC) on one Kelvin Simpson...whomever and wherever I
could get someone to do that. I tried the door to Deidre's classroom

and found it unlocked. Somewhere down the hallway I heard whistling.

Inside, the chairs had been stacked on the tabletops. The shades had been drawn. I looked for traces of my cousin.

Her desktop was clean, except for a solitary plastic apple and a calendar with marked-off meetings.

Each Tuesday of the month on the calendar was circled. I sat down behind the desk. This was Tuesday. The clock on a side wall ticked loudly.

A counter ran the length of the back wall. Miniature ferns had been situated in a row on it, apparently ready for a watering. On the wall behind the desk was the blackboard. A substitute's name, Ms. Campbell, was written on it. On the wall, just off the doorway, was a map of the world, along with a poster board with classroom pictures and cutouts of planets, the sun, and stars.

I rummaged through the desk drawer for some hint of foul play. Pencils, magic markers, a grade book; everything very well ordered. In the bottom drawer, under a stack of state teaching guidelines, was a blue journal with a small gold padlock, the kind a teenager would have to keep secrets in. I pushed the lock open. The inscription on the inside binding read "My Journal," with this year emboldened. *Open reading for anyone who bothered.*

I began with Deidre's comments from the first of January. "Today, worse than yesterday. K. was drunk all day again. And he had his friends over for some game watching. I wanted to call Mother, but he wouldn't let me. After his friends were all drunk, K. made me put on a show for all of them. I cried, which only made things worse for me. They all enjoyed seeing me suffer. But no one touched me and eventually K. and the rest all left. He took the car keys so I wouldn't leave. I made a big mistake marrying him. I am sick, too, for putting up with it all. He threatened to kill me if I leave. But he says I am no use to him if I can't give him a son. I want desperately to be out of this marriage. I am so scared."

I scanned the rest of the entries. Each recounted Kelvin's mistreatment of her. More than one entry said, "There is something in this town that is very sinister and Kelvin, I fear, is a part of it."

I got up, taking the journal. I had enough to lay out the guy. A big part of me hoped somehow I'd get the chance to do so. I snapped up the window shades. The playground, jungle gyms, and slides meshed with a small baseball field. On the pavement, inside what used to be called a dodge ball circle, was a drawing, worn with weather.

"Is you the new teacher?" a voice asked behind me. A beanpole man stood, grasping a mop sticking upward out of a bucket.

"No," I said. *No reason to lie.* Deidre's room had been open and so had the building, albeit the back entrance. "I am Mrs. Simpson's cousin and thought I might find her here."

The man wheeled the bucket into the room. "Oh, she's gone. They says she went to hep a sick relative. That you?"

I decided to play it straight with the codger. "It's not me. And I'm not certain who that might have been."

"You minds if I settle up this place," he said, not seeming concerned about what it was that I was doing in the room. "Forgot to spray in here. These kids stink up a place like you can't believe."

He pushed the bucket further inside and began whistling. "Excuse me," I said. "I noticed Ms. Simpson's calendar has Tuesdays circled. Would you know why that is?"

"That's because of the trains." *Just as Mom and Pop had said.* "But Ms. S. is gone because she has sick kin."

A bell rang.

He continued, not looking up from his mopping. "That's because of da train coming through and Sheriff say it best for everyone to be inside, what with the cargo and all. But the train not coming till tonight so I don't why he says school needs to be closed down now. He the boss of town, dough. But Ms. S. gone because of sick kin," the old man said again.

I took a last look around, then left with Deidre's journal, the old man fixed on his whistling. I walked down the hallway and to the dodge ball circle outside. This rendering on the concrete seemed to have a message about it. It appeared to be of a train with people standing by.

I looked up toward Deidre's window. The old man looked out at me. Laddie belted out barks from the other side of the building.

28

I Was Wondering If the Names
Are Familiar to You?

Deidre's journal confirmed that something was amiss in
Chapwell Falls, and likely with Deidre as well. What was it
with this town? And where was my cousin? No reason to
head back to Brookdale and Alice's yet, although I was sure she'd be
calling me soon enough.

Laddie let the breeze whip through his mane as I drove back
through town. At the same intersection where I'd seen and then lost
the black Focus earlier in the day, I turned toward the store where the
sign read "Estate Sale Auctioneers."

Penny said she was getting her aunt's condo ready for an estate
sale. And Cromwell and his sidekick had claimed as much in their
investigation. *Coincidence: a black Focus had led me to this place?* I cracked
the window for Laddie and entered the store.

Wall-to-wall collections of roll-top desks, chairs, couches, and
every imaginable vintage antique converged into the three small
browsing aisles, each running the length of the basketball court-sized
sales area. In the back, beyond the furniture, standing behind a
counter, a woman, fiftyish, wrote out something. She turned down the

radio giving a weather report as I walked toward her. She smiled. *The first friendly greeting I'd gotten in this town gone eerie.*

"May I help you?"

I hadn't thought about what I was really there for, other than to try to piece together some parts of the puzzle. "Yes. Possibly. I am a family friend of Margaret Johannsen, who died last year."

I waited to see if Penny's aunt's name rang any bells for the woman. *Apparently not.* I asked about Penny, also known as Margaret Theriault.

The woman nodded slightly, as if she either recognized Penny's given name or that the story just sounded familiar.

"Were they trying to sell their furniture?"

"Ms. Johannsen's niece was. Also a Margaret, but her last name is Theriault."

The woman raised her finger in a just-a-second gesture, left the counter, and stepped behind a large partition, which I guessed doubled as an office. Within seconds she returned with a large day log. "Now when would this have been? We do business with so many people in the area."

This is where it gets complicated, I thought. In my world it was several days ago. But according to my friend Cromwell it would have been last year. "It would have been last year, I believe, say April."

The woman flipped back pages, moved her eyeglasses some for focusing. "Yes. Last year, I have a notation of a scheduled auction of property for the estate of Margaret Johannsen, April ninth. But nothing noted as a follow-up. Seems I made this entry earlier than the April date. Contact person, Penny at 573-555-9387. You say you are a family member?"

"A family friend."

"Now I remember this young lady. Yes. She was a sweet girl. Came from down south somewhere I believe. She had taken a drive to see the countryside and had heard we handle estate sales. Just luckily found our place. She said her aunt's neighbor told her about us. She had a dog named, uh, Norris. Brought the dog in with her. Thought that strange. But she said he barked too much when she left him in the car. I remember the dog's name because that was the name of my father. I thought, odd, naming a dog after a person. My dad would have thought that funny, though."

I got a chill. Aspects of this puzzle were falling in place all too quickly. The dog tag at the makeshift burial read "NOR." I had finally hit on something, in addition to Deidre's journal, although the dates of the visit to this place only confirmed Cromwell's comment about the whens and wheres of it all.

Nothing to do with my reality.

"So what happened to your family friend? Looks like this young woman never got back with us.

Should I spill the beans or make up something? "Well, she had to leave town and I am following up. You have no record of any furniture being sold from the Johannsen estate?"

"No," the woman said, again looking at her logbook. "But it sounded, if I remember correctly, like the young woman had some nice pieces. So do you want to arrange a time for us to come down and look at the property?"

I gave a quick look around at the store. "Uh, let me take one of your cards and get back with you." The woman handed me her card, which said she was the proprietor, Eloise Hartwell.

"Oh, wait a minute!" she said holding up her hand. "Let me get the man who might have helped her with making arrangements for the furniture transport. Leon, are you back there?" she called. "Leon James. Leon James..."

From behind the partition a workman poked his head out. *Was it Kelvin's friend from the diner? I'm not sure I'd be able to identify him. In this part of the country there are a lot of Billy Bob lookalikes.* He quickly pulled his head back, disappearing behind the partition.

She shook her head at the man's abruptness. "Hard to find good help around here. If I think of anything I will call you. Do you have a card?"

"No, not on me. But I appreciate your time. One last thing. I'm clearing up some past bills for this friend. Again, what was the phone number Ms. Theriault gave you?"

Ms. Hartwell rattled off the number again.

29

Some Type of Weapon

A t Aaron Burr Fork, I made the turn south toward home. The sun was going down. I'd written out Penny's phone number and was about to call it, but felt the presence of a vehicle behind me. A truck. Kelvin, I thought. I tried to get its make. The driver was several car lengths back. Laddie detected my angst and whined. "It will be all right, boy," I said, giving him an ear scratch.

The road winded up ahead, then plummeted downward. As I tried to keep my speed constant, the truck slowly gained on me. At the next hill it caught up. I was expecting he'd try to run me off the road, but the truck just passed. Its windows were rolled up and were charcoal-tinted to keep out the sunlight. This truck was blue. Over the next hilltop, I pulled onto Country Road 225 and stopped. Laddie perked up. I let the Jeep edge some down a gravel road. I'd felt like I'd been on automatic pilot these past few days, especially in Chapwell Falls. It was a curious feeling, one I'd never experienced before or could easily explain; only that it was a pulling-forward sensation.

"Let's take a pee, boy."

I leashed him and got out. The car idled. There was a smell of the country in the air. Marijuana used to grow prolifically in the area at one time. In the distance I heard another vehicle idling.

Laddie and I did our business. We got back in. This was a time I wished I had a weapon of some sort. Learning to shoot was one of the things on my to-do list. But like most of those things, some useful, others of the Walter Mitty variety, I told myself I'd get around to them someday.

I turned around, still listening for any sounds of approaching cars, lights off. It was dusk. The gravel crackled as I turned into a makeshift driveway. Ten yards in front of me there was a gate latched with wire. Laddie sat up and sniffed. I heard a vehicle, its engine being gunned, as if it was trying to make it up the hill I had just come down. I eased my Jeep down to the main road and toward home.

30

Death Penalty

I t had been a long day and as I pulled into my place all I could think of was downing a few Beck's. Laddie hopped out to a nearby shrub as I unloaded myself and my thoughts. I hadn't called Penny's number, mostly out of fear that no one would answer. And that if someone did, that would only add more complexity to the puzzle. If Cromwell did have a trace on the number, my calling it would certainly implicate me more in this mystery.

"Hey, Mr. Riordan," a familiar voice called out. "Need me to take your new dog for a poop walk?"

I smiled. "Sure, Byron," I said.

I handed over the leash. I had Byron as a student at my previous school, Wolfcreek. He was now in middle school. He was one of four students whom I'd kept in contact with from my former school.

Byron's mom had died of an apparent drug overdose and over the past several years he had been relegated to group homes and foster care. His new foster mom lived two flights up from me and, in addition to Ms. Spragg, Ms. Cooler, and myself, was one of the older residents of the building.

She got money from the state for taking in the kid and as far as I could tell was doing an adequate job. She was fortyish and had a slight limp. I helped her carry up her groceries from time to time, usually at the urging of Byron, who'd knock on my door yelling that his mother needed help. It was a ploy by the boy to get me to play checkers with him, a game in which we had immersed ourselves when he had been a student of mine.

"We know you didn't take that woman, Mr. R.," Byron had offered up the day the news story came out. "I think she was taken by werewolves," he'd said, half believing such things existed. The comeback "It must have been taken by werewolves" was an inside joke of ours from our days together at Wolfcreek when something came up missing. I watched Byron let Laddie lead him down the block for a walk around the nearby campus.

I opened my door to the humming of my small clothes dryer and the sight of Issac Peterman standing in his undershorts folding clothes into a plastic basket. "Thanks for knocking," I said.

"Paddy, I tried to call you. Didn't think you'd mind. That crab-invested laundromat I go to is shut down for remodeling. You're the only one I know who has his own washer/dryer."

"How did you get in?"

He held up a small leather case and took out a metal screwdriver-like gadget.

"You picking locks for a living as a side job to painting murals?"

"It pays to be skilled in more than one area of expertise," he said with a sarcastic chuckle.

I deposited Deidre's journal in a kitchen drawer, remembering that the blue dress was under the seat in the Jeep.

"I'll take one of those brewskies in the fridge."

I grabbed two and let Peterman continue with his folding while I began to sort through the mail, which I hadn't opened for days.

"Paddy, what the fuck is going on with this missing woman shit? I read the newspaper story. I saw Mary McGibbons and Teresa Hogan downtown and they asked me about you. This place is too small to keep too many snatches," he said, again letting out a sarcastic chuckle.

"Just fold your laundry, fuck stick."

"Seriously, though. What the fuck is going on?"

I kicked off my shoes, sat down, mail strewn on the floor next to the rocking chair, and was about to lay out the past week's events for my oldest friend when there were two hard knocks at my door.

I looked through my peephole and saw Cromwell and his sidekick. "Cops," I said.

Peterman stepped into my bedroom. I breathed deeply and slowly opened the door.

The two men stood there, just staring at me accusingly. "You're not much of a stay-at-home guy are you, Riordan?" Cromwell said, about as antagonistically as he could, waiting for an invitation to step in. Detective Stephens-Christian moved forward enough so I could smell the onions he'd had with lunch. In his hand was a poster of some type.

"Can we come in, Riordan?"

I felt a confrontation coming.

The landline answering machine clicked on as the two entered. *Timing.*

Both men perked up to the voice. I immediately knew the caller. In broken English, the caller said she missed me and that I was the best teacher she'd ever had. Great! That's all I needed right now. I took a Mendota out of the fridge, leaving my Beck's on the floor next to the rocking chair.

I stood by the door hoping to urge the interlopers on their way. But both plopped down on the sofa. I took a seat in the wicker rocker.

Cromwell asked, eyes penetrating, "Who's that on the phone?"

I felt my dander rise. *This fucking prick.* I stared back, then glanced over at Stephens-Christian, who was examining an eight-by-eleven poster he had brought in.

"Sounds like Christina Morales, a student of mine," I said.

"You mean ex-student, don't you, Riordan," Stephens-Christian said without looking up.

Cromwell took the poster from his sidekick, stood up and handed it to me. It showed face shots of two pretty brunettes. The caption read "Missing, Tara Simon, 22, and Carrie Ann Lindsey, 22," with standard information about their last known whereabouts, the MK trail, along with a description of the clothes they were wearing.

"These women look familiar to you, Riordan?" Cromwell said, still standing over me.

I looked at the pictures and handed the poster back. "No. Should they?"

"You no doubt read the story about yourself in the paper."

I leaned forward some and got brave. "Sounds to me like you guys have your suspect and have everything neatly wrapped up for the fine citizens of this town."

"Smartass, are you, Riordan? Well, right now, we've certainly got one person of interest." He looked for his partner to join in, but Stephens-Christian kept his head down. "Margaret Theriault is missing and you were at her condo or her dead aunt's condo. These other girls are also missing." He flicked the posters of the girls with his finger. "And given your proclivity for getting into trouble with women, or at least that was your reputation with your former job out West, it stands to reason that you might be connected." Some seconds went by with a standoff of no one saying anything.

Stephens-Christian looked up. "Got a dog, Riordan?"

"Why?" *Lie.*

"Well, this Penny, we heard, had a dog. A golden, I believe. Just a puppy," Cromwell said. "At least that's what the condo people at her aunt's told us. Of course, that was last year. So we figure we find the dog, now bigger, and maybe we find her. Unless of course both this girl and the dog were snuffed together."

The phone rang again. I let the answering machine take it. It was Alice. I kept expecting Byron to knock on the door with Laddie. If that happened I might as well just put out my hands for cuffing.

Peterman stepped out of the bedroom dressed in jeans and a blue work shirt. Both cops looked at him and he at them. Glares shot back and forth. Peterman gulped his Beck's.

Cromwell said, "Didn't know you had a roommate, Riordan. We keep learning more and more about you. Thought you liked young girls, but..."

Peterman took the bait, just like Cromwell wanted him to do. "What are you implying, Mr. Policeman?" Peterman said, stepping into the living room.

Cromwell jerked a quick smile, looking at Peterman's laundry basket. "Well, looks like you are playing house, Riordan. Guess we caught you at a bad time."

Peterman set the Beck's down on the small coffee table. "Is that right?" he said, voice deep and booming. "Didn't know the police department was hiring father and son Book-'em-Danno teams now. Good to keep it all in the family."

Cromwell got red-faced. Stephens-Christian's glare narrowed.

"Gentlemen," I said, rising slowly, remembering my rights with these cops and walking toward the front door. "I appreciate your investigative prowess. But unless you want to arrest me or have some special information you want to share, I am now going to have to ask you to leave. It's been a long day."

Both cops stayed seated. "You a jogger, Riordan?" Cromwell asked, ignoring Peterman and my request for them to leave.

"I walk." *I needed these two out of my place before Byron returned.*

"I'm guessing you walk the Trail. That right?"

"Me and half the town."

Cromwell nodded. Stephens-Christian wrote out something in his small notebook, then pulled out his cell from his jacket and began scrolling.

"Right, Riordan. But half the town wasn't in a missing woman's condo, were they?"

I opened the door saying, "Unless you intend to take me downtown, gentlemen, I want you both out of here. Now." I glanced down the hallway for signs of Byron.

Both men returned half nods, looking at one another. "All right, Riordan," Cromwell said, flicking the coffee table top three times, getting up. "We understand that you and your boyfriend have important business to attend to and you have calls to return. But if you want to confess to this thing, it will make things easier on you in the long run."

He took one last look around. "Sad life you lead, Riordan. Prison might not be all that bad. We'll see if we can keep you from the death penalty. Stay in town."

Each cop gave Peterman a glare and Peterman reciprocated with a devilish grin, arms folded across his barrel chest.

They left. I listened for any shuffles or barks in the hallway.

Death penalty. I drew a hard breath.

"Motherfuckers," Peterman said as I shut the door. I sat down and examined the poster with the photographs of the two young women. Peterman looked over my shoulder at the girls' names and their former employer, La Torea's.

"We need to talk, Paddy," Peterman said with as much caring concern as I'd ever heard in his voice. Just then I heard my door creak open.

"Sorry we took so long, Mr. R.," Byron said. "But I took Laddie to ask my foster mom if we could get a dog like him."

Peterman looked at me, then Laddie.

31

So You a PI?

I jumped out of bed Wednesday with an energy level uncharacteristically high for a school day. But then again I wasn't a
schoolteacher anymore. Peterman had left the preceding night
with his laundry done and with the offer to help me get to the bottom
of this mystery. He believed in my innocence, or so he said, but then
again, with a news story and the police hounding you, even the most
loyal mate might lose faith.

I offered my roommates bologna and cheese for breakfast and
made myself some coffee. I stepped out on the balcony. Beautiful day.
Despite the fact that cops were giving me the distinct impression that I
was their man, I felt surprisingly alive. I checked my cell for messages;
only the typical fitness and travel notifications.

The girls' photos on the poster Cromwell had left said both last
worked at the restaurant La Torea's. That would be the first stop; that's
if I was in the self-vindication business. Would there be a tie-in to
Penny and her whereabouts? *What about Deidre?*

A HUNDRED THOUGHTS PELTED THROUGH MY MIND AS I DROVE ALONG. Laddie caught the morning breeze.

It was still early and no dinner restaurant would be open, if that was what La Torea's was. I drove in the general direction of where most of the dining establishments were located, hoping to check the place out anyway.

At Bearden, I exited and took a new roundabout to the city center and then headed toward Sanford College for Women.

After turning into a small strip mall, I pulled up in front of an eatery named La Torea's, written in italics on one of the tinted windows. I cracked a window for Laddie, got out and walked toward the door.

I peeked in the window for any sign of activity. None. I walked back to the alley to a red, steel door, the trash exit. The knob was grimy, but I tried it. The door opened easily. I headed inside and up three steps to the kitchen where a stench from the night before met me. Dirty dishes were stuffed in a large washer. *These guys better hope the health department doesn't show.*

A janitor was sweeping up in the main dining area. *Seems like I'd been running into custodians a lot.* He jumped back when he saw me, then cautiously asked who I was and what I doing there. A name tag said he was Theo. I didn't answer right away, just smiled, trying my best not to seem like any kind of a threat. I pulled out the folded poster and held it up for him to see. "I'm looking for any information I can find about these two missing girls. I was told that they worked here."

He studied me for a moment, looking at my maroon, island-print shirt and khaki Dockers. He leaned the broom against a table. "You a PI or something?"

I was a little offended he hadn't mistaken me for a cop. But then again my shirt didn't make me look like a straight-laced type.

"Unlicensed, but let's just say I'm interested in finding out what happened to these women who worked here. You know there's a reward for information leading to their whereabouts?"

He again looked at the pictures and almost blurted out something, but just as quickly caught himself. He resumed sweeping. "Yeah," he said. "A reward you say. The young ladies did work here. And the cops have already been by asking questions. I don't know much. I'm just here before opening. But nobody said nothing about no reward, nothing 'bout no money."

I waited a moment before going on, giving the man time to let the thoughts of dollars settle into his mind. "Well," I said. "If you know something, Theo, call me. Your information might pay off." I handed him my number written on a sticky note. I didn't want to give this guy my card with my name and the name of the school district on it.

The man took a deep breath as if gasping for fresh air as he pushed the broom past me. The odor of cigarette smoke emanated from him. He set the broom against a table and wiped off some dried salsa. I waited. If you can master the art of silence, it is surprising what you may be rewarded with.

He took another swig of air, then sat down at the table where I had left the poster. I guessed he was in his late sixties. He'd probably had a hard life and one likely relegated to subservient positions. He coughed. I sat down across from him. We both stared at the poster.

"She was a bubbly thing," Theo began, pointing to the picture of Tara Simon. "That one not so much," he said of Carrie Lindsey. "And the only reason I knowed them was that they both used to open the place up. And that one would pay me," he said of Tara Simon, "because he didn't come in till later."

I didn't ask who "he" was.

Thoughts of Penny came to mind.

Theo continued. "Then Mr. V. showed up, when the girls didn't come in. He sometimes comes in the mornin'. He was all bothered and just paid me. I didn't ask him about nothin'. And sometime later I heard about them missing. Afterward, the cops and all sorts of people were here when I got here in the morning. That was only, what, last week? Seems longer, though." He snorted again.

"So, Theo. What else do you remember?"

"People just call me Tommy."

"Riordan," I said. We shook.

"So you a PI trying to find these girls?"

I wasn't a liar. But then again there was no reason to elaborate. "Something like that. Let's just say, Tommy, that I have a family interest. And I'm wondering if there is a connection between these two girls and someone else I know. You ever hear of girl called Penny, could also be known as Margaret?"

Tommy coughed some more, then turned to the front window. "No. She missing, too?"

Before I could explain, Tommy got up. "There's Mr. V. coming in," he said. "Only I didn't tell you nothin'." He grabbed the broom and started slowly pushing.

Mr. V. swung into the restaurant as if he owned it, which he did. But not in the cordial, I'm-the-proprietor kind of way.

He smashed out a cigar in an ashtray and wielded himself right up to me and Tommy. His deep-sunken tar-black eyes were tired.

But he was primed for business.

Tommy pushed his broom away after giving a perfunctory "How you, Mr. V.?"

Giving me a hard stare, Mr. V. bit out, "And you are?"

I stood. He held his ground, then looked down at the poster and stepped back.

"Riordan. I'm working on the disappearance of these women."

I expected to be quizzed about my credentials, but Mr. V. didn't even ask whether I was legitimate or not, just said, "I fucking told you all everything I know, and if you keep dropping by my place I will have my attorney file a harassment suit!"

As if I were a tough cop, I held my ground, waiting to see if he was done. I was sure Cromwell would be proud of my technique. Mr. V. whisked through the swinging door to the kitchen without waiting for me to do my follow-up. Tommy had disappeared somewhere. I studied the surroundings, then walked out the front door.

Outside, Laddie clawed at the window. At first, I thought his excitement was at seeing me, but his eyes were cast beyond. Just as I opened the door and before I could catch him, he jumped out and followed someone with an auburn ponytail disappearing into the alley. "You should leave the windows down more for him," a familiar voice called back.

Laddie froze at the edge of the alley, barking and wagging his tail. I caught up with him and looked down the ten yards or so where the alley dead-ended. No one was to be seen.

Spontaneously, I yelled, "That's it, Penny! Play your games! But I am leaving town for good unless you come clean. You got me into this. Now help me get out!" I'd crossed over the bridge from disbelief to belief.

Two elderly ladies across the street stopped and stared at me. They shook their heads and walked on, concluding I probably resided in the nearby Dumpster.

32

THUMPING

Somewhere in the night she heard an owl hoot, or was it a dream? It was like the time she was selected for the cheerleading squad and for a time afterward, she had to pinch herself to be sure that it was all for real.

But this time she hoped it was a dream. The fear was nearly more than she could bear, a terror beyond anything she had ever known. She curled up. She wanted to scream out, but couldn't.

There was a thump, thump, thump above her. Then she heard laughter and the distant sound of a TV. More thumping. Boots. Someone was walking around upstairs. She must be in a cellar or basement. She curled up as tightly as she could.

First she was cold, then hot, then cold again. Except for the callus-handed one, nobody had touched her. She heard muffled voices, then fiendish laughter from above. How long would this last? Where was Tara?

33

COCHRAN

I pulled Laddie back in the Jeep and drove away from the restaurant. I was peeved at Penny, who, unless I was hallucinating, was not a figment of my imagination. With an emphasis, I told myself, on "my imagination."

My student Every Stout's comment, "My daddy says that fat cop is dirty," again played in my mind.

I needed to get with someone who could offer some clarification about the mess I was in, a mess that started with Penny, but was being perpetuated by Cromwell.

Cochran!

In my past life as a county investigator, my work pal Cochran, now DEA Agent Cochran, was the only person I could think of. He worked out of South Florida. I scrolled down the list of my contacts on my cell.

If he was around and if the number was still good, it was an hour later than where I was. A DEA agent doesn't have a public number. I was privileged to have his special private one. He'd said it was against protocol to give it to me, but he did so for old times' sake. I punched in his number and after a few rings, a gentle voice answered, "Hello."

"Is this Cherri?" I asked. There was a pause.

"Who may I ask is calling?" the woman said.

"This is Pat. Pat Riordan," I said in the most unthreatening tone I could muster.

First a slight giggle, then a heartwarming, "Well, Patrick. How are you? Yes. This is Cherri."

"I'm good."

"We think of you often. Sam just said last week we should have you down here for a weekend of golf."

"I'd love that."

"How long has it been?"

"Three years at least," I said.

Cherri continued the conversation, filling me in on their family happenings. Unlike Malone's wife, who was dismissive and just wanted my hands off her husband, Cherri was genuinely concerned, a trait Cochran also had, but sometimes disguised with cutting remarks.

"Sam pointed out three women who he said would be just right for you, at the grocery store last week. I told him to keep his eyes on the cart. You know how well he minds."

I laughed. "One of his better characteristics."

"You are still single, aren't you?"

"I am."

"So to what do we owe the honor of this call?"

"Well, Cherri. Uh. I'm in a bit of a jam here." I didn't want to elaborate or tell too much about my predicament. How does one explain such things? I could do so to Cochran. But I feared Cherri might not get it.

"You're not hurt or anything like that?"

"No. Nothing like that. It's just that some people are trying to link me to some things I don't have a clue about. I just need to talk to Sam."

"Oh. Well. Okay, Patrick."

There was a baby's cry in the background.

"Listen, Cherri, sorry to bother you. Is that little Sam crying?"

"Yes. Sam is out on assignment, but when I hear from him, I'll let him know that you called. If he can, he will call you back, I'm sure."

"Thanks, Cherri." We shared the silence.

"Patrick, be careful."

"I will."

"Godspeed, Patrick"

"Godspeed, Cherri."

I knew Cochran would call back and could do a record check on Kelvin and Cromwell, whatever good that would do. Who could I turn to about the other matter that was giving me an increasingly spooky feeling?

34

SENSEI

I t was still early in the day and I decided to drive over to see Sensei. Cochran could help with practical cop matters if I wanted to find out a history on someone. But as to encounters with the supernatural, if that was what my reoccurring contact with Penny was, I knew Sensei could shed some light on the subject. I left Laddie in the Jeep, this time with the window lowered more, and entered the dojo, giving out a loud hello.

The office was empty. Sensei appeared from his living quarters with a cleaning rag in hand. "Ah, Master Pat, what bring you here on this fine May day? Come, we have tea. Business slow so far."

I followed him into his living quarters. Spartan and well-scrubbed with an oak floor, the main furniture feature being a black potbellied stove that sat in the middle of the room. Two antique rocking chairs were situated in front of it, separated by a small coffee table.

A futon was neatly placed along the back wall under a bay window with an adjacent wardrobe. Two pairs of nondescript shoes were situated in front of the closet next to the small shower room. A sink and small refrigerator extended out along another wall. There was no TV.

The only visible sign that Tom San was connected to current

events was the map of the world hanging just inside the entrance to his bedroom. Colored pushpins decorated the map, each pin signifying a country Tom San had visited.

"Sit. Tea ready for the talking," Sensei said.

I sat and sighed. I hadn't discussed the news story with him yet and I knew Sensei wouldn't bring it up even if he did know about it.

"Beautiful day, but your mind a tsunami," he said. He handed me a mug. "Tea help purge bad spirits," he said.

I rocked slowly, the heat from the stove relaxing me. He kept a fire going despite the mild weather outside.

"I'm in a bit of a fix and I wanted to know your thoughts about some things," I said sheepishly.

Sensei's dark eyes were glued to mine. He leaned forward. His black hair was cropped short. His neck muscles were taut, I guessed from years of proper stretching and basic good living. "Go on, Patrick."

"A week ago or so..." I stopped, contemplating what direction to take. *Should I talk about Penny, the chief reason I was there, or relate my fears about being a suspect, or both?*

"Uh. Well, the fix I'm in relates to the police believing I had something to do with some missing women in the area."

He waited for more. I stared into the stove and sipped the tea.

"Ah. Yes, I hear about that. Some of the customers were talking about a news story. And you say that someone believe you did this. But you tell me about a missing woman several weeks ago. Remember we say a lot like a movie. Same woman you run into three different times."

"I remember. Well, since that time, a policeman, name of Cromwell, has come to think that I'm a person of interest in this case because I was in one of the women's condo. The really strange thing is that the cop says this woman, Penny, has been missing for over a year."

"Um. Yes. Seem very strange."

"It is."

"But now other people missing too, you say?"

"That's what the newspaper story said. I'm sure the reporter's source was the policeman."

"This all mysterious."

"Well, here is why I wanted to talk to you. I have been with this Penny woman on three different occasions, one quite recently. I don't mean in the biblical sense, but just in contact. Also, and even more strange, is that she appears to me almost out of nowhere."

Sensei nodded and smiled and took another sip of his tea. "Go on."

"Just several hours ago, I was doing some investigation of my own at a local restaurant and had Laddie with me. I forgot to tell you about the dog."

"I think you talk about the dog when you here earlier."

"I don't remember. But when I came out of this restaurant, the dog was in the car, whining. At first I thought it was just because he was glad to see me."

"What you say you call the dog?"

"Laddie. When I let him out, I caught a glimpse of a woman's hair, a ponytail, and heard a voice saying that I should leave my window more open for the dog or something like that. Laddie followed the voice. So did I, but no one was there."

Sensei got up and put his palm on my forehead.

"I'm serious, Sensei."

He laughed lightly. "I know, Master Pat. You are serious. But with serious things, sometimes better first to put laughter to it." He poured more tea and let me continue.

35

ALL SO EASY

M ama, can I go look at them?" the little boy asked, not raising his head up from the toy boxcar he was playing with. His mother stared at the man sitting across the table from her.

"This got to stop, you all hear?" she hollered to the man.

Leon stared into his coffee cup. On the table was a cell phone.

"They's just tramps anyway," he said. "And those that ain't are working on it." He dialed a number. The woman shook her head. The boy ran the toy car into the man's boot.

"Quit, you little varmint," he said, thumping the boy on the forehead. The man asked the person on the other end, "What time can we expect it?" He nodded, then said okay and clicked off the phone.

"I ain't just hooting about all this, you hear?" the woman hollered as the man exited the back door to his pickup. He opened the cab door and scooted his bulk in. He pulled the blanket to uncover a stack of DVDs and examined them with his big callused hands. He lifted one of them to his nose, smelling it as if to relive the moment he filmed it. He turned on the ignition and slowly backed the vehicle down the driveway and toward town and the hilltop.

He'd have just enough time to get his jollies before this batch was taken away. He'd come close to losing control the other night. The new one was a dish. He'd made a DVD of her and kept it for his own library. The sheriff said the whole thing was foolproof. Still, he and Kelvin were being cheated out of money for all the risk they were taking; especially since what had happened with Kelvin's wife. They did what they had to do.

Leon stopped at the four-way. The town had closed down early even though it was Wednesday, not Tuesday. The train hadn't arrived last night, so the sheriff told the school and businesses they needed to close down early today. It seemed all too easy. The sheriff had ordered everyone to stay in their houses for their own protection due to the fact that bio waste was being transported. Stupid people. How long these people would believe such a thing was anyone's guess. But it was working so far. The only way that little varmint nephew of his knew about the girls was because his stupid sister brought the boy up to the hilltop with her hoping to educate the boy about trains. She always got mixed up in his business. If she didn't cook and clean for him, he'd have offed her, too.

He stopped the truck. Kelvin had been concerned about his wife's cousin, the professor type, who was at the diner nosing around. He eyeballed the rearview mirror. No one following him. With the sheriff covering their tracks, everything would be okay.

Leon let the pickup climb the hill. At the top he eased into the parking area just off the loading zone where the train would stop. Each car was marked according to its destination, but their car would wind up south of Brownsville, way down south.

He and Kelvin would shoot up the women with just enough dope to knock them out for the trip and then put them in the ventilated boxcars. They'd only give each one a single old quilt. If those women shivered for the entire trip, who would care? Once they got inside Mexico, it was off to whoever paid the highest price for them. Kelvin and the sheriff had said they weren't the only ones in the girl-trade business.

He slogged up the ramp to the front door. It was quiet. He kicked his boot against the jamb, paused, and checked his cell phone. Nabbing the girls had been the easiest part of it all. They'd paid those illegals to grab these last ones. When the wetbacks had come off the train, they'd threatened to report them and their families if they didn't do what they were told.

Only problem had been that when the job was done the illegals would disappear into the woodwork, so you couldn't get the same crew to do repeat jobs. Crews. That was a good name for the wetbacks that helped. He should have crews. He was entitled to have crews. They'd taken one of the women from that wooded trail and the other from a parking lot. They'd followed both from their workplace, some restaurant in the city.

The sheriff had said it was not good to frequent the same place for the kidnappings. Throw off the scent, he said. Leon thought about how the transactions had taken place. When the train pulled in, someone looked for the boxcar marked with the poison symbol. There'd be Mexicans in it. Get them off. Take the Mexicans to town for a nabbing. Store the product in the depot cellar until the following week when the train came back. All nice and tidy.

They'd told the Mexicans they'd be paid for the job, but they never did pay them. Being from Mexico, they understood corruption. He and Kelvin each made a cool three grand, all for fun work. He didn't know what the sheriff got out of the whole deal; or for that matter what the bozo detective in the college town made. Neither one had to do the dirty work.

He'd just take a peek at the merchandise.

36

Our Friendly Ghost

My meeting yesterday with Sensei had been a venting session. And it also gave me a lead. He told me that an acquaintance of his, a visiting professor, might be able to shed some light on my puzzle. He said, "Japan have many ghosts and spirits. We not fight them. No resistance to them. Sometimes they can be teachers."

I appreciated his grasp of my situation, but I was becoming distraught. And couldn't quite adopt a "let it be" attitude, especially since I was being hounded by Cromwell.

~

I took the expressway toward the scene of the accident with Penny. Retracing my steps might help clarify things.

At Clyde's Garage—*now I was certain it had been vacated*—I turned off the ignition, patted Laddie, and got out. I snapped photos of the surroundings, not knowing the purpose other than reassurance that I wasn't seeing things. The last time I had been here seemed eons ago, but in actuality it was only last Saturday. Had I left my trusty crowbar back in Chapwell Falls at the depot? I checked the back of my Jeep. Somehow in the hurry of yesterday I had remembered to take it with me. It's funny how the mind sometimes operates on automatic pilot.

I grabbed the tool and walked around to the back of the garage, hoisted myself up over the wall and into the backyard that had become a small wasteland of once-roadworthy vehicles. I had gradually acquired a no-nonsense boldness, which in part was scary, but necessary if I was going to find my way out of this mess.

On closer look around the back lot, it was evident the cars had been there for quite some time. But still no Ford Focus in sight. I was thinking in terms of my reality, assuming that the car had been towed here only last week.

Laddie barked from the Jeep. The back office windows were cobwebbed. I twisted the doorknob. Locked. I cracked the windowpane with my crowbar, cleared the broken glass out, reached in, and unlocked the door.

A toilet directly inside the door reeked of urine. In the front office, a solitary bell, the kind you use to summon a clerk, sat on the front counter. A small desk was nearly hidden behind the counter with piles of weathered paper lying on top it. On the wall above the desk was a girlie calendar, the type popular in the 1950s. A blonde with sweeping locks in a bikini and high heels stared upward to the advertisement, which read Coca-Cola.

I looked out the front window through the greasy glass. I had followed the wrecker to this place, I knew that. And I had seen Penny hand her keys over to the big-bellied mechanic. And that was only days ago. So why did the place look like it had been abandoned for months? Cobwebs and rusted cars in the backyard told the story of a business dried up and gone south. The young detective, Stephens-Christian, had said the garage had been closed at least a year.

I scraped off what appeared to be some hardened breadcrumbs from an old plastic chair and sat, staring out. Across the street in a strip mall was a laundromat and a Chinese restaurant, Wang's. The name conjured up images other than eating, but I thought someone there might have some answers to my questions. I unlocked the front door and walked to my Jeep, opting for an early lunch.

~

"IF OUR FRIENDLY GHOST, OR WHOMEVER SHE IS, COMES BACK SAYING YOU need the windows rolled down some more, tell her she can find me inside," I told Laddie, cracking the windows for him. The smell of deep-frying blasted out when I opened the door to Wang's.

A diminutive middle-aged woman with coal-black hair asked in broken English if I wanted lunch. "You first of the day," she said, leading me to a booth, which was one of a half dozen meshed with the wall. A mirror ran the length of the room on the opposite wall. I checked myself out. Stubbles.

Tea was brought by a young Asian girl, who asked, also in broken English, if I wanted the lunch special. I said fine, along with a Diet Coke. My real mission here was to find out about the auto body shop. Within minutes a hefty plate with side dishes of all anyone could ever want for lunch was arranged neatly in front of me. I asked the young waitress what she knew about the auto body shop. She gave me a hold-on gesture and scurried back to the where the older lady was arranging some napkins. Both returned.

"A lady want to know about that place, too. She say call me if I ever know anything about them," the older woman said, laying down a business card of one Cynthia Crystal, reporter for *The Echo Times*. I recognized the name of the reporter who wrote my nemesis piece.

"She wrote story about our business and about the Chinese in city. That last year. But she want also to know about auto place." The younger girl nodded along with the older woman, interjecting that men who worked there had frequented this place for lunch, but not recently.

Both women pointed to the story about their restaurant framed and hanging across the room on the wall. I smiled approvingly. I breathed a sigh of relief that at least there had been men at the auto body shop and that I wasn't completely delusional.

A middle-aged man showed up at the table. He said something gruff in Chinese to the women. They hurried to the back. The older woman said something in a caustic tone back to him as she left.

The man smiled at me. "Mind if I sit?" he said. "Hope you enjoy our food." He played with a napkin ornamented with symbols of animals and years. "What year you born?" he asked. I think he might have been embarrassed that he had been so coarse with the women. I told him.

"Ah, year of the rabbit," he said.

I read the description of that year and what I could expect of myself as it played out in the cosmos. Then he talked.

"I have to send women to the back. They not understand about the men who used to come in here from across the street." He tore at the napkin some more. "They were very bad men, I think. And when they start asking young Lee Sun about herself," he said, pointing to the young waitress who'd just left, "then I take over the table. And I did that whenever they come. And enough of me they not want. They stop coming in. That business close down. Men might have gone to prison. I don't know. But glad they gone."

I asked him about the card and why Ms. Crystal asked about the auto body shop.

"After she write article on our business, she ask questions about men. I tell her what I tell you, about men being too friendly here. For a while she come in a lot."

He asked about the soup I had started and asked if I had been in before and said I should bring my family for a dinner special. I said I would.

"You take Ms. Crystal's card and tell her to come by some time. We miss her. We not see her for long time."

I said I'd do that. I finished what I could of the feast and asked for a doggie bag. Outside I laid out the leftovers for Laddie. I was ready to make an alliance with this Ms. Crystal.

37

CYNTHIA CRYSTAL

I called *The Echo Times* from my Jeep and asked to be patched through to the editorial department.

A moment later, a self-assured voice answered, "Cynthia Crystal."

I returned with a confident tone, "Riordan here. Person of interest in the case of the local missing women."

A pause told me she melted some at my ID. "Oh. Uh. Yes." I heard some shuffling at her desk. I expected she was probably signaling to her brethren to be quiet since she had a criminal suspect on the line.

"Yes. Mr. Rierman."

"Riordan," I said.

"Yes, of course. What, uh, can I do for you?"

I wanted to say, "If you are going to write a news story and lay out in print someone's name as a suspect in a criminal case, especially if that someone has not been formally charged, you need to try to get the suspect's comments about such accusations."

But I didn't. By the sound of her voice I guessed she was somewhere in her mid-twenties, tops.

Although she may have been schooled in town, where we have one of America's leading journalism schools, a fair and balanced story she had not written.

"I just ate at Wang's. And the owner there said to say hi."

"Yes," Cynthia said. "Again, what can I do for you, Mr. Riordan?"

"Well, Ms. Crystal, I am obviously a bit concerned about the situation you made public by writing that article and would like to talk to you about it sometime."

"That can be arranged. I'm free now. Would you like to come here? Or should we meet somewhere else?"

I was impressed with her customer service response and that she was not fearful of meeting a criminal type like me. She obviously had a hard shell. "How about Wang's? I just had lunch there, but they will be glad to see you again."

"Twenty minutes?"

"Sounds good," I said.

I got back to Wang's ahead of Ms. Crystal and sat out in the Jeep for a while with Laddie. When I headed back inside, I was greeted with curious smiles. I walked over to Mr. Wang; at least I presumed he was Mr. Wang. Earlier he hadn't bothered to introduce himself. I told him that I'd taken his suggestion and called Ms. Crystal and she was on her way. That news prompted special treatment. "You come and sit in owner's booth," he said.

I followed.

Mr. Wang escorted me to the first booth off the bar, larger and more sequestered from the main dining room. "I give you drink."

I ordered a Tsingtao to settle my nerves and played with my cell, googling news stories, hoping I'd not find anything with my name on it. I wanted to be calm and not act as if I saw myself as a guilty party. I knew Ms. Crystal wasn't seeing me because she had a caring concern for my welfare, but was rushing over with the hope to get some story out of the meeting.

CYNTHIA CRYSTAL ARRIVED QUICKER THAN THE TWENTY MINUTES SHE promised. She was immediately greeted by the two waitresses and Mr. Wang, who once again pointed to the story she'd written about the restaurant. She cordially acknowledged their appreciation and was directed to the solitary figure in the booth.

38

I Got Suspicious

Cynthia Crystal walked over with an air of "I will get to the bottom of this." She had a smart but very masculine 'do, cut just above the ears. Black-rimmed glasses added to her countenance as a truth-finder. She wore a black double-breasted jacket, white blouse, and black pants. She was not dressed for success, more for functionality, probably because of the pauper wages paid to small-town reporters and also because her sole intention in this life was not to sugarcoat anything, much less herself.

She stuck out her hand. I stood and we shook. We sat. In unison, we said, "Thanks for meeting with me."

"Since you called me, why don't you go ahead?" she said, taking out a reporter's notebook.

"Okay." I reminded myself not to get off track with some tirade about the injustices of her story, or worse, begin to talk about how I was getting an eerie feeling that a spirit of some sort was directing me in this investigation. I told myself to stay focused on the auto body shop. I placed my cell to the right of me on the table and patted it twice, hoping to imply I was tapping the conversation. I expected

Cynthia to do the same, but she pulled out an old-school reporter's spiral notebook.

"I was visiting the auto body shop across the street and came over here to ask when the shop went out of business. That's when Mr. Wang told me about you." The older waitress poured us water and waited for our order. "I'll have another," I said holding up the beer bottle.

"Oh, I'll have one, too. What is it you are having, Mr. Riordan?"

"Tsingtao."

"I'm celebrating," she said more to herself than me.

I waited for more. She didn't elaborate.

"I'm sorry. Go on," she said.

"As you know, Detective Cromwell considers me a suspect in this missing person case, which led in part to my dismissal from my teaching job."

Cynthia Crystal primed her pen for investigative scribbling by writing the date with my name below.

Two beers were laid down with a basket of some type of oriental chips. The waitress gave a submissive nod, then left.

"*Slainte*," I said.

Cynthia didn't reciprocate.

"Where was I?"

"Visiting the body shop across the way."

"Right."

She waited.

"Well," I continued. "Mr. Wang said you know something about the body shop, or at least that's the impression he gave me."

She took a sip, surveying the room as if for listeners. "I guess this town is behind me now." She didn't elaborate. "But this whole issue of missing women began last year, when I had taken off a Saturday to do some shopping and happened by an estate sale being held across the street from Margaret Johannsen's condo. She is the aunt of the woman the police have implicated you in."

"I am aware."

"Yes, I guess you are. Sorry. So, anyway, the elderly widow who was having the sale and I started talking about the neighborhood, and she mentioned Margaret Theriault's sudden disappearance. She thought it was strange because the 'poor dear' was going to help with her aunt's estate sale. After browsing a while, I brought an antique vase from the woman, then left."

I took several gulps of my beer.

"But I got nosey," Crystal said. "Probing is something I like to do, as you might guess. My dad was a Chicago cop. Anyway, I'd asked this lady what kind of car Margaret drove and she said it was black, with out-of-state plates. She didn't know the make. She said she thought Margaret came from Kentucky. Right after I interviewed Mr. Wang for the story on this restaurant, I was getting in my car and saw a black car with out-of-state plates, blue trim like Kentucky, being towed around back of the garage across the street. Well, bells rang!

"I went back inside and asked Mr. Wang about the garage and he got jittery. He told me how the men from the place came in for lunch and had become overly friendly with his young waitresses. It was then that I became fixated on Margaret Theriault."

I felt goosebumps crawl up my back.

"When I went back to the newsroom that day, remember this was last year, I made some calls about abandoned vehicles to find out where they go. I found out the police have an impound yard, although not all impounds go to a city lot. But I called the one that the city uses. There was no record of a black sedan. I called the neighbor lady to see if Margaret had returned. She said she still hadn't seen her and had reported her missing. She gave me the name of the policeman who interviewed her."

"Detective Cromwell," I said.

"Right. Anyway, as things go, I got caught up in other stories. And my dad got sick back home, so I had to be there for a while. When I returned, the freshness of what could have been a story had worn off, until out of the blue, I get a call from Detective Cromwell telling me they have a suspect in the case of the missing women. You."

Cynthia Crystal looked around. She suddenly seemed to want to reach out to give me a consolatory hand pat. But she said, "So, I apologize for not getting with you to ask for your side of the story, but here we are." Her cell phone rang. She looked at the caller ID, but didn't answer it.

The waitress returned and asked whether we wanted to order another beer. I waited to see if Ms. Crystal was game. But she said she had to get back to the office. "I can meet you again, say Saturday, here. That okay?"

As she got up I asked, "What was the name of the neighbor lady?"

"I don't remember. Probably have it in my notes. I'll bring it to our next meeting. You playing Sherlock?" She looked around and left.

It seemed like Ms. Crystal had wanted to talk about something bothering her, which she didn't get to this day. Even though she no doubt wanted quotes from me about the mess I was in, our meeting seemed to be as much about her need to talk as to get any scoops from me.

Just as I knocked down the last of my beer, Cynthia returned, seeming harried, as if she'd forgotten something. She walked straight up to me, head tilted as if something had clicked and said, "I forgot to mention that Margaret Theriault had a dog. Same kind as the one sitting in your front seat. That is your Jeep outside, I take it?"

"It is, and what I really wanted to talk about—"

Her look stopped me midsentence. She was staring into my face as if looking for lies and began to sit, but hurriedly pulled out her cell phone.

"I need to get going," she said with irritation in her tone, as if somehow I had betrayed her by not telling her about Laddie. "If I can make it before Saturday I will call you. Oh, I remembered the neighbor lady's name. Struger."

39

STRUGER

A t home I made a pot of French vanilla, more to stay awake from the lunch and the beers than anything else.

Laddie had situated himself across the bottom of my bed. "If only you could talk, boy."

The dress!

I raced down to my Jeep, having visions that just as I did, Cromwell would pull up, sirens blaring, cuff me, and alert the world that the case was closed. Physical evidence found.

The sundress lay where I'd left it, under the front seat. Should I take it inside, dump it, or just keep it hidden under the seat?

Somewhere in my past working life, I learned about forensic scientist Edmond Locard, who was instrumental in starting crime scene evidence analysis back in the 1920s. He had said that every criminal leaves a trace of something at a crime scene. Locard supposedly was a pioneer in forensics before DNA had ever been discovered. The dress would offer evidence as to who had worn it as well as who buried it. Now it had my DNA on it, too.

I decided to take the evidence inside. I got a plastic garbage bag, deposited the dress in it, and put it in my bedroom closet behind some empty boxes.

So, where should I focus my investigation at this point? I should probably talk to the neighbor lady who lived across the street from the Johannsen condo. She was the same person who called the cops on me for the recent Saturday-morning investigation of Penny's whereabouts.

I googled on my cell for local last names... Struger. Two listings, one of which was for the Bluff Drive area. I breathed deeply and dialed.

Three rings later, an answer, voice eightyish, female and friendly, but cautious. "Hello."

"Ms. Sturger?"

"Struger. Yes."

"This is Detective Stephens-Christian." *Did she know him from Cromwell's visits with her?*

A pause. "Oh, yes."

"I'm calling about the incident last Saturday. Have you got a few minutes?"

"Oh, yes," she said. "So glad you called. About the break-in across the street? That scruffy-looking man?"

Hardly a break-in. Scruffy-looking? I hadn't looked that *bad.* "Yes. We had another question. We're trying to track Ms. Johannsen's furniture, and you said you were working with the niece on a kind of cooperative estate sale. Is that right?"

"Yes, last year. And I still haven't gotten myself around to it. I was hoping that dear child would help me. But like I told you, when she up and left, I just didn't have the energy to put it together myself. Have you found her?"

"No, still working leads. When was the estate sale to have been scheduled?"

"Oh. Let me think. Time goes by so quickly. Well, it was about this time last year. No, earlier. I remember having to start up the lawn service again. And thinking the other day, why haven't they come by this year yet."

"Ms. Struger, do you know what happened to the furniture? Was it taken, or moved out?"

"Well, I think Margaret Senior owned her place. So I don't know why her furniture would be moved without family consent. But I meant to tell you men when you were here, I did buy some pieces of Margaret's. Not much, but a few nice pieces. I just loved the way Margaret decorated. Very elegant."

"Ms. Struger, did you happen to buy the French secretary in the hallway?"

"Oh my, yes. How did you know?"

"Just hoping that might be the case. Will you do me a favor? Would you check the drawer? In the very back of it, possibly in a small compartment, see if you can find any documents or papers there."

A minute later. "Yes, Officer, I have a paper. It says... let me adjust my glasses. Yes. It says, Hancock Family Insurance. Yes."

"And any name on the paper?"

"Oh. I can't really read it. It looks like a signature. But there is a license number written down."

"Read it to me, please."

"Z-B-eight-Y-two-Z. Yes, that is it."

"Anything else?"

"The date. April eighteenth of last year."

"Ms. Struger, you have been very helpful."

"Will you let me know what you find out about that poor child? And also about that scruffy man who was trying to break into Margaret's house last week?"

"We will, ma'am. Thanks."

I quickly hung up.

40

Against My Better Judgment

All night I had rapid-fire dreams of pickup trucks, women I had known, and grocery stores. According to the information Ms. Struger found in the French secretary, I was working with events that occurred a year ago. I wasn't proud of my con job on the old lady. Then there was the matter of Penny's phone number. Call it or not?

And the matter of the furniture store helper. Was he the same man at the diner with Kelvin? Is that why he did a disappearing act when asked to comment on the Johannsen place?

After cereal and coffee, I called _The Echo Times_ and asked for the editorial department. I realized I was a day early to get back with Ms. Crystal, but I needed someone to clear up some of the unanswered questions. When I was patched through, a young male voice informed me Ms. Crystal was not in, but that I could leave a message on her voice mail. I left the message to get back with me ASAP.

I was also expecting to hear from Sensei, and hoped to get a call back from Cochran about any dirt he might have found on Cromwell. He, if anyone, might shed some light on tracing phone activity, even though doing so was out of his jurisdiction.

Laddie snoozed, refusing to get up. Pig was calling for more break-fast. I looked out the window at the swimming pool. A solitary figure on a lawn chair lotioned herself. Two maintenance men watched her as they were half-heartedly clipping the shrubbery.

I needed an itinerary. But I first needed to call Alice. She answered and immediately asked what I had found out about Deidre. I didn't relate my gut instinct, which was that Kelvin had done something to her. I just said that it appeared there had been a matrimonial spat. I could just imagine Alice shaking her head, exasperatedly.

"She never should have married that boy. He didn't come from her world anyway. And it's all been trouble since they were married."

I lied and told her I was sure she was fine and would get a hold of us when she felt better. "Likely with a girlfriend," I said. The tats on Kelvin's arm flashed across my memory. Why indeed had she taken up with the guy?

I let Alice ask me questions about my predicament, which I said I was taking care of. I told her not to worry, and that when I found out more I'd call. She said she'd try to call Deidre's sister, Maureen, to see if Deidre had contacted her.

I headed to the bedroom closet and got out the bag with the sundress in it. I knew all too well that killers commonly retained some property of their victims. My phone rang. I put the dress back in the closet for safekeeping.

I let the answering machine take over. It was Christina Morales. I picked up.

"Oh, Mr. R., so glad you answer. I call last night. Something that I want to talk to you about."

"Is this about you wanting to work at the bagel shop I go to?"

"Oh, yes, I do want to work there. But is about something else. My family."

"Where are you now?"

"Home. Can you come by my house, uh, apartment?" she asked. "It is very important."

Against my better judgment, I said I would. She told me how to get to her place. And with that, Laddie and I took off. Why was she home on a school day?

41

CHRISTINA

The area of the city called Pelster Heights typically housed both the long-term disenfranchised and immigrants who had just arrived from points east and south. There was constant friction between the old guard, who had lived for generations in the tenements, and the new residents, usually Hispanics or Asians.

Laddie sniffed the morning air as I made the drive along the street known as "Drive-By Boulevard" due to recent shootings. Even though we were sequestered away from the big-city lights in what the coastal elites would call flyover country, crime was on the upswing.

Christina had been somewhat lucky in getting to attend the newest of the high schools, due to recent school redistricting lines. But being one of two Hispanic girls enrolled, I was sure, weighed heavily on her self-esteem.

I really didn't know much about her family, other than she had a cousin, a brother, and a mother. I had heard no mention of a father, or any mature male figure. Despite the good principal Rivy's certainty that I had some kind of improper relationship with Christina, it was really no more than a superficial dad-daughter bond.

Christina had told me that her brother and cousin were working day labor, and that was why she was always early to class. She was really a good kid. Given her dutiful work in my class and her helping nature, I had recommended her for a part-time job at the bagel shop.

∿

I CHECKED THE NAPKIN WHERE I'D WRITTEN DOWN HER ADDRESS. AT THE red-brick five-story, I slowed. Third floor, she had said. I checked out the surroundings for a suitable parking space near her building. Two teenage boys with hoodie sweatshirts dropped their skateboards, then hopped aboard the contraptions. More adolescents not in school. I parked just down from the apartment and cracked the window for Laddie.

Smells of onions cooking blasted out from the walls as I climbed the steps. I knocked. A middle-aged woman answered. She wasn't over five feet tall, and immediately stuck out her hand. Christina jumped in from behind her with the introduction of her mother and then a "Come inside." Two boys, late teenage years or maybe early twenties, sat looking remorseful on a well-worn red couch. Christina took my hand and sat me down across from the boys in a La-Z-Boy. Her mom joined the boys.

"Mr. R., thank you so much for coming," Christina began. The mom nodded, although I wasn't too sure she understood what her daughter was saying. The boys just looked on. "This is Jesus, my brother," she said, pointing to the bigger of the two. He nodded. "And this is Roberto, my cousin."

Her mom nodded attentively. For a moment there was silence. Then Christina told her story. She started slowly, almost ashamed about what it was she had to say. The boys bowed their heads. So did her mom.

"Jesus and Roberto are good boys," Christina said. Her mom nodded, either agreeing, or just confident that anything Christina said was okay. "But something bad happened when they first arrive here." This time the boys nodded, ready to admit to some foul deed.

Christina told the story, and with each passage she explained what she was saying to me to the boys and her mother, in Spanish.

"When I heard about you having to leave school because of a newspaper story and told my mama, Jesus and Roberto told me about it all."

Roberto nodded again, but in a far-off, haunting way. "You see, we can't go to the police because they will send the boys back. They have no papers," Christina said.

"La policia, no!" her mother cried out.

Christina related the story, checking her facts in Spanish with the boys, as she told how Jesus and Roberto had arrived on a train at night, but not in this town. They and a handful of other illegals had been given water and sandwiches, and were allowed to take one suitcase with them when they were hustled onto a twenty-car freighter in Brownsville. The boys had saved their money and they gave the "train coyotes" three thousand dollars each to be smuggled into this country.

Sometime in the night of the following day, the train stopped. Two men hopped aboard. They shined flashlights onto everyone. The others were herded off and loaded into a truck. But Jesus and Roberto were told that they were to go with the two men. The train, they guessed, had stopped in the country somewhere, not a city.

"They didn't know why, Mr. R., so they did what they were told."

I got up and checked on Laddie from Christina's window. He was sitting, staring ahead in the passenger seat. The two boys with hoodies had skated on.

Christina continued, while I watched my car. Roberto lit a smoke. Ms. Morales quickly took it from him and doused it out.

"They were hurried off the boxcar," Christina said. "And into a van by the two white men." I let her tell the tale without asking for descriptions of the two men. I'd do that later.

She continued, and said the boys were told that unless they cooperated with the men, they would be turned over to the police. The boys were driven for some time, and then finally the van stopped in a parking lot of a grocery store in this town.

For an hour they waited with the men. The men drank whiskey, but didn't offer any to the boys. The men watched women go in the store and out again. Finally, when the traffic had thinned in the lot, they pointed to a young woman who had parked her car. Both boys were told that when she came out, they were to grab her.

I asked Christina if the boys understood what it was the men were asking them to do. She said they did. The men shook their fingers at the boys and said if they told anyone about this, they'd be turned into immigration. Once this woman was in the van, the boys were let out, she said.

For minutes we all sat in silence. Christina then asked me what I would do with the information. I assured her I would do nothing for the time being. I hadn't collected all the information I needed and wasn't too sure what I'd do with this information. When I left, Christina hugged me. Her mother gave me a kindly nod.

In my Jeep, Laddie looked to me for our next move.

42

SWING BY THE TEACHER'S PLACE

Cromwell eased his girth out of the passenger side of the black sedan. His sidekick threw out a butt, then turned off the ignition and followed the senior cop into Crispies Donut. Inside both men began their daily routine of flirting with the girl behind the counter.

Cromwell told the young woman she'd better use that pretty smile sparingly or every Tom, Dick, and Harry will be asking her out. The girl tugged at her hair. Stephens-Christian said if he were ten years younger he'd be one of those boys. The girl blushed and handed over their orders. Each man stuffed a dollar into the tip jar, smiled, paid, then exited.

"Nice ass on that little one," Cromwell said, looking back into the bakery window. He took out his cell phone and scrolled for messages. "Should have taken a picture of that sweet thing for my library," he said.

Stephens-Christian gave a half-hearted chuckle. "She could be your daughter, old-timer."

Cromwell downed half of his pastry before he got into the car and put his phone back in his pocket. "I've still got what it takes. Besides, haven't you heard that older men take more time under the sheets than you young bucks?" He moaned as he eased himself back into the passenger seat. "Let's take a swing by that faggot teacher's apartment and see if his piece-of-shit rattletrap is there. We may just fucking pop the sucker for hampering an investigation, if we find that he's left the area again. We already got him on burglary at that condo. We should just haul his ass in and see if women stop turning up missing." He gurgled out a laugh.

Stephens-Christian didn't bother to reciprocate this time with his perfunctory chuckle.

43

CROMWELL AGAIN

I n my apartment, my roommates snoozed on the bed, while I stretched out, contemplating what Christina had shared.

I'd asked Roberto and Jesus if they could describe the men who met them at the train, but they only said they were white and middle-aged; or, as Christina had said, about "your age, Mr. Riordan." But she said the boys noticed one had a tattoo of letters, which ran up his arm vertically.

Three hard knocks on my door. Laddie didn't budge. Pig bounced off the bed.

Through the peephole I saw my new friends. I looked to the heavens for help, realizing I had damaging evidence in my bedroom: Laddie, the same make and model as the missing Penny's dog. I opened my door. I said curtly, "Good to see you gentlemen."

Ms. Spragg, my ninety-year-old neighbor, peeked her head out over the guard chain of her door. I needed to get with her about my predicament, just to ease her soul that she wasn't living across the hall from a serial killer.

"You're not scaring old women, are you, Riordan?" Cromwell said, chuckling. "Oh, I forgot, you just like the young ones."

"If I am scaring them, Officer, it's with your help," I said. I let the two in, hoping the gods would keep Laddie asleep, and hoping Cromwell didn't have a search warrant. I quickly invigorated myself, knowing, despite what might appear as incriminating evidence, I hadn't done anything wrong. Pig tried to be friends, but both looked at him like he was some rodent.

"Where's your boyfriend, the bruiser type?" Cromwell asked, plopping down on the futon as if he'd come to watch a game and eat chips.

Stephens-Christian walked over to the porch window and looked out. I casually shut the bedroom door to a crack, so as not to be obvious I was hiding something. Laddie was still dead to the world. If he barked, I'd have to come up with some logical reason I had the dog, of which there was none.

"What is it you guys want with my time today?" I said softly.

"Well, we were wondering where you were, for starters. Like, yesterday?" Stephens-Christian said.

"Well, this is Friday. And you are asking what I have been doing for the last day?"

"That would be about right," Stephens-Christian said, still looking at what I guessed were some early-morning sunbathers, who were braving the coolness to get a head start on their summer tans.

Cromwell busied himself with a copy of *Golf Digest* I'd left on my coffee table. I walked around the kitchen counter to retrieve a water from the fridge, nonchalantly, feeling a surge of panic about the dress, not to mention Laddie snoozing.

"What have I been doing, is what you guys want to know?" My voice went up an octave. "The thing of it is, gentlemen, you might say I was doing some investigating myself."

Pig returned to the bedroom, bumping open the door. Stephens-Christian left his post at the porch, paused, seemingly thinking about having a look-and-see with the cat, but then took a seat next to Cromwell. I took a swig of the bottled water and sat in the rocker to cordon off the bedroom from the interlopers.

I left out my trip to Christina's and the restaurant, but told the two that my cousin Deidre was missing. I didn't offer up Deidre's journal as evidence of Kelvin's abuse.

After my very short replay of my recent activities, trying to speak slowly with eye contact so as to give the impression I had nothing to fear, Cromwell took Alice's phone number and said that if Deidre was missing, then a report needs to be filed.

Whether they believed a word I said or not, I didn't know. But, I was saved by Stephens-Christian's cell phone text chime going off. "Fucking thing," he said, reading the message. "We're going to have to answer this."

Cromwell stared deeply into me, not in a way that said *We know you did it*, but with something more sinister. "Well, Riordan, we can get a warrant issued for burglary. You know that, don't you?"

"Yes, that is what you've said." I opened my front door. "But I guess you are saving me for bigger things." I stepped outside. Both cops followed. Cromwell scratched his shirtsleeve, and as he did I saw the tattooed lettering.

"Don't leave town, Riordan," he said, flushed.

44

HEY, OLD MAN

A s soon as the door shut, I checked on Laddie. He was belly-up as if someone had been scratching his stomach, atop a made bed, which wasn't of my doing. A slight smell of something sweet emanated from the pillowcases. I looked about for more traces of my intruder, and as quickly dismissed any further investigations, counting my blessings that Cromwell and crew hadn't checked the bedroom.

Both animals followed me to the living room futon. I grabbed a Beck's and stretched out. Laddie melded himself into my feet as if to say, "Let me continue my nap here." Pig jumped up, nestling into my armpit.

Outside, giggles from poolside had started. The college crowd, which the complex was mostly made up of, congregated around the pool in anticipation of Memorial Day weekend, when the pool would actually be filled.

Laddie's slowed breathing tranquilized me. Then an overall sense of peace enveloped me. A petal fragrance... sleep.

A figure appeared in a blue dress. She smiled. Penny? I'd almost forgotten what she looked like. Hair color, eyes. Then she was atop me, hair hanging, falling about my face. She kissed the nape of my neck. Her thighs were velvety smooth.

When I awoke, the curtains were fluttering. My tattered blanket lay atop me. It was midafternoon.

I shook off the fear that I was losing it. There was still racket from outside.

Time to attack the day again. I grabbed a dirty towel from the laundry basket.

A shower gave me a new lease on the day. I let my beard stubbles stay; maybe not the best idea, since I was considered a crime suspect. I tried to put the unexplained on the back burner for a while, but I couldn't stop thinking of my dream of Penny. During the recent visit by my cop friends, had she intervened by keeping Laddie quiet?

Persons under duress can develop quasi-hallucinations, seeing things and hearing voices in the night, so to speak. In the world of dream analysis, according to Jung's voluminous text entitled *Dreams*, hypnagogic or hypnopompic states, those waking states just before sleep and when awaking, can be confused with hallucinations. I hadn't experienced some fugue state when I had my experiences with Penny. I was very much aware of my here and now—or I thought I was.

LADDIE AND I TOOK THE STAIRS DOWN INTO THE COURTYARD. I LET HIM do his constitutional by the pine shrub just on the other side off the pool area. The chatter inside the gate stopped as I neared. Two stud types stared over at me. The two girls they were with turned away from me, as if to say, *We have our bodyguards.* Had they read Ms. Crystal's story about me?

The bigger of the wannabe studs got up and staggered over to the fence. Laddie pooped. One of girls called out, "Brian, don't." Brian chuckled.

He looked down at Laddie. "Your master murders young girls." He gave me a glare. I didn't have to get too close to recognize that he was in the fourth stage of inebriation, much too early in the day.

I kept my cool. It had been less than a week since I had been canned from teaching and a newspaper story had implicated me in a missing woman case. I didn't need more trouble.

Laddie let out another log on the far side of the gate. I'd forgotten to bring a poop bag with me for pick-up. The other wannabe followed the big one to the pool gate. One of the girls again called for the two to behave.

My heart thumped. I was just frustrated enough that if either young Sir Lancelot took a swing from across the fence, I'd likely reciprocate. Laddie tensed up on the leash as the two neared. I remembered a show I'd seen on the nature of canines, that dogs feel the emotion of their masters and, as protectors, act accordingly. Laddie was a golden, though, and hardly of the Doberman variety.

I didn't look up. Only the fence separated us. "Hey, old man, where you hiding those young snatches?" the big one said with a devilish laugh.

"Come on, boy," I said to Laddie. Just as we backed away, the big one honked a spit our way. It landed on Laddie's snout. The dog didn't bark, but tried to wipe at it with his paws. The two let out roars. I dropped the leash and in a lapse of judgment, took three giant steps to the fence, reached over, and grabbed the wrongdoer by his T-shirt. It tore as I pulled him toward me. Instead of his buddy coming to his aid, he backed off. I fully expected the big one to throw something my way, but he too shrank back.

"Hey, man," he said, almost whining. "I was just kidding."

I was shaking. I didn't say a word. But I knew if I took a jab at him I'd be talking to Cromwell, who would be all too excited to show me the way to his workstation. I let the kid go. I looked over at the two girls, who were skedaddling away from me.

As the bigger wannabe caught up with his group, his buddy said, "Man, you shouldn't have spit on his dog. He'll probably cut your throat in the night now."

45

ALICE

Now more than ever I needed a second Beck's. I climbed back up my stairs, shaking. I called Alice.

She answered on the first ring, as if she were waiting for my call. "Oh Patrick, honey. I just got a call from a..." She paused and shuffled some papers. "A Detective Cromwell. He wants to know all about Deidre. He said you said she is missing. What is going on?"

I patted Laddie, mostly to calm myself with the hopes that I could offer a soothing explanation about what I thought was happening. "Well, I didn't want to get you all upset," I began.

After I had told her that Kelvin seemed to be behind the whole thing with Deidre, Alice unleashed a torrent of tears. I let her wail. When I hung up, I concluded I would visit Chapwell Falls again, Cromwell or not, and do some more investigating, then drive by Brookdale and sit with her.

∼

JUST AS WE WERE GETTING IN THE CAR MY CELL PHONE JANGLED. No caller ID appeared. I half hesitated, but answered.

"That you, Paddy?" the familiar voice asked. Cochran. In the background a loud humming.

"'Tis."

"Why are you hassling my wife? You know she doesn't like you, fat boy." Snide chuckle. "Actually you are one of the few people she does like. What's this about someone trying to link you to some crime. You're not smuggling in heroin, are you? I'll have to arrest you."

"No. Well, Sammy, things are getting very complicated here."

"Give it to me."

I told him, as briefly as I could, about Cromwell, Kelvin, Penny and my recent history with her. I wasn't sure if he got it all, but thought he got the gist of it. I left out the paranormal, other than to say Penny had been missing a year, according to Cromwell.

"You know enough not to talk to cops, Paddy," he said. "Cops twist things around to suit their needs."

"I know how this sounds. But I am feeling like some scapegoat."

Cochran raised his voice over the apparent roar of a plane engine. "Guess where I am?"

"Uh. Not anywhere close."

"I am somewhere south of Cuba. I'm going to have to get off. But first give me this Cromwell's full name and DOB. And the same for this Kelvin character."

I gave him Donald, with a guesstimate on year of DOB, and the last name on Kelvin, with a DOB somewhere in the neighborhood of 1971. I also asked for anything in any database about the Greek letters sigma, epsilon, chi. ZEX.

"Sounds like a good fraternity to join. I'll see what I can do. I'm not sure when I'll be able to call you back. I might even need to get someone else to call you with the info. Godspeed, Paddy. It will work out." He hung up.

For whatever it was worth, there was comfort in having a friend employed as a federal agent. I sat for a moment, not feeling as defeated as I had before talking to Cochran. And I had played to my instincts with the two young bucks at the pool, something Cochran and I had talked about as the best course of action in times of trouble.

46

Sarah Augustine

M r. Popular," I said as my phone rang again. I put the cell on speaker and answered.

"Master Pat," Sensei said excitedly. "I talk to my friend, who teach at college, and I tell her about you. She say you can drop by now. She just leaving dojo and be at her office berry soon. She say now good time. Her name Augustine. She study odd feelings. You no need to call before going over."

~

At the campus I found a vacant parking space in the Art and Archeology Building faculty lot and left the window down a bit for Laddie. He'd contented himself with a chew toy I'd made out of an old shoe.

I entered the building from the backside and immediately was greeted by memories of the place and sitting with Peterman, who meticulously painted eight murals as part of the diorama depicting the evolution of man.

"Are you Pat?" a well-coifed, middle-aged woman asked from the switchback stairway.

"I am."

She stepped down. "Sarah Augustine." We shook. She pointed upward. "We can talk up in my humble abode."

"I am parked in staff parking; my dog's inside my car. Think I'll get a ticket?"

"You are fine. Parking guy doesn't come in the afternoon much. The semester's ended. All quiet until summer school. Dog's window's down, I hope?"

"It is."

The stairway creaked as I followed her up. She spoke over her shoulder. "You could have brought him in, new school policy, I'm told." Her small office was wall-to-wall bookcases. She pulled out a wooden, high-backed chair from the corner, home to a stack of weathered books, which she set on the floor, then pulled the chair toward her desk. "Excuse the mess. Have a seat.

"Sensei San, uh, Tom, didn't share a lot about you or your concerns, only that you are his closest friend and are having...how did he put it? Having some experiences of another world." She looked at me for my reaction.

"That is putting it mildly." *How much do I tell? It was time to spill the beans about this mystery to someone.* "Where do I begin?"

"Begin from the beginning. I should tell you I am a professor in anthropology. But my area of interest is in folklore. And within that, an interest in the evolution of man's interactions with the paranormal."

"Sounds all very esoteric."

Dr. Augustine waited silently, like a therapist does with a patient. I began.

"Well, several weeks ago, I met a woman on the Trail here in town. She seemed to be in a confused state and asked me to walk with her for several minutes. She had been jogging and said some men had scared her on the way up the trail. She was afraid to jog back in that direction alone. There were other people around; not sure why she asked me."

Sarah Augustine nodded, casually crossing her legs.

"So, I walked with her back toward the place where she said these men were. I took a look at some nearby underbrush, but didn't find a trace of anything suspicious. I climbed back up this little embankment where I had left her, only to find her gone. And me standing there like some crazy man talking to himself.

"It was late afternoon. I felt odd. And I remember smelling something sweet. Nice perfume, I think like flowers. At the time, I didn't particularly remember the smells and everything else, but when I met her on two other occasions, this all came back to me. Should I continue?"

"I trust you haven't gotten to the good stuff."

"I don't know if that's the way I'd describe it. A week or so later I am at the grocery store and smelled something similar to the scent I had smelled on the Trail. I turned to glance at the person in line behind me. I thought, *Is it her?* I looked down at the *People* magazine on the rack and became puzzled at the cover, which was dated a year ago. I remember thinking, *Misprint. Doesn't* People *magazine have better editors?*

"I paid for my stuff, then stepped to another counter to buy a lottery ticket. I remember hearing a TV show broadcast from the small coffee area nearby. A sports announcer was saying the NFL draft is coming up. I thought, *What's the deal with that? The draft was last week.* The announcer said that Johnny Football is predicted to go in the first round. Again I thought, *Must be a broadcast talking about an earlier draft, last year, or before.*"

Sarah Augustine wrote something down on a legal pad. "Go on. This is getting interesting."

"I left the store and saw the woman who had been in line behind me heading to the parking lot. I followed her. Within several seconds I heard a car horn go off in the direction of my car. It was coming from a black Focus parked right next to my Jeep. I walked up. It was her. She had on the same jogging outfit she'd worn that first day on the Trail, except now she was wearing a blue sundress over it. She handed me the keys, saying 'Stupid thing,' and I pushed the off button to silence the alarm.

"I identified myself as the guy she had met on the Trail. She tilted up her sunglasses, said she remembered me, and told me her name was Penny. Then she said, 'This place isn't safe.' She got into her car. I stood, wanting to say something to her. But she drove off. Disappeared just like she had before, this time into traffic.

"I tried to see which direction she went, but there were two large trucks blocking my view, and when they turned onto the thoroughfare there was no trace of her car."

Sarah Augustine nodded gently, as if she were finding my story credible. "So do you remember how you felt during this interlude at the grocery store?"

"Felt?"

"Well, you said when you were at the Trail, you were in a kind of trance."

"Right. Uh. I don't remember that so much at the store, just more a feeling of puzzlement over her, the smell, and the NFL thing."

"And the outdated *People* magazine."

"Right."

"There is more, I trust."

"Did I mention that, both times, I think the weather changed quickly when I was around her? The final straw, so to speak, is what followed a week after the grocery store."

"So this is, what, two, three weeks after your first meeting?"

"Yes."

Sarah Augustine listened as if she had heard my story before, or one like it, as I told her about the accident, the garage, now vacant, and my taking Penny to her aunt's condo. I related the mystery of the blood found at the condo, as told to me by Cromwell. And I also told her Penny has been missing about a year. Finally I let her know that, according to the police, I was considered a person of interest in the case.

Sarah Augustine adjusted the blinds slightly to cut down on the westerly sunlight. "I like this old office. Will be a good place to do some research over the summer; just gets kind of warm in the late afternoon," she said. "So is there more?"

"I've hit the high notes, I believe."

She thumped a pencil on the desk three times and said, "Mr. Riordan, have you ever heard of a time slip?"

"Time slip? Uh, sounds familiar."

"Well, it's also known as a slip swing, meaning slipping or swinging into another dimension." Her soft voice was reassuring, as if she were about to perform hypnotism.

The sunlight coming through the blinds caught the speckles of gray in her hair. "What you have just described suggests you have experienced it." She pulled down a large textbook from the shelf, authored by her and someone else. She opened it quickly, so I didn't get a look at the book's title, and found the right page. She perused the paragraphs.

47

An Interactive Personality

S arah Augustine closed her book and ran her fingers along the cover proudly, remembering the words she'd written. She began: "A time slip is really not as rare as you might guess. Perceived experience is a key word, because little in the paranormal world is as evidenced-based as we scientists want things to be. Do some research yourself on the Internet. Throughout history authors have tackled the subject. Mark Twain in *A Connecticut Yankee in King Arthur's Court*, Dickens in *A Christmas Carol*, and Woody Allen's movie *Midnight in Paris* all refer to the time slip.

"Sometimes the person traveling has an active encounter with those they visit, most times not. Most accounts say the time spent in history is brief. People might slip for a moment and call it deja vu.

"Jung wrote about it in his work on synchronicity. He said we all get messages and dismiss them as coincidence, again, déjà vu. But, he said, these thoughts might be something more profound. That is not to say that when a person has a déjà vu moment, they necessarily experience a time slip. But in the grocery store, you heard a broadcast about a football draft from an earlier year and saw a magazine that was dated a year ago. Those sensory experiences make me think you were probably in a slip swing. What do you think about that?"

She stared into me like some Rogerian clinician waiting for me to come up with some *aha* to my mystery.

I said, "Let's say that what you are suggesting—"

"Good choice of word, suggesting," she said.

"What you are suggesting is that I went somewhere back in time, roughly a year ago, to places where Penny was in distress."

"In my study of folklore, ghosts and other manifestations are ever present. They appear as far back as biblical times, as when Saul tried to speak to a dead Samuel. The Greeks also made references to the spirit world. In fact, as a cultural anthropologist I am hard-pressed to find any culture that doesn't. Actual sightings really don't become prevalent until the eighteenth century, though, helped along by the advent of the camera.

"I got into studying this as a purely academic pursuit when working on my dissertation one summer at Trinity College in Dublin, when I came across the mysticism of the Druids and the time slip. Anyway, I won't bore you with my studies. Just know that messages, warnings, suggestions come in all dimensions. Do you understand?"

"Uh, I suppose."

We heard barking from outside. "That your puppy?"

"Speaking of time, I need to get going. He's okay being alone for a short while, but then gets bored."

"Where does your dog fit into all this?"

Was Laddie's bark a paranormal prompt to introduce him into this conversation? I followed with the story of how I found him, and then related the incident at La Torea's, when Laddie barked at the brick wall. I also told the professor about Laddie digging up the dog collar at the makeshift grave by the depot.

Sarah studied me, nodded, and then said, "So that is one more connection to this Penny?"

"I am starting to believe so."

"You said there were sudden weather changes during the days you had contact with her."

"When I was entering the grocery store that day, there were storm clouds, and rain was predicted. But when I followed her out, it was bright and sunny."

Sarah adjusted the black reading spectacles on the bridge of her nose. "Tell me more about your conversations with her."

"We never had any intimate conversations. It was like she was always trying to hurry me along, even though in all three episodes I came to her aid, so to speak. I have another question. I always thought ghosts had to stay put in the environment where they died."

"The ghost we're talking about, if we can assume Penny is that, is called an interactive personality and would be very capable of interacting in our world, the linear world. She can make herself visible and is even capable of touching. You say you smelled something wherever she was around?"

"Petals. Flowers. A sweet smell."

"These interactive personalities can conjure up emotions. Some are playful, others are fearful. It sounds as if Penny was very much fearful of something or someone.

"The fact is, Mr. Riordan, conditions were ideal for you to experience what Penny had experienced one year earlier. And this town is on the thirty-seventh parallel, actually the thirty-eighth. Are you aware of the theories about that?"

"About the thirty-seventh parallel?"

"Some investigators who track paranormal activities claim there are more sightings and occurrences on the thirty-seventh latitude line, especially through this part of the country."

"But there are a lot of people living on this latitude line. So why me?"

Augustine again looked out toward the campus through a slit in the blinds. "Something in your unconscious, or perhaps subconscious, has stirred up the events from a year ago. But, why you? That is an interesting question, isn't it, Mr. Riordan?"

48

AN EMPATH

By the time Sarah Augustine finished with me, Laddie had summoned me at least a half dozen times. It was too late for a drive to Chapwell Falls, so I took the long route home, stopping by Sonic for a large milkshake. "I am an empath, boy," I told Laddie. "That's what the good doctor said I am. Is that why you found me? You could be an empath dog."

~

PIG AND LADDIE LAY IN THE COOL AIR FROM THE CEILING FAN TWIRLING above us. *Good to have a family. The lady at the furniture store said the dog with Penny was called Norris.* "Will the real Norris please stand up," I said. Laddie raised his head.

Sarah Augustine had offered me information on what exactly an empath was. "You are sensitive to the feelings of others," she had said. She also said certain ghosts, the interactive personality type, do impart emotions, but not many of the living are able to detect those emotions in the dead. I guess I was just lucky. Penny had found that quality in me.

I wondered, was Penny just hanging out a year after these encounters happened for some unsuspecting empath to happen by? Was I summoned back? Had I been near her the preceding year and was now somehow recalling these episodes? The whole empath/time slip thing was a real stretch. But then again, Sarah was a professor, and she said she was going to teach a course in the paranormal this summer.

I googled an article about empaths. It said they can read emotions, can feel vibrations and psychic energy of others, and, most surprising, their traits are passed on from generation to generation. The article was written by a Ph.D. and cited a seemingly credible source, a biologist who talked about there being preliminary evidence that one's DNA has something to do with being an empath.

I didn't know who in my gene pool might possess such esoteric traits. Maybe Alice, always very caring, or my recently deceased Aunt Hanna, who died at ninety-eight. The good Dr. Augustine had left me with more questions than answers. All she had said when I left was, "Sign up for my summer school class. And bring your dog."

49

Amos

The cooing of the doves on my window ledge acted as my alarm clock. Despite my current circumstances, I was feeling good. I was on a mission. *Follow the path before you.*

My bank balance wasn't overflowing, but I would have enough to make it if I withdrew money from my teacher's retirement. That plus the pittance of savings I had should cover the rent. Someone—I suspected Peterman—had sent me an email about how to live under aliases, overseas.

I fed Pig and leashed Laddie. Chapwell Falls was on the agenda, but first a stop by the department store to see if I could find out who purchased the dress. Had I mentioned the dress to Dr. Augustine? I'd have to make up a story about why I was bringing some woman's dress in, especially a soiled dress. But the real concern was that I was playing with fire, tampering with possible evidence. But I had the dress and it was too late to turn it over to the authorities at this point. *Ditch that plan.*

Cochran hadn't gotten back with me about my inquiries regarding Cromwell and my cousin-in-law. It was against the law to give official database information to anyone not in law enforcement. But I knew Cochran would find some plausible way around that.

Cynthia Crystal was supposed to call me today to schedule a follow-up meeting. Maybe before I left for Chapwell Falls or checked about the dress, I'd take a drive to my student Every Stout's trailer and talk to his dad, Amos, about Cromwell.

IT HAD BEEN A YEAR SINCE I'D BEEN TO EVERY'S TRAILER PARK. I KNEW HE still had the same residence by his address on the school roster. All year, Every had made a point of asking me when I was going to visit him. Just before I'd lost my job he reminded me. "Last year you brought me home before a snowstorm, remember, Mr. R., and told my dad and Uncle Fran how well I was doing in school. How come you don't come by this year?" he'd asked, forgetting I had taken him home the previous year after he had been suspended from class.

No doubt by now he'd told his father about me being fired. And if Amos Stout read the newspaper, he'd probably seen the article about me. But in his world, being a person of interest could give me insider status.

I turned off the expressway past the advertisement for bail bonds and into the mobile home park. Just as the previous year, loose canines nipped at my car. Laddie stared down without barking back at them.

At a speed bump, I stopped to get my bearings. The second lot down was Every's place, same rusted Chevy Impala parked outside as last year. Broken steps to the front door hadn't been repaired. It was Saturday morning, but late enough for Every and family to be up. I parked. The nipping dogs vacated the area. I lowered the window a bit for Laddie and got out.

A loose tire rim lay upright on a barbecue grill. Empty beer cans and cigarette butts were strewn about. To the side of the trailer was a makeshift horseshoe pit. I took a deep breath and knocked.

50

Egg

A mos Stout opened the door judiciously, then said with a big grin, "Well, teacher man, to what do we owe the honor?" He flipped a dangling cigarette butt toward the horseshoe pit. "Come in. I sent the boy and Fran to the store. You remember Fran. The boy's uncle?"

I said I remembered, also recalling that Fran and Amos were not related, but were intimately involved. "Unless he gets arrested for being a dummy," Amos said, "he should be roundin' the corner pretty soon. Have a seat."

I sat on a kitchen chair with red flowers decorating its seat. Amos sat with a groan on a stained white couch. He muted the TV and said with an uncomfortable air, "So the boy told me about your troubles. Not that it's any of my business."

I paused, nodded cordially, and waited a second before beginning. "Well that's why I dropped by."

Amos looked me over, nodding back. "I twelve-twelved my sentence, but if you get to headin' to my former residence, I can make things easier for you, if that's why you came by. Just kiddin'." He chuckled. "I'm sorry, but I forgot your name. The boy just calls you Mr. R."

"Riordan. Pat."

"That's right, a Mick name."

"Yes, it is at that."

"Beer, Pepsi, water?"

"I'm good."

He deftly rolled a quarter from his thumb to his pinky and back, more, I guessed, as a nervous habit than for show. "Well, I don't suppose you came by for a social visit."

"No," I said.

I didn't begin by spewing out a rendition of "I'm not guilty," which he'd heard countless times as an inmate, but got to the matter of Cromwell and what Every had said in class about him being a crooked cop.

"The boy told you that, did he? I see." Amos got quiet. He scratched at a tattoo on his forearm, which was mostly hidden by his dark, curly hair. He shook out a cigarette, lit it, and blew out with a reflective exhale. "Yep. Well, guess that's accurate about Egg. That's what we called Cromwell back in the day." He got up and looked out the window onto the trailer park. "You got a dog out there?"

"He found me."

"Been promising the boy a dog. You ever want to give that one up, I'll take him."

"I'll keep that in mind."

He sat again staring at the muted TV. "Egg, is it? Now anything I tell you is between you and me, 'cause I just got off parole. And I'm tired of going back every other year. Sets a bad example for the boy. If I ever go back, I'm going to have you and Uncle Fran split the boy's raising." He chuckled.

"Back in the day, me and Egg played ball together. I wasn't too bad, neither. Played fullback, that's what we called the short-yardage back. That's before I got this gut. Anyway, Egg—we called him that 'cause he liked to crack skulls like he was breaking an egg. I seen him do it more than once. He always provoked the thing. But then that ain't what you want to hear, I'm guessin'."

"Not exactly."

"Well, the boy heard from me and Fran that Egg is crooked."

"Right."

"Anyway, Egg never busted me for nothin'. I work in the area of property reallocation, so to speak. Nothin' perverted enough for Egg, I guess. So he's always stayed away from me. But with you, I'm thinkin' Egg has been on your case 'bout these missing girls. And if I know him right, he been showin' up at your place uninvited-like."

"Yes. And it's becoming more of a routine."

"Sounds like him. Always pressing. He hopes you'll say or do something, give him an excuse to smack you around, and if you react and lose it, makes his case stronger. Like if he can get you to whack him, he can retaliate with an impeding investigation or charge you with assaulting a cop. That opens the door to what he thinks you done, or is trying to pin on you. Don't let his marshmallow body fool you none. He sucker punches plenty hard, even after all these years."

"I don't doubt that."

"Now, I ain't sayin' you done nothin'. I hated to hear the school let you go. Shit, you're the only teacher the boy likes. I think he cried when you was let go. And I didn't slap him for it, neither. The crying, that is."

"Good to know, Mr. Stout."

"Amos. Shit, we's almost family, 'specially since you got a criminal case hanging over your head." He doused the smoke. "Just givin' you a hard time. Hope they got nothing against you. But missing women, that's rough shit."

I looked down at his forearm tattoo. "I've seen that tattoo before."

Amos looked at it. "Glad I am part ape. All that hair hides it. Not too proud of it. Hell, I got a prison tat on my shoulder, 'AB'. I'm none too proud of that, either. I'm still part of it. Can't get out. But this here is a boyhood thing. Me and Egg and a bunch of other wannabe thugs got them back in the day. Most of us didn't put much store in it, but I think Egg took it seriously."

I leaned forward slightly toward the couch. "If I'm right, the tattoo has the Greek letters ZEX? Sigma epsilon chi?"

Amos belted out a laugh. "Shit! I never knew. We had sweatshirts with it on them, too. But to us, it just spelled sex. We called it Boys Club."

"You said Cromwell might have taken the meaning of the tattoo too far?"

Amos got up and went to the refrigerator. He took out a can of Coke. "Want one?"

"I'm good. But thanks."

He spit in the sink, then sat back down with another groan. "Well, this club was just an excuse for us boys to have keg parties and run around naked if we wanted. The older boys would initiate the younger boys by giving them one hundred swats. And we was selective about who we let in, or we thought we was. Hell, who would want to be in a club where you had to get one hundred swats to join up? But we was stupid. Anyway, as I said, Egg and me and some others played ball pretty well. Egg was popular with the coaches.

"When he was a senior, hell, I'd dropped out by then, but I still came to the keg parties. Egg was the president of the club that year and he decided that we needed a new initiation. He made the boys get younger girls to come to our parties. Some of those girls wasn't even out of junior high. And I don't have to tell you some bad stuff happened at those parties. I didn't get involved, believe it or not. I got stupid later on in life.

"Anyway, Egg and some of his followers—and Egg always had followers, mostly, I think, because people was scared of him. Still are, the best I can tell. Anyway, that night, two of the girls got drunk and pulled a train. Bad shit. And one girl was in foster care, and didn't really have no one to complain to, without getting herself sent somewhere else.

"But the other girl had parents, and her old man went to the school when he found out, which was a week after things happened. He stormed into the principal's office with descriptions of the boys, one being Egg. Anyways, they all was pulled into the office, but the coaches intervened for Egg and got him off. Egg's ol' man owned an automotive shop. Think he gave the coaches discounts or something. But two other boys were turned over to juvie, and finally did county jail time. But good ol' Egg walked. Egg always had a way of creating layers. You know what that means?"

51

LAYERS

Amos gave me the once-over to assess whether I was capable of understanding the meaning of layers.

He started, "With any crime, what you want is a low profile. And the way to do it is to put layers in front of you. Blankets. Creates a diversion away from you. Shit, listen to me like I know. Been down two times because I was stupid, forgot to put blankets on. But the more people you have up front, the less likely the police are going to trace anything to you. Least gives you time to get out of town, anyway.

"With this party thing that night, Egg got the young boys to bring the girls. And he got others to get these girls away from the party into the woods, so all he done was show up. If the girls talked, his thinking was that his would be the last name mentioned, if at all. But this insulation theory, if you want to call it that, works mostly with dope and property business. Might work with kidnapping. The crime he says you done.

"Wouldn't be surprised if Cromwell's just using you for insulation." Amos looked at some report on CNN about missing planes, then said, "So, yes, you could say Egg took this ZEX tat seriously. And from what

I heard about him to this day, he is about the same as he was back then."

He drew a deep breath, nodding to himself. "I always heard that there was something real bad that the club did. I mean, most of us boys was just wild and wanted something to belong to. There was a rumor that some of them, well, done worse things. Don't know if Egg was a part of that or not.

"Shit, ZEX has been around since the 1950s. And it was since that time that bad things happened here in this town that went unsolved by the cops. But in the eighties was when I was in it. You and me, teacher, are 'bout the same age. You'd been in it if you was running with us."

Amos shuffled some newspapers on the table. "I heard after Egg got out of the service, he got on with the PD. Heard that when I was doing my first bit in the joint. Couldn't believe it then. Still can't believe he been there all these years. What is he, a sergeant?"

"I believe."

Outside, car doors slammed. Laddie barked. "The boy and Fran are home. I don't want to talk about this 'round him. But let me just say that it is a joke having Cromwell work a missing woman case. Fran even said so. He said if truth be known, Egg is probably the prime suspect himself. But you didn't hear it from me.

"Tell the boy you were here just to check on him. It will make his day. But teacher, I'd watch myself around Cromwell. Guess you know that. Don't surprise me none, him trying to pin something on you."

At the door, Uncle Fran nodded at me, grocery bag in hand. Every followed him inside.

"Hey, Mr. R.! I been wondering about you!" Every said, setting a sack of groceries on the nearby kitchen counter. "You picked up a case, huh?"

"Boooy," Amos wailed, "that none of your business. Mr..."

"Riordan."

"Mr. Riordan come by to check on you 'cause he cares. Show some respect."

"I'm sorry, Mr. R. All the kids at school miss you."

For a moment we all were quiet. Laddie barked. I asked Every what his plans were for the summer. And he said he was going to try to find a job, which his juvenile probation officer wanted him to do.

"I don't want you quitting school. Promise me that," I said.

"Yeah. I won't. But you ain't comin' back, are you, Mr. R.?"

"Not this year, anyway." More silence.

"Me and Terrance miss you." I thought I saw a tear shaping up. He took off toward the back of the trailer.

I shook Uncle Fran's hand.

Amos walked me to the door. "Teacher, be real careful. Egg is not someone even the worst of us would mess with."

52

PROBABLY NUCLEAR

A mos Stout had given me confidence that my gut feeling about Cromwell was correct. But knowing something and being able to do something about it were two very different things.

Sensei's encouragements helped, and the good Dr. Augustine's assessment of me being pulled into this incident by something paranormal was also good information.

But I doubted any of it would exonerate me of wrongdoing if Cromwell had his way.

It was early. Laddie and I headed to Chapwell Falls for some investigation of our own. Technically I had been warned not to leave town. But staying put wouldn't help me build a case to counterbalance the one Cromwell was building against me. Had Cromwell put some trace on my cell? I was not a techie, but knew there was some way to track a cell if you had a person's number.

I smelled the breeze. May was a good month in this part of the country. The humidity of summer hadn't set in. I put in a CD of the Mills Brothers and sang along to "The Glow-Worm." At the Aaron Burr Fork I turned onto the two-lane toward Deidre's.

~

CHAPWELL FALLS SEEMED MORE ALIVE WHEN WE ARRIVED; AT LEAST there were vehicles in the streets. I stopped at Mom and Pop's.

The door chimes rang out as I entered. Just like several days ago, Mom was at the front counter.

"Hello," I said, beaming as much as I could.

Mom nodded in a bothersome way. Pop appeared from behind the back curtain like before. He walked over to me and looked out at my Jeep and Laddie.

"Still got that dog?" he asked.

"I still haven't found who he belongs to."

Both waited as I retrieved a Diet Coke from the cooler and a Snickers bar from the shelf. Mom said, "Three dollars and twenty-eight cents."

"Can you tell me more about the train that comes in?" I asked Pop. "The one you mentioned the other day."

Mom immediately got a stay-out-of-it look on her face. Pop studied me for a moment. "Not much to tell," he said, behind his spectacles, eyes darting to the door. "You thinkin' that dog of yours might have found her way off one of the boxcars?"

"He," I said.

"He."

"The dog is a he," I said.

"Oh. Well. What do you want to know?"

Mom gave Pop a small shake of her head and shuffled something about behind the counter. "We don't know nothin' about that train, mister," she said, jumping in. "Only that it comes in late at night, stops to let off salvage or pick some up. We been told to stay inside because some of the cargo is poison."

"Nuclear," Pop said. "Or some hazardous cargo, that's what the sheriff said. Don't want no one near it."

The door chimes once again jingled. A boy walked in, possibly ten, but with the continence of a younger child. "What's you looking for this fine day, Billy Ray?" Pop said.

The boy pulled two ice cream bars out of the freezer and plopped them down on the counter near me, then placed an assortment of coins on the counter without saying anything.

Mom counted out the change. "Sorry, Billy Ray, you only have enough for one." His hair was tangled and needed a washing. There was a musty odor from his clothes.

"I'll spring for the other one," I said, forking over the extra change.

The boy quickly looked up at me, then walked out, unwrapping one of the ice creams.

Mom got a forlorn look, shook her head again, this time as if to say *pitiful child*. "You have a nice day, mister. And I hope you find a home for that pup," Pop said.

I had been dismissed. I took a swig of my Coke and walked out. Outside the boy was standing at Laddie's window, trying to stick part of the ice cream through to him.

Laddie was helping himself to licks through the partly open window. "He likes ice cream," I said. The boy kept the feeding up, unperturbed that I might scold him. Most kids his age should be cognitively developed enough to know you don't stick something into a person's car, especially if you don't know that person. Of course, if you are impulsive and have no training in boundaries, you do.

Laddie licked the last of bar. The kid stood and watched the dog, mesmerized, as Laddie cleaned himself with his tongue. I said, "You live around here?"

He unwrapped the second bar, took two large bites and started to send the bar through the window again. "He is probably okay now," I said.

An off-white, rusted pickup pulled into the next space over. From its cab came an order. "Boy!" For a second, the boy didn't turn, but kept staring at Laddie. "Boy!" the voice growled again.

"He found a new friend," I said. The man had on sunglasses and a hunting cap pulled down over his brow. "Get in here, boy!"

The kid obeyed the order and climbed in the truck. The man thumped the boy's ear.

I'd had one too many episodes with pickups. Was the driver Kelvin's friend from the diner? Or was he the man at the furniture store? I needed to sharpen my observation skills. He backed out. His truck backfired several times. He crossed through the intersection and up a hill.

I finished my Snickers, took a swig of the Coke and got in my Jeep. Another look-and-see at the depot was in order.

53

MISSING WOMEN AND NO CLUES

C romwell and Stephens-Christian contemplated the dry-erase board. On the left column were the names Margaret "Penny" Theriault, Carrie Lindsey, and Tara Ann Simon. Next to each name were the dates of disappearance. Penny was the first to disappear, in April one year ago, followed by Carrie and Tara this month. "He's getting hungrier," Stephens-Christian said.

"Especially since he is now jobless." Cromwell gave a devilish laugh.

Stephens-Christian shut the door and pulled out an ashtray from a drawer. He shook the pack and let a smoke pop out, then threw the pack over to Cromwell. Both men shared a light and took in the nicotine.

"Well, it's a fine mess you've got us into, Ollie," Cromwell said to the younger cop, showing a rare side of levity. "Three missing women and no clues, other than a faggot teacher who likes young girls."

Stephens-Christian sucked in another drag. "We've never asked for a warrant to search that place of his."

Cromwell flatulated. "Fucking pantywaist liberal judges in this county won't issue one." He scrolled down his cell phone screen, seeming to check something of importance, then texted someone.

"The blood on the washcloth from the condo should do it," Stephens-Christian said.

"Fucker admits it's his, though. It's too much of a coincidence that the man was in the condo. He's got some bullshit story about being with this Theriault woman the day before. And she's been missing more than a year."

"Well, technically, no crime has been committed, just women who are missing," the young cop said, trying to figure an angle. "I mean, we got no bodies or ransom requests. We got squat. No bodies, no case. All we got is this working theory."

"Direct physical evidence with the DNA of one of these young bitches would do it," the old cop said. Stephens-Christian flinched at the man's description of the missing women. In this college town, several missing women cases, all of young coeds—some had gone unsolved, as had two murder cases of young women.

The town had three colleges, so kids came and went. And if some student went missing, parents or friends would report it. Usually a kid would turn up, with an explanation that they'd taken off with a boyfriend or took a hiatus to Mexico.

Following Riordan being pegged as a suspect due his visit to the Johannsen condo, Cromwell had contacted reporter Cynthia Crystal. She'd obliged his request for a follow-up story about Riordan being named a person of interest in the missing woman case of a year ago.

Cromwell was surprised how cooperative the school administration had been in canning the teacher: no hearing or union intervention, the way these matters are usually handled.

"So what do we have?" Cromwell asked. "Three little beauties missing and a teacher who had visited the Johannsen condo, who claims he did so with the owner's niece. And let's not forget about our teacher's connection to that trail in town, the last known whereabouts of at least one and maybe two of our missing vics."

Stephens-Christian interjected that both Simon and Lindsey were employed by La Torea's. Another link. "But who reported the girls missing? Does Riordan have any connection to the restaurant?"

Cromwell looked at the names on the board. "One way to find out."

54

Seamy Types

B oth cops showed their IDs to the new hostess at the restaurant. "Just a minute, please," she said, putting a check by a name in the reservation book and leaving for a back room.

"How long can this place stay in business?" Stephens-Christian said, taking a gander at the mostly empty tables.

The hostess returned. "Mr. V. will be up in a minute. He asked me to seat you." Cromwell and Stephens-Christian followed her into a rectangular-shaped room with a long table. Both men took seats.

Cromwell watched the young woman exit. "Mr. V. knows how to pick his help."

Stephens-Christian opened up the folder with photos of Tara Ann Simon and Carrie Lindsey. "We need a photo of Margaret Theriault," he said.

"See if DMV in...what state was it? Tennessee or...Kentucky, might have something," Cromwell said. He knew for protocol's sake that should have been done last year, but then again, with the woman's aunt dead, who really cared?

Through the walls, dishes clanged and someone cursed. Quietly

Alfredo Vianellia took a seat across from the two men. He just nodded, having seen both before.

Cromwell began. "Mr. Vianellia. It is Vianellia, isn't it?"

"Yes."

"That's right, you told us that last time," Cromwell said. "An Irish name."

Vianellia didn't bat an eye at the man's snide remark. Stephens-Christian quickly took over from the older cop. "We aren't here to keep you from your business, sir; only that we need some clarification about two of your employees." He showed the man the photos of the women. Stephens-Christian continued to ask the questions. "Did either Tara Ann or Carrie have a boyfriend?"

Vianellia curtly said he didn't know and had already been asked that question.

Secondly, Stephens-Christian asked whether the girls were friends, to which Vianellia again responded that he did not know. Finally, Cromwell asked if the name Riordan meant anything to him. He showed the man Riordan's DMV photo.

"That guy was in this week, asking questions. I was in hurry. Thought he was one of you." Cromwell studied the man for a moment.

Some more dishes clanged. Vianellia looked at his Rolex.

"Thanks, sir," Stephens-Christian said. "Anything else, Detective?"

"I guess that's all. But if you think of anything, you will tell us."

"Like I said, I told you everything." All three men stood. Cromwell shook Vianellia's hand. The two cops followed the man out of the room.

At the hostess station two seamy types were standing, waiting to be seated. Like hounds watching prey, they bore down on her as she situated herself on a stool and crossed her legs. As Stephens-Christian passed by the men, he had a fleeting feeling about something, but let it pass. One of the men rolled a quarter over his knuckles. Cromwell followed the junior cop out, but not before giving one of the seamy types a light grab on his upper arm.

PART II

55

Young Girls Jog Alone

K elvin and Leon gassed up and headed for the blacktop. Even though they had been told that the takings were to be done by the illegals, they wanted to sample the merchandise themselves. Kelvin and the director of this operation, the sheriff, had said the girls had no families, so no one would be checking on them.

Leon had heard that the kidnapping of the woman last year went badly. He undid the cap of the whiskey flask with his teeth, took a swig, and passed it over to Kelvin. "We ain't going to get into trouble with the sheriff, is we, K.?"

Kelvin shook off the first shudderings of the alcohol. "Fuck that old man. We do what we want. Anyway, he is the law and if we want, all we have to do is tell on that fat fuck. And he is history."

Leon hooted out a laugh and took back the flask. The two drove toward the city. It was still early evening. They had a van, a rusted-out Econoline, 1970s vintage, the same one used for the other takings and the one he'd kept in storage at Clyde's salvage yard just for these special occasions. The same yard, now closed, where the woman's Focus from last year had been taken.

The snatching game, as Kelvin had come to call the kidnappings, had to be done just at the right time. He had told Leon that most women didn't bother to look around when they were out. Young girls jogged alone, at all times of the day and night. Housewives shopped and were more concerned with putting their groceries in their cars than paying attention to who was standing behind them. And all were preoccupied with their smartphones, unaware of their surroundings.

56

He was Part of a Team

Kelvin parked the van off the grocery store lot. "We can get a better view from here," he said, easing back in the captain's chair and surveying the area. It was dusk.

Leon surveyed the parking lot too. *He was part of a team. The sheriff had said that this was business.*

A sedan drove by. An older couple looked at the two men in the van.

Despite spending the entire day getting up the courage to do this thing, they hadn't even talked about how they would nab the victim. Would they ask her a question or just grab her? He put the van in gear and let it ease down the small incline toward the main parking lot. The old couple had driven by and parked in the handicap space. Both were hobbling up to the supermarket door.

Kelvin felt his heart thump. This boob Leon was stupid, which served him well, because he never seemed to get uptight. Although he did seem more jittery tonight. Leon didn't have all the things at stake that he had, like people asking about his missing wife and her busybody mother and nosey cousin.

Kelvin let the van move itself slowly toward the space one spot over from a Camry. A woman, brunette, got out and hurriedly went into the store, talking on her cell phone. They'd wait until she returned.

57

A HUFFY VOICE ANSWERED

Cromwell hated working late nights. It was Saturday. He was getting too old for all this. He talked himself into believing that his two marriages had gone belly-up due to his rotten schedule, but he knew the reality was that he had been abusive to his wives, not so much physically as emotionally.

The first one couldn't give him a son, so he ditched her. The second one tried, but got fat, so he got rid of her, too. Basically all women were whores and the few that weren't, well, they couldn't understand a man like him. He wasn't a go-to-bed-early type of guy. After this shift was up, he'd drive down to The Ambrosia and pay for table dances.

He stared at the board that still showed the names of the missing women. If they didn't conclude this thing soon, outside help would be called in and that would mean real trouble.

"Let's put a wrap on this thing for the night, Detective," he said to Stephens-Christian. "I hadn't planned to spend all day doing paper-work." He reminded himself to thank the kid for all the tidy house-keeping, dotting all the i's and crossing all the t's.

"I'll stick around and get back with the Colorado family about our newest victim," Stephens-Christian said.

"Suit yourself." Cromwell groaned and waved a goodbye. "Don't stay too long. You don't want to keep that young snatch at home wanting it," he said. Stephens-Christian forced out a smile.

At the street, Cromwell lit up and walked across the lot to his Buick. There needed to be some tying up of loose ends. He leaned against his car and flicked open a burner phone and dialed. On the other end a huffy voice answered.

58

Siren Eyes Calling

Cromwell shut his phone and stamped out the cigarette. "Idiot," he said out loud. The small-time sheriff on the other end was going to fuck up the whole deal. He'd ordered him to move the cache. He got in his Buick and turned on the oldies station, feeling inside his coat pocket for his smartphone. He turned it off for the time being. He'd check to verify whether he'd ever made a call to that boob in Chapwell Falls. Fucking world, every move is trackable.

The Ambrosia was the best club in town. And the dancers he'd come to know liked it when he showed them his badge. He parked, put the pack of Basics in his coat pocket, and walked up.

The bouncer at the door waved him on through, knowing that it was good to have a cop around, despite the fact that he was as much into the girls as every other deviant in the place. "Good to see ya again, Detective," the bulb-headed bouncer called out. "Table up front just for you."

The cop surveyed the surroundings for anyone familiar. He took the table that bumped up against the runway. On the floor was a young thing spinning on the pole to some bumping and grinding music. She gave him a come-hither look and let her legs spindle down the pole. She flipped back her hair and sat cross-legged, with the pole between her thighs.

Her contorted position revealed a tattoo of a skull. Cromwell thought the marking odd. But never mind, he wasn't at the place for any kind of investigation. He scratched his own tattoo unconsciously. A lanky cocktail waitress with three-inch heels and flowing red locks touched him on the shoulder.

He inhaled her.

"Glad you could drop by," she said. "You been a stranger lately." He tucked ten dollars in her garter. She told him he was cute, then skirted slowly away, telling him she'd return to give him a table dance.

The dancer pulled herself up the pole and gave one last sweeping look at the audience, which clapped lazily at her performance, but only at the disk jockey's prompting.

On the runway waiting to be introduced stood a buxom newcomer. "And ladies and gentlemen, help me welcome Mary from St. Montrose. She's kind of shy. Let's give her a big hand."

The new girl stepped out onto the walkway, head bowed slightly. She had on a plaid Catholic-schoolgirl skirt, strap heels, and a tie-around blouse, which she dropped at Cromwell's feet, exposing her gyrating pasties. She bent over and he reached up and deposited ten dollars in her stocking. At the table directly behind him, two drunks yelled something about the color of the girl's nipples. The bouncer immediately moved in on them; his presence caused them to hold up two five-dollar bills.

Cromwell motioned a girl over who had just gotten off the runway and was carrying a cocktail tray.

"What'll it be, handsome?"

He wanted to say, "Come home with me, sweet thing," but knew the rules, which required any extras, such as behind-the-scenes arrangements, to be set up through the bouncers.

She set the tray down. "Table dance, handsome?"

He stuffed twenty dollars into her garter and nodded yes. Another girl quickly brought up the rear and picked up the tray. He stretched out his stubby legs and perused the woman's crevices as she began to grind to the music. The girl danced around him, her siren eyes mesmerizing.

59

BEAUTIFUL

T he woman set her purse in the grocery cart and dialed a
number on her cell phone as she pushed the cart into the
parking lot. Leon and Kelvin sat still as cats ready to pounce.
"Wait till she hangs up that fucking phone," Kelvin said. He could tell
Leon was getting excited. The woman shut the phone and pushed the
cart toward her car. "Now, K.?" Leon asked.

"Go," Kelvin said.

Leon took a deep breath and opened the passenger door, then
slowly slid open the side door as if he were getting something out. The
woman busily set the bags in her trunk, oblivious to it all.

Kelvin slowly backed the van out and let it drift back to the trunk
of the woman's car. Leon followed the van back. As she set the last bag
in and shut the trunk, Leon took a quick look around. No one. The
woman looked up. Her eyes met Leon's. She immediately sensed that
something was wrong and drew back, but it was too late. Leon hit her
across the chin, which knocked her back onto her car. He didn't look
around. From inside the van Kelvin yelled, "Come on, man, get her in
here!"

She groaned and tried to get up. He picked her up like a sack of groceries and threw her in the back of the van, dazed. A car entered the lot. "Come on, man, get in," Kelvin yelled.

Leon hopped in the back, slamming the van door. "No, no," she whimpered. Leon slapped her across the face. "Shut up," he said.

"Quiet, man," Kelvin said, backing out. "Be cool!"

Before Kelvin got the van out of the lot, Leon had the woman's sandals off and was on top of her, pulling at her blouse. She tried to struggle. He turned her over and bound her hands together with duct tape. He tore off a shorter piece and plastered it across her mouth. She was somewhere between consciousness and passing out. "Throw out the fucking cell she has," Kelvin ordered.

Leon pitched out the contraption, and hopped up to the front seat, panting. He grabbed the flask and took a swig, let the liquor drift down his throat, then yelled out the window, "Hee haw! We gots a catch!"

"Shut the fuck up, you idiot!"

Kelvin slowed down at the stoplight and searched in the rearview mirror for any signs of cops or good Samaritans. The woman was whimpering.

Leon stared at her thighs. "Where we going to take her? She is all ours, right?"

Kelvin nodded and sped up through the light. "County Road 225."

60

This Time Some Investigating

It was Saturday. I had parked the Jeep and waited for nightfall. The depot looked unoccupied, just as it had been several days ago. "This time, boy, we are going to do some inside investigating," I told Laddie. The cicadas began their nightly serenades, too early for this time of year. How long had it been since they last visited? I tucked my cell under the car seat, turning it off, opening the door. Laddie bounded out.

I did a creep-up up the hillside with my Eveready flashlight. Along the tracks were several candy bar wrappers. I couldn't remember if they were there last time I'd visited. Laddie caught up with me and sniffed for leftovers. Other than lights from scattered homes in the village across the river, there was no sign of life.

I hadn't bothered to stop at Deidre's on the way in. I feared the worse.

I flashed the light on the depot door and walked up the ramp. Laddie followed, not bothering to revisit the site of the buried clothing. The deadbolt, which I'd seen Kelvin unlock from my hiding place of a couple of days ago, had another deadbolt resting above it.

Laddie and I again took the porch around the building to the rear. I flashed a look down the wall to the window where I had entered my previous trip here. A board had been nailed up to prevent reentry. I listened for any traffic coming up the hillside. Laddie whined and, just like our last visit here, he clawed at the back door.

I had forgotten the crowbar. I heaved my shoulder into the board and heard a slight crack. Five, six more times, then the board loosened. Laddie tried to straddle the wall on his hind legs. "Back, boy."

I pushed the two-by-four into the building and eased myself through the window. Laddie barked. I reached back and pulled him up, all fifty-plus pounds of him. He sniffed his way around the periphery of the inside, corner to corner. He suddenly stopped and began clawing at the floor. He'd found a latch nearly meshed with the flooring. I flashed the light one more time around the whole area, then lifted up the small door. An accordion stair with wide steps fell downward.

Cold air gusted up the shaft. Twelve or so steps down into the darkness. I opted to let Laddie be the brave one. "Go on, boy." He slowly took the first step, then scrambled the rest of the way down. I followed, my flashlight's beam steering the way. At the bottom I felt along a brick wall to my right. Laddie disappeared into the darkness, but I could hear his whines close by.

I flashed the light at the floor first, then to the walls on both sides of me. This was definitely a storage area. Some wooden doors with locks lined the right side of the hallway. Ten yards or so down the narrow corridor, Laddie sniffed, then clawed at one of the doors.

The dankness gave me a shiver. Laddie bade me to help. I shined light on his discovery. This door only had a lift-up-like latch. I quietly raised it. Laddie moved through the door as I carefully eased it open.

At a time like this, a weapon, even my crowbar, would have settled my jitters. Laddie stopped just inside the room, sniffing. The room was cold and appeared empty, except for a small bed. Dangling from the four bedposts were nylon ropes. Immediately Deidre came to mind, and then came a memory of Kelvin unlocking the depot front door.

Laddie exited to the hallway, then stopped at the fourth door. I followed and lifted the latch, trying to jimmy it against a deadbolt. No luck. I peeped through the fingernail-sized keyhole into darkness.

Laddie sniffed his way to the last door. I followed. At that door I again lifted up on the latch. Locked with a deadbolt, too. "Hello," I yelled.

I waited for some response. A new smell overtook me, medicinal, not customary for a storage cellar. "Hello," I called out again. Laddie sat. "What do you think, boy?"

I heard a stir from inside, then, "Help!"

"Hello," I yelled. Laddie barked, then took off toward the stairway.

"Can you open the door?" I said, pulling up on the latch. Then a sharp crack to the back of my skull and blackness.

61

CALLUSED HANDS

T raffic had thinned on the expressway. Leon's eyes were glazed over from the whiskey. Kelvin grabbed the flask and took two quick swigs. A sign read "Carrolton Lake Preserve ~ 1 Mile." Traffic thinned even more.

The woman's cries died down to whimpers. Kelvin signaled left for County Road 225. He slowed, continuing to check in the rearview mirror from time to time.

"This where we took your old lady," Leon said, as if the killing were but a vague memory.

"Of course it is, you fuck," Kelvin said. "Billy Bad-Sheriff says no one ever looks out here for anything." He slowed. The road narrowed. He turned onto a gravel road and stopped at a gate. "Open it up," he said to Leon.

Leon stumbled out of the van, hobbled over to the gate, and undid a wire hitch. He moved the gate back. Kelvin eased the van over the cattle guard. "Hook it back up," he ordered.

The woman tried to calm herself and listen, to try to figure out where she was, but all she heard was the crackle of the gravel. Minutes later, the passenger door opened and slammed shut. The van side-door slid open. Her mouth was covered with the duct tape. Her wrists and ankles bound. Then she was being dragged out.

His hands were callused. She felt faint. Could she pass out? Was this a dream?

She could smell the alcohol and tobacco as both men got close. She could hear tree frogs with their mating calls. She wanted to beg, but knew it wasn't likely to do any good. Would they take money? It wasn't money they were after, she knew that. At the top of the small knoll in a clearing was a small shed. It was cold. The door to the shed was opened. She was pushed inside.

AFTER BOTH FINISHED WITH HER, SHE LAY, TRYING TO CRY. BUT THE tears wouldn't come. She breathed deeply so she wouldn't lose consciousness. They were just outside the cabin, laughing, still drinking their whiskey, smoking. She needed to block out what had just happened and figure out what to do.

Slowly, and as quietly as she could manage, she got up. She slipped on her skirt and blouse and put on her sandals. She had to get out of this place. They would kill her.

The window, a few feet away, was open several inches. She tiptoed over to it, slowly lifting it, not daring to look around. Up and then out. A small shrub broke her fall and muffled the noise. She caught her breath. So far, so good. She crept down the hill. Soon they would check on her. She crept deeper into the night. Her heart pounded. Keep going, she told herself.

Then from the shed, a roar, which echoed through the trees. "Bitch is gone!"

She fell down the hillside through some briers. *Please*, she prayed, *let me get away.*

She could hear them behind her, not close, but on her trail. She fell, over and over. A sandal came off. Her skirt tore. Now she was spinning in air. She closed her eyes. From high above her, her eyes still closed, she could hear one call out; then the breath went out of her.

Both men stood in the night air and stared out into the darkness. Both listened for any sign of life below. "Should we check it out?" Leon asked.

"She's dead," Kelvin said. "That's too long a drop for anyone to survive. By morning, the coyotes will be eating her for breakfast. Don't say nothin' to that fat shit sheriff about this, understand?"

Leon followed the bigger man up the incline. He was thinking about Kelvin's wife, Dee.

Kelvin had strangled her at their home. That had been several weeks ago. He had called Leon to help move her body and together they had taken her to this place and buried her, just down from the shed. Both men were silent during their climb to the shed. The flask was drained.

"Let's take a gander at the depot," Kelvin said. "Make sure our product is ready."

62

I Called Out

I awoke in a daze, trying to get my bearings.

"Laddie." My voice was scratchy. I tried to rise up to scout for the dog. Nothing in the room but me. Nylon bindings secured my hands behind me; my ankles were tied together with a rope, which ran to the bedpost. For the time being, unless the divine intervened, I was helpless and going nowhere.

If Kelvin had appeared at the door, I wouldn't have been surprised. My thoughts went to Laddie. The dog had taken off just before I was knocked out.

"Laddie," I called out again. No scratching or whimpering at the door.

What would James Bond do?

63

HE FLASHED HIS BADGE

Cromwell was drunk enough that he should have called a cab, but instead, he climbed into his Buick and headed home. He had spent more than he should have on dancers, but they served their purpose. The streets were empty. He stopped at the red light and took out a smoke. The light changed.

To his right, on the sidewalk, a young woman was walking, her arms folded around her in typical victim posture. He signaled, crossed lanes, and pulled over just in front of her. She was twenty if a day. He stopped and got out. She picked up her gait. Cromwell stepped in front of her and flashed his badge. She froze.

"Got some ID?" he said. For a moment she looked puzzled, but then let her black imitation leather purse drop off her shoulder. She dug inside and produced a billfold. Cromwell took a glance around to check for any cherry tops. He looked at her driver's license.

"This says you are twenty-one. Guess you don't have a curfew, do you?" She gave him a quick smile. He could feel himself getting excited at the interrogation.

"What is this about?" she asked, with a degree of assertiveness in her voice.

He moved a little closer to her. She was petite, with almond eyes, and underneath those tight jeans he was certain had quite a nice body. "We've had reports of a rapist in the area."

The woman looked up and down the empty street. "Oh. I didn't know."

"I'm going to have you come with me and I'll drop you where you want to go. Sally, is it?"

The woman put her billfold back in her purse, looked up and down the street again, wondering if this middle-aged, overweight guy really was a cop.

"Oh, I don't live too far away. I'll be fine. But thanks anyway." She began to walk away, which only incensed Cromwell.

"Ma'am, I'm not going to let you walk away with this man loose. I am going to have to insist that you come with me."

Again she looked around. The street was still empty. Cromwell opened the passenger door. "Please," he said.

She sighed as she got in.

He felt the urge intensify as he moved around to the driver's side. No one on the streets to say they had seen him. She hadn't even read his license plate, or for that matter even looked at his badge number.

He got in. He'd have to warm her up some. He offered her a cigarette. She refused. "Now, you said you live nearby."

"Just off The Circle," she said pointing.

At the next alley, he turned in. She quickly looked behind her and frantically said, "What are you doing?"

He pulled the car down in front of a Dumpster. She grabbed for the door handle. Cromwell pulled out his handcuffs and quickly snapped one over her left wrist. She struggled with the door with her right hand. He pulled her hair and blared out, "This can be quick or we can do it the hard way, understand? Understand?"

She nodded.

Ten minutes later, he threw her clothes out next to the Dumpster, undid the cuffs, and told her that if she reported what happened he would hunt her down. She sorted out her garments and spit out what she could of him.

Cromwell eyeballed his rearview mirror to make sure the woman hadn't produced a cell phone and snapped a photo of his vehicle.

64

I was Attacked by One of You

S tephens-Christian had stayed at the office after his mentor departed for the evening. He stared at the dry-erase board with the victims' names scribbled in red. He wrote out what he knew on his legal pad.

Three missing women; all single; one from last year, the other two more recently; all without any relatives locally; two with the same place of employment; the one from last year had been seen with a dog. All within the age range of twenty to thirty.

He then wrote out aspects about the newest missing person, a woman in Chapwell Falls, reported by her mother in nearby Brookdale —Deidre something, cousin of the schoolteacher suspect.

He scribbled out "connection to others?"

He listed the only suspect's characteristics: single, fired teacher, history of too-familiar relations with a female student. But was that accurate? According to Cromwell it was. The suspect had no family residing in the area, except the mother of the last missing person. He wrote "dog" next to Riordan's name, with a question mark.

Since he had been Cromwell's understudy, he had come to realize his boss was becoming nothing but an old, burned-out cop, angry at life. Stephens-Christian was uncomfortable with the man's rush to judge the teacher.

The DNA on the swab of Riordan's mouth would conclude that the blood on the towel at Margaret Johannsen's residence was his. Riordan had said as much. But whose blood was splattered on the wall in the Johannsen condo from last year? That evidence, along with hair samples from the condo bathroom, had been catalogued a year earlier when the Theriault woman was reported missing.

Stephens-Christian hadn't checked in the evidence room to verify whether the evidence still existed. Would it be degraded by now? The reality was that he didn't understand all the processing features of DNA testing. Could you compare hair DNA to blood DNA for a match? All the physical evidence needed to be preserved, he knew that much.

He switched off the overhead light and headed to his car. He texted his wife, alerting her he was on the way home. The street was empty except for a sweeper scooping up trash. A clean street was a work of art, he thought. He stopped at a traffic light. Just then a figure stumbled out of an alleyway. He pulled over. She immediately backed up against a department store window, then turned and began a fast stride away.

"Hold up, ma'am," he yelled. He got out, leaving the sedan door open. He quickly caught up to her, but she turned and swung her purse into him. He deflected the blow. From his jacket he pulled out his badge.

"No," she screamed. She again swung the purse at him.

"Hold on, miss. I'm a police officer," he said. She tried to wrestle loose. He lightly pushed her up against the store window. She kicked him in the ankle, then spit on him. Stephens-Christian backed up. The girl fell to the concrete and began weeping. A black-and-white pulled up.

Stephens-Christian threw out his badge to the uniforms. "She was stumbling out of the alley," he said, nodding in her direction. The two cops looked at her, then at Stephens-Christian.

"You need us to call it in?" the cop in the look-out position asked.

Stephens-Christian took a deep breath. "I'll find out what's going on with her, and if I need to, I will. Thanks."

"I was attacked by one of you," she sobbed.

65

THE GIRL DESCRIBED HER ATTACKER

The girl graphically described her attacker, down to the ZEX tattoo.

Afterward, Stephens-Christian knew he had a choice to make. He'd long felt that his partner had problems. For the girl to come up with such an accurate account of Cromwell's dress, even his tattoo, she had to have been near him at the very least. She hadn't claimed rape, only fellatio.

He helped her up and grasped her elbow. She sniffled. He steered her into the passenger side and sat her down. Minutes later they were edging down her street of brownstones, which, given her age, he was sure was out of her price league. His first thought, unfortunately, was not to follow protocol and take her to the ER for an examination, but to protect one of his own.

"Parents' place, miss?" he asked, as she pointed where to pull over. She nodded. He did a quick Q and A, with the intent of lightly persuading her to hold off on any rash moves. "What do you want me to do, ma'am? We have several choices here." She continued sniffling, half opening the door. A mist fell.

She looked at Stephens-Christian, then down the street, then up the steps at her home, and asked, "Do you have a card?"

He was about to offer her one of his, but said, "No. If you want to call this in, talk to your parents and then call 911." She got out.

On the ride home, he contemplated taking the short detour to Cromwell's. Should he confront the cop, or wait? Chances were the girl wouldn't make a report. Her parents, though? The girl couldn't trace his car or him to the incident, which would give him time to figure out what to do about Cromwell.

Stephens-Christian pushed the remote to open his garage door. He would let the remaining hours of the night take care of itself with his wife's cheesecake and a peek in at his sleeping daughter.

66

YOU BAD MAN

I lay bound and listened to my surroundings; a whimper from an adjoining cellar room. Rooks cawing. Whoever had knocked me out and decided to tie me up had plans to teach me a lesson, albeit a perverted one. The nylon tie dug deeper when I tried to manipulate the bindings. Finally I heard some commotion from the room next to me. Had that been where the voice had come from? What was being said? A door creaked open. I waited.

"Shut up" came from the hallway, then silence. The voice was authoritarian, but not gravelly like Kelvin's. Even if Laddie were with me, I knew he was no Rin Tin Tin and wouldn't have a clue about how to gnaw off my bindings. I heard a thump. Was it the trapdoor to the depot shutting? Was someone coming or going?

I had heard about people channeling energy during inopportune times to get out of tight fixes. If only I could get a sudden surge of adrenaline. According to Dr. Augustine, I was an empath. But seemingly one with no apparent special powers except how to be suckered into following a ghost's wild-goose chase. Will the real Penny please stand up?

In the hallway there was some more shuffling. I tilted my chin toward the keyhole and waited. The latch moved and then the door squeaked open. Two small pupils stared at me. A leash extended out from his fingers and around the edge of the wall. The figure yanked the leash. Laddie appeared. The dog squealed with excitement at the sight of me.

A boy stepped inside and pulled Laddie through the doorway. He gaped at me, then took a step over. Laddie bolted to me, but the boy yanked the leash back.

"You stay, dog!" he commanded.

"Hey, dude," I said, as brightly as I could. He just stared. He looked familiar. *The boy from Mom and Pop's?* "Can you help me out of this?" I said.

The boy stepped up to the cot. "You have ice cream?" he asked.

"Untie me and you and I will go get you some."

He then shot out some order to Laddie in what appeared to be some type of rhythmical tongue.

"Betta you, Betta too, Betta do, symbolo moo." He cowered down a stare at me. He poked my chest. The kid needed a bath. Again, "Betta you, Betta too, Betta do, symbolo moo."

Clangs. Gibberish. But when in Rome. "Mecom door, Mecom roar, dem dol dem some more," I called out.

The boy froze. "Mecom door, Mecom roar, dem dol dem some more," I chanted, this time looking him straight in the eye.

My response seemed at first to confuse him. But on my third go-round, he stepped back from my cot. I lowered my voice an octave. I repeated the chant, not remembering exactly what it was I had dreamed up. And then yelled out, "Untie this rope, young dude. And let's go get some ice cream."

Laddie barked. The boy darted a glance at the doorway.

"Undo this rope, young man, and I'll buy you some ice cream." I said, this time nodding.

The boy bent over. Without hesitation he began untying the nylon binding.

67

It Was a Blood-Brother Thing

Stephens-Christian paced the small cubicle until his mentor waltzed in, sipping his customary morning brew. The first thing out of his mouth, Stephens-Christian knew, would be some vulgar comment or question about whether he'd gotten any from his "old lady" last night.

"You and your little sweetness have an all-nighter, S.C.?" he said, lumbering into the cubicle. "I hate fucking working on Sundays." Stephens-Christian might have left any inquiries about the night before and the woman in distress to a later date, but the old cop's sarcasm was beginning to wear thin.

"Just another night," the young cop said, trying to withhold any direct affront. "But I did have an interesting encounter after you left and before I made it home."

Stephens-Christian waited for a response. "We need to check out that faggot teacher again," Cromwell said, not looking up from the legal pad. "We need to push him more."

Stephens-Christian took a sip out of his coffee. The man had heard him, he was certain. "I said, last night I had an interesting encounter."

Cromwell scooted his chair back and looked up. "I hope it had something to do with all this shit that we have in front of us."

Stephens-Christian sat down. He bounced the pencil eraser several times. "I hope it doesn't."

Cromwell glared up. "What is it?" he said, challenging Stephens-Christian to spit out whatever it was that was irritating him.

The younger cop breathed in deeply. "Well, I was headed home, and at Broadmore and Tenth I came upon a woman. One of our homey hookers stumbling out for the last score of the evening, or so I thought. So I pulled over."

Cromwell bent himself over the paperwork on the desk, quickly disavowing his interest. "Anyway. The woman had been assaulted."

Cromwell nodded indifferently again and followed with a chuckle. "Big surprise. One of our fine ladies of the evening," he said, scribbling something with the pencil that Stephens-Christian had discarded.

"Not quite. She said that she had been assaulted by a cop."

"Who did she say assaulted her, Thomas?" Cromwell said, with the doubt of a dad who was about to hear a tall tale.

Stephens-Christian got up, fidgeted with some loose change in his pocket, then walked up to the dry-erase board. He hesitated before turning around and dropping the woman's description of the perp.

"The cop had a tattoo, uh, just like yours."

Stephens-Christian waited for his partner to glance up and defend himself. But the man just grunted as if the connection to him or any cop was purely coincidental. Stephens-Christian took his seat at his desk, across from his partner.

Cromwell got up, walked over to the coffee pot, and poured himself a refill. He poured a second cup and brought both back to the table and set one in front of the young cop.

"A tattoo like mine, you say." The seasoned cop stared into his partner as if he was about to begin an interrogation of his own. "So what do you think, Thomas? You think it was me?

"I was in a club, when I was a teenager. Bunch of us got these tats. Kind of a blood-brother thing. Still some of the old boys around. Nothing would surprise me about them. One of them probably got some dime-store police ID he flashed the whore. I'll check around. This so-called abused woman get any badge number, or vehicle make or model this supposed cop was driving?"

Stephens-Christian again walked up to the board. He wasn't up to confronting the man, despite his gut feeling that the old cop probably did assault the young woman. "Uh, just a coincidence, I guess," he said.

"Lots of those in our business, Thomas."

68

I Stepped Up the Stairway

I shook off the ropes. Laddie jumped up on the cot. The boy stood, seemingly half waiting for another chant from me.

I moved to the doorway. Laddie followed. The boy stayed behind, staring at the cot. The hallway was empty and dark. The door to the room where the "help" came from was open. I checked inside. It was empty. I edged along the wall in the darkness. Every few feet I stopped and listened. Nothing.

I stepped up the stairway and listened for anything topside. Was it morning? The door creaked as I pushed it up. Laddie whined. I stepped back down and heaved him up enough so he could walk up to the top.

The depot was empty. Sunlight was streaming through the cracks in the boarded-up windows.

69

WE NEED TO FIX OUR TEACHER BOY

Cromwell harangued on about his pension, dismissing Stephens-Christian's questioning about the assault on the young woman. He had hoped the old cop would oblige him with a confession that he had, in fact, committed the assault due to some lack of judgment. But nothing.

"Let's do another drive-by to that faggot teacher's dive," Cromwell chuckled. "He should be in this morning, unless he's at confession. If he ain't in, we're going to get a warrant," he said, flipping out a cigarette from his pack.

Stephens-Christian drove and listened as the man bellowed on about how the case needed to be closed before the suits brought in outside help. "In my day, just the fact that this teacher boy had relations with his students would have been enough to book him for probable cause."

"Boss, I don't figure it that way," he finally said, timing his interjection just as he pulled up in front of Riordan's. The old cop didn't offer any rebuttal, but stared at the younger cop. Cromwell threw out the smoke he'd just lit. The two walked into the building and up the two flights of stairs to Riordan's apartment.

Cromwell pounded on the door three times, then another three times.

"Open up, Riordan, if you're in there," Cromwell called out loudly, enough so the door across the hallway opened. A small figure peered out, then quickly closed the door.

"Check and see if the guy's car is parked across in the university lot," Cromwell said. "And if not, check in the back of the building. Our boy might try to be inconspicuous, parking away from this place."

Stephens-Christian disappeared down the stairway. Cromwell tried the knob. *Locked.* He waited until he was certain the junior cop was gone and the old lady had shut her door, then took out the lock-pick case. Quickly he selected the right tool, slipped the small metal piece into the lock, and with a twist, opened the door.

Inside he surveyed the surroundings. Pig tried to make friends, but was shooed away with a light foot jab. On earlier visits he hadn't noticed how spartan Riordan kept his surroundings; just the bare essentials. Where would Riordan hide the murder weapon?

He moved quickly into the bedroom and slowly opened the closet door. On the shelf were scattered assortments of shirts, sweats, and boxes. There was a garbage bag on one shelf. *Probably the teacher's old clothes.* He didn't look in it. He pulled a cell phone box down. Just some cardboard and a user's guide inside.

Out of one of his coat pockets he pulled a nylon rope; out of another, some blue panties; "Courtesy," he said, smiling to himself, "of Tara Simon." He coiled the thick nylon like a snake and situated it in the box and laid the panties atop it. Then he closed the closet. He made it to the front door and met a startled Stephens-Christian, just entering.

"What's going on, boss?" It was the second time Stephens-Christian had used "boss," which was uncharacteristic for him. Since the talk about the assault the previous night, the young cop had become more deferential.

"That was quick."

Stephens-Christian waited for an explanation about why Cromwell had entered the apartment without an invitation.

"Just making sure our faggot teacher wasn't hiding under the bed," Cromwell said. "Stupid teacher didn't lock his door. Nothing in there.

Faggot's probably out buying a suitcase for his getaway. We'll check later."

In the sedan, each cop waited for the other to say something.

70

THEY GUESSED SHE WAS A HIKER

L eon stood over the two women calf-roped and in gunny-sacks on the floor. He was alone with them. The sheriff had brought them to his place overnight from the depot. That was after the sheriff had knocked out the trespasser schoolteacher and tied him up. They'd have to do away with him. Put him where they'd buried Kelvin's wife. Neither he nor Kelvin had mentioned the kidnapping of the woman they'd taken from the grocery store. If Kelvin was right, she'd been dinner for the coyotes.

The earlier nabbings had been pulled off like clockwork, the women shipped off to points south. Then after those two, there had been the woman from out of town, who'd struggled so hard she had to be wasted, the woman with the dog.

Cromwell, the city cop who put the whole operation together, claimed they needed to change the distribution from rail to truck. The interstate was nearby. Only drawback was that truckers were always on the alert for trafficking women. But then again, it shouldn't be too hard to get some desperate long-distance hauler to cooperate, especially if the price was right.

The two women in the gunnysacks whimpered. He could feel their terror. He rolled one woman over onto her back. Just then, he heard a car pull into the driveway. Kelvin. Kelvin would stay with the merchandise while he went to look for his nephew.

71

I GOT MY BEARINGS

No trucks, cars, or people were outside the depot. My rescuer stayed behind. I figured the time to be midmorning and that his dad, Leon, or whatever the bubba's name was, would be returning for him.

Laddie took off down the ramp and darted around the corner of the building. A faint smell of fish blew up from downstream. Laddie joined me at my Jeep. I checked under the mat where I usually dropped my keys. Nothing. Laddie begged to hop in. My Jeep had obviously been spotted, but not moved. It was only a matter of time.

I pulled the spare set from the inside of a small magnetic bumper box. Gas enough to get out of here. But where to? How long had this whole nightmare been going on? Weeks since I had met Penny on the Trail. One week since Principal Rivy had fired me, and at least that long since that fat shit Cromwell had been on my tail.

Oddly, I was famished. I hadn't seen any fast food the last time through town. I checked my console for cash, then for my cell under the seat. I set it atop the console, quickly scrolling for messages. Only a call from Alice. In desperate times, I had no one to call. I'd stop at Mom and Pop's. Would they be open on a Sunday? Was it Sunday?

~

AT MOM AND POP'S PLACE I LEFT LADDIE IN THE JEEP AND WALKED
through the doorway to an empty store. Mom came out from the back
room and got shaky when she saw me. But then again, I was gaunt-
eyed and smelled. She called for Pop. "We are closed until noon," she
said.

"You still hanging around our little town, doctor?" Pop said, setting
a Coke bottle down, then burping. "Only thing that helps my acid
reflex. It's okay, Mom, looks like the doctor just needs some attending
to."

Mom went over to the door, looked out, then busied herself
straightening merchandise.

"Uh, I was wondering if you remember that little boy who was in
here the last time I was."

"Best I remember, that was Leon Whatley's boy."

He walked over to the cooler, pulled out a bottle, and handed it to
me. He motioned me toward the back of the store, seemingly to get me
away from Mom. I followed him to the small office.

I stood. He sat and took a gulp. "By now, doctor, I'm guessing you
are on to something in our little hamlet."

I waited. A normal interaction would have me telling Pop I had
been knocked out and escaped from a dungeon where I believed
missing women were kept. And would Pop call the police? I knew this
town, and guessed Pop would not be cooperative.

He confirmed my suspicions. "I wish I could help you out. But if
you know what's good for you and that hound out there, the both of
you will chalk up this place to a bad experience and hightail it out of
here."

I took a chair nearby and scooted closer. "My cousin is the missing
schoolteacher here."

He nodded, empathetic-like. "I seen her, but never got to know her
any."

A short bark, then three longer ones, came from outside.

"You are being summoned. Sometimes canines have a sixth sense
about things. Better listen to your friend and go back where you came
from." Mom poked her head into the room with a frightened look.

In a different time, Pop would have laid out to me his assessment of what was going on in this town. But he was scared. I took the hint, and bid him good day.

Laddie was jumping from the front seat to the back when I arrived, and nipping at the glass toward a familiar figure. Cutting across the street and into an alleyway was my rescuer, chanting to himself.

72

CALLING THE LITTLE SQUEEZE

Back from planting evidence at Riordan's, Cromwell busied himself with examining a file of old cases. His own record-keeping system, he had told the young cop several years ago. "Keeps me from having to be married to that fucking computer." He got up, grunted, and said, "I got to drain the lizard."

Stephens-Christian had the eerie feeling the old guy was planning something sinister. If he had assaulted the woman, what was he capable of? Nearing retirement and alone in the world might breed desperation in a man.

The young cop contemplated the victim list again. Cromwell had left his file open to the Gibbons-Fein murders. He remembered the killings, two coeds at the college who were strangled with nylon ropes. Case unsolved. He returned to his desk and called his wife, just to vent about his day. Although he said nothing specific about Cromwell, his young wife sensed his misgivings enough for her to give him a cautionary, "Be careful."

He hung up, saying to her, "I don't know what to do, but I'll figure it out," as Cromwell entered the room.

"Calling the little squeeze?" Cromwell said, with a fiendish grin. "It's Sunday and you still got a chance to go to church."

73

Just in the Neighborhood

Both men called it quits at seven and parted to head to their respective homes, Stephens-Christian to a wife, an infant, a toddler, and babysitting duties, Cromwell to his customary night alone.

When the young cop yelled, "I'm home," he was greeted with instructions. "I shouldn't be long at Mom's. Just make sure Andrew is fed and changed before you put him down. You can read to Katherine. She should be fine. I'll be home by nine."

Stephens-Christian followed his directives, and by eight o'clock all was quiet. He sipped on a beer and channel-hopped with the remote to drown out thoughts of the day. A few minutes later he heard a knock on the back door and instinctively reached for his weapon. He remembered he'd already locked it away in the hallway closet, not useful for quick access, and not protocol for his line of work, but a demand his wife made of him, given their two young children.

Who drops by on a Sunday night? On the other side of the sliding glass a familiar figure stood, a bit disheveled, but par for the course. Stephens-Christian slid open the patio door.

"Sorry, guy. I had to take your alley in. It was closer than walking clear around to the street side. My car got a flat. My cell's out of charge. You were the closest phone in town. Need to call Triple A. You look surprised. Thought you'd have seen me on video with your new burglar-prevention camera."

"I need to get one."

"Never know. No cameras anywhere? You alone?"

"No cameras. And yeah, wife should be home in half an hour or so. Kids are asleep upstairs. Phone is in the kitchen," Stephens-Christian said, leading the man through the living room. "Want a beer?"

In the kitchen Stephens-Christian bent down to retrieve a beer from the bottom shelf of the refrigerator and was about to ask the visitor why he didn't call Triple A on his cell phone. Cromwell pulled on latex gloves. Suddenly Stephens-Christian felt something cut into his neck. He tried to turn, but Cromwell's knee was moving up his back. He gasped, arms flailing at his attacker, who now had him on the floor.

Cromwell was on top of him, knee square in his back, pinning him down. Stephens-Christian gurgled, the rope cutting into his neck. He kicked. The killer maintained the pressure. More kicks, gurgling. Finally the young cop was motionless.

After a minute, possibly longer, Cromwell got up, inhaled. Sweat poured out. Did any drop on the floor? He looked around the small room. Should he check the whereabouts of the man's kids? He stepped out of the kitchen and looked up the stairway. Nothing.

He returned to the kitchen and Stephens-Christian's lifeless body; head twisted sideways, eyes bugged-out like a gigged frog. The kitchen curtain was open. He looked through the window. The sun was down. Better check for any witnesses from across the alleyway.

He backtracked his entrance, stopping to pick up an antique clock off the mantel. He didn't see anything else in the house worth grabbing. He kicked over a small end table next to the patio door before leaving, hoping the missing clock and the upturned table would suggest a burglary.

Outside, the smell of newly cut grass met him, which he hadn't noticed earlier. He walked over to the fence and stood on his tiptoes, looking over for any witnesses. In a kitchen, across the alley, a young woman was washing dishes, oblivious to him.

Against his better judgment, he lit a smoke. He could use that beer inside to settle him. The rawness of the kill exhilarated him. Just like the first time. But then he felt a numbness set in, telling him not to second-guess what he had just done. What to do about the young cop's dish of a wife? Had Stephens-Christian alerted her about his suspicions? It seemed by the way he ended the conversation just hours ago that he had said something to her.

Just then he heard the garage door opening. Fuck! He stood in the night and waited. Bloodcurdling screams came from inside. Cromwell casually opened the back gate and disappeared down the alley. He took out the murder weapon from his coat pocket and dropped it in some weeds. What had he done with the smoke he'd lit? Around the corner, he took one last look back, then got into his sedan.

What to Do About Mr. Riordan

C hristina hadn't heard from her former teacher since his visit earlier in the week. The rumor had gotten around school that despite his general likeability, Mr. Riordan was guilty of something really bad. The newspaper story said that he was a suspect in the disappearance of a woman.

Could it be the same woman her own brother and cousin were involved with? No, the woman in the story had disappeared over a year ago, and her brother and cousin had just arrived here. Her mom had gotten upset after Mr. Riordan left their apartment and feared that if the boys told their story to the police, they would be deported.

It was night. The weather was balmy. Almost like her native Hermosillo, before the heat of the summer set in. She was the stable force in the family, what with the two boys whose English was poor, and her mother's lack of interest in learning a new language. She was the voice and ears of the household.

She sat down on the stoop and sipped on a Coke. What to do about Mr. Riordan? Where was he? He wasn't guilty of the things Mr. Rivy and the rest said he was. She would walk down to the Casey's, where the pay phone was, and call Mr. Riordan. One day soon she'd get a cell. She checked her pockets for quarters then walked to the convenience store phone.

75

HE WOULD HAVE MADE A GOOD COP

Two squad cars squealed out of the garage as Cromwell parked his sedan in the space reading "Detectives." He punched in his password at the garage entrance and was on the way to his cubicle when a sergeant grabbed him by the shoulder. The swing shift had just started, and they didn't know him as well as the day shift. Would they ask why he was at work? It was Sunday, after all.

Who snuffs someone, then goes back to his day job? The sergeant solemnly related the news. Cromwell played the part of the stunned partner after hearing the details and took a seat on the nearest chair.

It was too bad the kid had to show signs of suspicion. He would have made a good cop. Cromwell got up after hearing about Stephens-Christian and somberly walked back out to his car. He took the long way back to the young cop's home. He needed to show up again so if his DNA was found, the forensics team would assume it was from this condolence visit to the widow. What had he done with the gloves? He'd smashed the clock he took from Stephens-Christian's mantel and distributed the parts about the town. His cell phone? If his actions were ever traced, his cell would show his proximity to Stephens-Christian's house on or about the time of the kid's death. No worries, he had turned it off and had told the kid his cell had run out of juice. A cell turned off couldn't be traced. He should know the answer to that.

IT WAS A TYPICAL CRIME SCENE: POLICE TAPE, FORENSIC GUYS, ambulance, gurney, and the dead detective zipped up in a black body bag. A dozen or so neighbors were now standing in their driveways, and more than the usual black-and-whites were parked up and down the street. *When one of their own dies, it always amused him how panic sets in and every black-and-white shows up, destroying the virginity of the scene.*

The kid's wife was sitting dazed on the couch when he entered. The daughter was with a female officer, whimpering. Some older woman was holding the infant. Cromwell gave the wife a superficial pat on the shoulder and said, "We'll find out who did this." She didn't make eye contact, just nodded. A female community service officer sat down next to her.

76

All Quiet

After my escape from the depot dungeon, exhaustion set in. I'd found a shade tree by the Watchahoo to nap under. I suspected the blow to the head was telling me to slow down. Laddie needed a rest too. The nap turned into an afternooner and when I awoke, the sun had set. It was risky to stay in town. I should have sought out a better place to hide myself, but my body needed replenishment, regardless of my predicament. One can go on automatic pilot for only so long. It was mid-evening. The tree frogs were arguing amongst themselves.

I let my Jeep do a crawl up Redmun Hill, where Pop had told me the Whatley boy lived. Some of the homes, most of which were nearing the century mark, might have been candidates for the state historic preservation marker had they been kept up. But now each resembled a shanty. Laddie was curled up in the passenger seat, still out of it from our ordeal.

This was one of those times when I wished I had a pistol. Although, when contemplating using one, there was always the fear of doing a Barney Fife on myself.

The gravel driveways of some of the homes led off the street and jetted into the backyards. I needed to be out of the way. I found a home with the lights off, lawn unkempt, with a For Sale sign in the front yard. I pulled over in a tree grove and walked up to the house and peeked into the front window, curtain open. Empty.

I looked around for anyone, traipsed back to my Jeep and Laddie, then backed into the small garage, 1940s vintage. Inside, we sat and waited. A lone truck made its way up the street. An Edgar Allan Poe breeze blew through the trees. I looked for ravens.

77

WHERE ARE YOU NOW?

The desk sergeant patched the call through from the young woman to Cromwell. He had just returned to the station, after showing enough remorse at the crime scene for his fallen brother. He nodded into the phone as the girl related a story about her brother and cousin and how they had been forced into doing some dastardly crime, which involved kidnapping a woman from a shopping center. And that despite newspaper accounts insinuating that her former teacher was a suspect, she was certain he was not.

"Have you told anybody about this?" Cromwell asked the girl.

"Just you." She was talking from what seemed like a pay phone. One of the few left in the city.

"Are you sure? No one?"

"I try to call my teacher but he's not home." Again, "Just you."

"Where are you now?" he asked.

Cromwell hung up after telling the young woman to wait for him. He got up and looked about the cubicle as if to detect any bugging devices that could have been planted, even though he knew that no one was suspicious of him, at least not yet. He checked his watch.

Despite the hour, the precinct was a-flurry with the news. On his way out, several uniform boys stopped him and offered condolences. One of the younger female cops who had been in the same academy class with the victim was sitting on a bench. She tearfully looked up as he passed by. He didn't make eye contact, no time for that now. He hustled himself out to his car and past small little groupings talking about the recent tragedy. Inside his sedan he checked the location of the girl on the phone with a new city map. No GPS for him. The area of the city called "The Projects." Not far.

As he made his way through traffic, he measured his options.

Cop work had trained him to take command of a situation. The girl from last night jumped into his thoughts. *If he hadn't stopped and let his urges overtake him, at least his young partner would still be alive. But then again, sooner or later, Stephens-Christian would have gotten too curious about everything, and when he did, he would start asking questions. This was the perfect time to get rid of him.*

This young Mexican girl hadn't left her name with the desk sergeant. He had asked her about that. No name to trace her to him. And she said she hadn't told anyone else about the kidnappings that her brother was a part of.

Cromwell flipped open his burner phone and dialed up the Chapwell Falls sheriff. He shouldn't have started communicating again with the guy this way. But then again, they went back a long way. And in this type of business, history meant everything. He pulled up the sleeve of his shirt and looked at the tattoo that bonded him to the sheriff.

He pulled off at Ryland and the expressway and saw a demure young brunette sitting at a city bus stop sipping on a soda and nervously shaking her foot. He looked in his rearview mirror to check for any followers. *Paranoid.*

He pulled his sedan over into the lot just down from where the girl was sitting and left the car running, but stayed seated. The girl looked up. He flashed his lights on and off. No one was watching. She deposited the soda in a garbage can and cautiously walked over, her arms folded in front of her.

She stayed back from the car window on his side. "Ms. Morales?"

Christina looked at the man as he flashed her his badge. Her immediate thought was that he looked spooky and had devilish eyes. But the car he was riding in, although not marked as a police car, looked official. He told her to get in and she did. She glanced over quickly at him again. He was old. Older than Mr. Riordan, and fat.

She could tell he didn't have a wife, because he was unkempt. Wives were supposed to help their husbands dress and look good. He said he needed to take her to identify a suspect who was responsible for the kidnappings of the women. It didn't make any sense for her to ID somebody. It was her brother and cousin who could do that. He told her all she had to do was look at a man from a one-way mirror.

He seemed in a hurry. She asked to go home. But he said that the whole ID would take "no time at all." This man was a policeman, but just like so many in her country, she had a feeling, a bad one.

78

WE'RE ALL IN THIS TOGETHER

L eon Whatley pulled into his small garage, got out, and stomped off mud from his boots at the back door. He slogged into the living room and beamed a look down at the two women, then at Kelvin, who was jumping up from the floor, beer in hand. Leon had been downtown, to no avail, looking for that nephew of his. He guessed he should check the depot next. He'd heard the sheriff had found the teacher nosing around the cellar where the women had been kept, and had knocked him out.

His sister wouldn't be back until tomorrow, which gave them plenty of time to get the product on the train. Leon called out the boy's name to check if he'd somehow made it back to the house.

He glanced at Kelvin. For the first time since they had taken that woman from the grocery store, he looked like he wanted to sample the product. The sheriff, though, had said absolutely no touching these two.

"What the fuck you looking at, dirtbag?" Kelvin said.

Leon bellowed a laugh. "It don't make no difference, Kel. We all in this together." Since both of them had had sex with the woman they took from the grocery store, Leon had become bolder with his comments around Kelvin. He'd taken Kelvin's word that the woman had died from her fall off the cliff.

Kelvin set the beer down on the coffee table. "That fat shit sheriff dropped these two off. Said he'd be back once the train was getting near. Where's that boy of yours, anyway?"

"He ain't mine. He's my sister's." Both men leered at the figures frozen on the floor.

79

THE SUSPECTS ARE AT THE POLICE STATION

The trip to Chapwell Falls had been a quick one. It was odd the policeman wanted her to travel to a nearby town. He'd said the suspects, as he called them, were at a police station there. She thought about jumping out of the car when he slowed down. She hadn't told her mother anything, only that she was going for a walk. Her mother only called out, in Spanish, that it was too late. In the policeman's car, she'd ask to call her mom, but he'd said that wasn't necessary and that he'd have her home soon.

Cromwell exited the highway. He had tried to ease the young woman into feeling more comfortable with him at the beginning of the trip by asking her questions about her homeland, but he had run out of things to say.

"It won't be long now, sweetheart," he said to Christina. "The suspects are at the police station just up the road." Christina moved herself closer to her door. She knew something was not right.

And Cromwell knew that she knew. He could waste her. That would be the simplest thing to do. She said she hadn't told anybody about her call to him. But she was cute and young, just the kind of thing perverts want. And the train was due in tonight.

Christina thought she could hear her heartbeat. Her mouth was dry. She looked at the small town down below as the policeman followed the winding road downward. There were scattered lights in a few of the homes. She glanced at the small clock on the dash. Almost midnight. She wanted to run, but to where?

She missed Mr. Riordan. This whole thing was about him. Somehow she had gotten involved with his predicament. But then again, her cousin and brother had been forced to take that woman. She got a sick feeling that she would never see her mom and family again.

LITTLE SAVIOR

After seeing Leon disappear into his home, I deposited my cell under the seat, too cumbersome to lug along, patted Laddie, and got out of the Jeep and slowly moved in that direction. Squeezed inside Leon's one-car garage was his truck. A shovel and hoe were the only tools in the truck bed. There were no traces of blood, no women's garments.

"Betta you, Betta do, Betta moo; Betta you, Betta do, Betta moo," came the familiar chants from the backyard, directly behind the garage. I squatted down in front of the vehicle and peeked through the garage slats at my little savior, head bowed downward, walking through a backyard gate, toward the house. A second later, the back door opened.

"Boy, where you been? I told you to stay put!" The man, whose face was now familiar, slapped the back of the boy's head. "Get upstairs to your room and stay put. Any peep out of you and I'll whip your butt. Understand?"

The boy didn't say anything, just hurried inside, rubbing his head.

Leon followed him. "You supposed to be in bed hours ago.

I Want to Call My Mother

Cromwell checked the dashboard clock. The train was to arrive after midnight. He listened for a whistle. The girl was shaking her foot. She was suspicious. "Won't be long now, darling," he said.

He drove by the sheriff's building and quickly did a U-turn, remembering that the women had been moved to the shanty side of town to one of the hillbilly's houses. Christina did a look-back at the building. "I thought we were going to the police station?"

"Uh, no, hon; the suspects are being held at a house."

"I want to call my mother," Christina said. "She will be worried. She 'spects me home by now."

"In time, sweet thing. We just need you to ID these perps. You want to be a good citizen, don't you?"

Cromwell accelerated up the hill. He thought that the sheriff had done a good job of scaring the shit out of the town folks. Some talk of dangerous waste being transported through town. Although he'd told the city fathers that Tuesday was the usual day, he alerted them that, this week, the train was coming through tonight.

Cromwell checked the address to the holding house. Until now he had stayed out of the actual taking of the women. His Billy Bob friend who ran the law out of Chapwell Falls had employed the two boobs who did the dirty work. He had history with one of the boobs, just as he had with the sheriff. No one needed to see him. Let them do the dirty work. Both the boobs had come too close to the action, visiting the restaurant in his town where these last two snatches had worked.

82

WE NEED TO ID THE PERPS

I took two steps up to the back porch, slowly opened the screen door, then let it ease shut. The best time to enter a residence, if you want your entry undetected, is when the resident has just come from where you are. When I was an investigator, a career burglar gave me that piece of advice. I was operating now on that force pulling me, versus good sense.

The smell of moldy clothes greeted me as I stepped into what appeared to be a laundry room. I moved into the kitchen, keeping myself close to the wall.

Beyond the kitchen, a dim light flickered. Leon was there. Was Kelvin in the house too? I didn't notice his truck outside. But then again, I was on edge and hadn't been all that mindful of my surroundings. Just then I heard the crackling of gravel. A vehicle stopped. Two doors opened, then closed. Footsteps moved to the front of the house. The screen door opened and two persons stepped outside, letting the door slap shut.

Voices outside. I glanced into the living room. Two figures were lying on the floor, one covered in a blanket, a gunnysack loosely covering the other.

The voices at the front door were Leon and Kelvin's. Who were they talking to?

"We need to ID the perps, ma'am," a familiar voice from the front steps said. "I told this little darling that once we did, she could call her mama," he said.

I moved back into the darkness of the laundry area, but was still able to see the parties coming inside. Yoked to Cromwell's side was Christina.

At the sight of the two women on the floor, Christina jerked back from Cromwell and toward the front door. Immediately Cromwell yanked her back into the room. My heart sank.

Kelvin chuckled and grabbed Christina's other arm. She kicked at Cromwell, who only seemed to get off on the ordeal. The women on the floor squirmed at the sound.

I searched for some weapon. I picked up a wooden chair. It would have to do. Who had a gun? Cromwell likely. Kelvin and Leon, unlikely.

"Let's take a look at this little beauty," Kelvin said, hovering over Christina.

She cursed something at him in Spanish.

In light-switch speed, Cromwell handcuffed Christina and threw her on the couch by the window. "Shut up, you little whore," he said.

The men froze over her, their backs to me. Cromwell seemed to be contemplating whether he would let Kelvin have his way.

Who to go for? Three against one. Bad odds. But if Cromwell had a gun and I could get it...

I moved quickly out of the darkness, chair in front of me like a lion tamer. The men turned.

Cromwell, who was closest to me said, almost half smiling, "Teacher man!"

I plastered the chair across his head. He fell back onto the couch as Kelvin threw a right jab into my cheek. Leon, to my right, froze. I stumbled back, still gripping the chair, but caught myself before I tripped over the women.

Christina called out, "Mr. Riordan!"

Still grasping the chair, I moved back as Kelvin tried a follow-through with a left hook. He missed. I shoved the chair legs into his chest and heaved him back onto the floor. For a moment, both men were at my mercy. *Finish the job, quickly! Where was Leon?*

Cromwell was hobbling back up, reaching for his firearm. Just as he got the .45 out of his holster, I kicked the gun out of his hand. It landed in front of me. I let the chair drop and kicked him in the shin, which sent him back across the couch and onto the floor. I reached down for his weapon.

I picked up the .45 and lifted it toward Cromwell, bracing my right wrist, which was shaking. Then a crack to my head! *Leon! Blackness.*

83

KNOCKED OUT

I awoke to exhaust fumes and an aching skull. My hands were bound with what felt like duct tape. A jolt, and voices somewhere above me and beyond. My head scraped against a tire iron. I'd been thrown in a trunk.

The duct taping was done in a hurry by the feel of it, but nevertheless securely. My legs were free. Odd. I had to strategize what my move should be once the trunk opened. I doubted we'd be having a gentlemanly chat.

I guessed that Cromwell had engineered depositing me in his trunk, as he had likely engineered this whole scheme. My head pounded as I tried to think. The car finally slowed again, this time to a stop. I heard some talk through the backseat. Steps outside. An order from what sounded like Kelvin. A moment later the car continued down a gravel road and stopped again. I opted to pretend to be out cold.

The trunk opened. I kept still, eyes closed.

"Okay, teacher man, time to meet your maker," the devilish voice said. I moaned.

"The faggot's still out, Kelvin."

I let out another groan. *Better Kelvin and Leon than Cromwell.* They pulled me up and I stayed limp.

"Do we take him to the cliff like the bitch last week, Kelvin?"

I groaned, but let the two buffoons drag me over the gravel, then down a hill.

"Yeah. No one found that bitch, even though she spoiled our fun by jumping off herself. We'll make sure with teacher boy to throw him out so he'll hit rocks."

"Teacher man must work out some" Leon said. "Still got some biceps."

"Don't make no never-mind now. His days are over."

I opened my eyes just a little. The moonglow lit the path. Tangled weeds grew out from a barbed-wire fence to my right, just off the narrow path. At about ten yards away there appeared to be a drop-off.

I moaned again.

"We gonna throw him off with his hands tied, Kel?"

Kelvin huffed some. "No. We need to make it look like he went off on his own. Like some kind of suicide. Cromwell said no one will miss him anyway. Got no family who cares, except for some ol' aunt. So everything will work out."

At the cliff's edge they let me drop, limp, and began to untie my bindings. I moaned louder. I felt the wetness of blood from the back of my head trickle into my neck.

"Give me the cutter," Kelvin said. With that, he bent down to cut the tape, straddling me. Just as he sliced off the bindings, I grabbed his crotch. "Motherfucker," he wailed. The carpet cutter fell into the grass. I squeezed as hard as I could, then let go. Kelvin fell back. I grabbed the blade as Leon came at me.

I raked the blade cleanly across his cheek to his chin. Another "Motherfucker." Both men down, but only momentarily. I backed up and hobbled as fast as I could through the weeds and into some woods. The tree frogs stopped their serenade.

"Get the fucker," Kelvin yelled.

"He cut me. He cut me!" Leon wailed.

The moonglow lit my way, but also theirs. Into the bushes. "Get the fucker," Kelvin yelled again.

As far as I knew, neither of them had a gun. I kept my dash up, down the hillside, through the brush. I dove into some shrubbery and rolled up against a tree trunk. Somewhere up the hill there was movement.

"I'm going back to the car, Kel," Leon called out, somewhere back up the path. "The fucker cut me bad."

"Get your fat ass back down here!"

"No, Kel. I'm going to tell the sheriff and that city cop."

Kelvin panted. "Fuck!" he said. "You get back here now, you dumb shit!" he yelled again.

"No, Kel! Come on. We need to get out of here. We supposed to be at the depot to help with the product."

"Fuck!" echoed through the trees.

84

A Train Whistle

I waited to hear the car start up, surprised Kelvin had given up on me so quickly. I hoisted myself up slowly, pressing my back against the tree trunk. I followed the trail back up to a wooden gate. Surprisingly, the pain in my shins and thighs had gone away, as had the throbbing in my head. I walked back up the gravel road, half expecting one of the boys to jump out. Somewhere I heard a train whistle.

I started jogging toward the sound. The whistle got closer. Just around a bend, more chugs. What had Pops at the grocery store said about the cargo? I knelt down. Then another whistle, this one a blare.

I could see it now, slowing at the crossroads. Three whistles, some fumes from the diesel, more clangs. I hunkered down as the engine neared. A lone figure stood behind the gears. He stared ahead, fixated on the track. Did he see me? Half a dozen boxcars followed. The doors were bolted. Each had ventilation slats.

I'd hopped a freight train in my college days when Malone and I hitchhiked to L.A. The secret was to get on board while the train is in the depot, or at the very least, just as the last whistle sounded. Or you could reverse the process and board when it slowed for a stop. I waited, crouched, as all cars clacked by.

There! The caboose, rusted red. It was likely past midnight. A night glitter cast light into the car. No one was in it. I took a last deep breath and scurried up the small hill. I grasped the railing for the steps, then up one, two, three, onto the caboose. I quickly looked inside for signs of life. Nobody. All things considered, I was in good shape. I slid open the small door.

85

I'LL DO THE TALKING

Kelvin took the curves on the country roads like a sixteen-year-old.

"You stupid motherfucker," he shouted to Leon about what he had claimed was the man's ineptness. "You should have been standing over me." But after venting, he quieted himself and began to consider what to tell Cromwell and the sheriff about the incident of letting the teacher get away. The immediate concern was to get the merchandise onto the train.

Leon pressed the dirty towel against his cut. Blood trickled down his neck onto his lap. No doubt, some of that blood landed on the seat of Cromwell's car. Kelvin slowed the Buick down at the city limits and pulled over. Leon waited. An image flashed through his mind of Kelvin pulling out a gun and blasting him in the head. But the man calmly turned and told him the plan for dealing with Cromwell.

"First, I'll do the talking. Understand?"

Leon nodded, still pressing the blood-soaked towel against his chin and cheek.

"On second thought, get out. Just get out!"

"But, Kel," Leon said. "I want to see the girls get loaded on."

"I can't take you up there like that. Too many questions. I'll tell the cop I had to take you home to check on the boy."

Leon cursed, but got out of the car after Kelvin threatened to hold back his share of the money if he didn't listen and do as he was told. "But how will I get home?" Kelvin sped off.

CROMWELL AND THE SHERIFF GLARED AT THE BUICK AS IT CAME TO A stop at the loading dock ramp. Three gunnysack-covered bodies were neatly laid side by side. Slits had been cut into each sack. Bundles of grain were stacked in front of them, ready for loading.

86

CHRISTINA HADN'T RETURNED HOME

Ms. Morales had paced the floor. La policia or not, it was after midnight and she had to do something. She had lain awake since ten p.m., far past the time Christina was supposed to have been home. Now she would go out into the night with the boys, or if she had to, she would go to the authorities.

She looked at the card which had been lying on the table for the past week. It was the card from Christina's teacher, Mr. Riordan. He had been her favorite. What a shame he had been fired. But was it all related to the stories the boys told about the taking of the white women?

She called out to wake the boys. Both shouted back at her to let them sleep. But when she said that Christina was gone, each shot up and quickly put on his flannel shirt and jeans. Roberto pulled a small firearm from underneath his bed. Ms. Morales screamed at the boy to put it away, but he ignored her. Jesus threw him the weapon's clip. Roberto fitted the clip into the gun, with an ease that showed he knew what he was doing.

In less than ten minutes, all three were outside. The moon was full.

The courtyard was empty, except for four boys, two black, two Asian, sitting on the stoop of a nearby walk-up. A cigarette dangled from one of the boys' mouth. One of the Asian boys played with a cell phone. They watched as the immigrants walked toward them. Roberto felt the handgun tucked just inside his jeans. Both boys wore their shirts out. If they had wanted, they could have easily passed as gangbangers.

Roberto walked over to the four and gave the customary knuckle high-five to each boy. He told them Christina hadn't returned home. In some cities, a gathering of Asian, Hispanic, and Afro-American teenagers would be a recipe for a rumble. But the four boys attended school with Christina and liked her.

Roberto asked if they knew the whereabouts of a train depot. One of the boys, DeCarlos, readjusted his ball cap, moving its bill from the side to the front. "What that got to do with my girl Christina?"

"Because we think someone might have took her there," he said.

One of the Asian boys stood up and asked, "Why you think Christina is there?" Ms. Morales turned to Roberto. He, in turn, looked at Jesus, who nodded to go ahead. Roberto related their story about riding to America on a train and the piece about the depot, not explaining why Christina might be there in another town, only that Ms. Morales believed it to be the case. "Mal hombre," he said. "She knows she has been taken by a bad man."

For a moment the boys let the story sink in, then DeCarlos nodded and gestured for a smoke from the Asian, who shook out a smoke for him.

"Yeah that be Chapwell Falls. Used to be a lumber town. My grand-pappy used to cut logs up there."

Ms. Morales jumped into the conversation, saying in Spanish to Roberto that they needed to get going. Roberto asked DeCarlos how far away it was. One of the Asian boys showed DeCarlos a rendering on his cell of directions to what appeared to be a depot. He smiled. "Gentlemen, for a hamburger on Tuesday, I'll take you there today."

Within minutes, Ms. Morales, Roberto, and Jesus were scurrying across the courtyard with the others to an old Chevy Roberto had just bought. At the parking lot, the boys flipped a coin to see who would join DeCarlos and the Morales family. The Asian boy, John Wee, won the toss and hopped in the backseat with DeCarlos. It was just past one a.m. Monday morning, according to the car clock.

Roberto kept the speed down as DeCarlos gave directions to the countryside and, hopefully, the whereabouts of Christina.

Train Cargo?

Now was a time to light up, if I hadn't kicked the habit. I sat down at one of the tables in the caboose. There was a map on the wall, which told the story of this new connector line and how it ran from the Midwest to points in central Mexico, some three thousand miles. It brought goods in from everywhere west of the Mississippi and east of California and delivered them south of the border.

The train slowed. I stood up and saw we were entering Chapwell Falls. I had tucked Leon's carpet cutter into my belt. It was my only weapon. Underneath the table I was sitting at, I kicked something. A lighter. I flicked it. Still worked. I stuffed it in my pocket.

I opened the back door and waited as the train made its way through town and over the Watchahoo, toward the depot. I was back to this place where I started, not by choice but circumstance. At a Norway spruce, I jumped from the train and did a tumble-roll, landing under the tree.

A Nylon Rope

T he county coroner was at work on Stephens-Christian's corpse when there was a page over the PA. Dr. Ben Lee turned from the gurney, flipped up the plastic goggle gear he was wearing, and stepped over three paces to a cluttered desk and to the phone.

"Lee here," he said.

"Dr. Lee, this is Detective Wellsley. I'm looking for Detective Cromwell. Thought he might be there."

"No. I haven't seen him. He, uh, in fact, hasn't been in all night." The doctor scratched a tickle in his nose with the surgical gloves. There was a pause on the line.

"If he comes by, tell him to call us."

"Will do."

Dr. Lee returned to the gurney to continue with the autopsy report. He studied the laceration on the man's neck. He took out a pair of tweezers and gently lifted off a miniscule piece of what appeared to be nylon rope. He switched on the mic and continued with the report.

The time of death was established, which was just a few hours earlier. He methodically described the victim and other perfunctory matters specific to all homicides. Dr. Lee nodded to himself, determining that the victim's cracked nose came not from fisticuffs but from something like a fall. A struggle and the vic went down? Likely, thereafter the perpetrator tied the nylon rope around the victim's neck. Broken hyoid bone. Consistent with strangulation.

Strangulation can take up to a minute and a half. But how would someone get the drop on this man who was over six feet tall and quite muscular? Dr. Lee rolled the man over. Putrefactive gas exploded. On his back were bruises and some sort of indentation. Not from a weapon. What would cause the indentation? He stepped aside and tried to play out different scenarios that might have caused the damage.

A knee in the back! He simulated a strangling position. Man in front of him. He tightened the make-believe rope around the victim, squeezed harder. What if the man wouldn't go down? Dr. Lee lifted his own right knee into the make-believe victim's back. Could he do that if the victim were standing erect? The perpetrator would have to be taller that Stephens-Christian.

But if the victim were kneeling down or squatting, then what? Easily done. The victim was found by the refrigerator as if he were retrieving something there, maybe from a bottom shelf. That scenario made sense.

Just then the morgue door opened and two cops walked in. One of the cops handed the doctor a bag. Resources for the crime lab were extremely limited in this jurisdiction, so Dr. Lee doubled as a CSI, as well as coroner. He shook out the bag that contained some broken glass, a cigarette butt, and nylon rope.

"Found these in the alley, might be something," the cop said.

The Moonglow on the Watchahoo

The bed of pine needles I tumbled into offered a safe haven for me. The moonglow on the Watchahoo lit up the train in front of me. A rushing image of Laddie came across my mind. I hoped the derelicts hadn't shot him. I'd left him in my Jeep, windows open. How long ago was that? I thought about Aunt Alice. What had she been told? I suspected that Cromwell had set her up for believing me guilty of something. I checked to make sure I still had the carpet cutter.

The engine slowed to an idle beyond the depot and down the other side of the hill, at about the same place I'd parked my Jeep on past occasions. The caboose banged into the last car as the train discharged some steam from up front.

The depot ramp was still hidden from my view. On the road to my right, driving up the hillside, was the Chapwell Falls sheriff. I had thought it odd, the times I had driven by the police station, that his vehicle, a Chrysler town car, had been parked in front. Usually the sheriff handles county business, not city matters. But in this place, all signals were crossed anyway.

The sheriff parked to the side of the depot and moved his girth out of the car. He stretched as if he'd just gotten up, adjusted his belt, which had the typical cop accessories, gun and cuffs, and slogged toward the depot. He called out to someone on the other side of the cars. "Got our product ready?"

I edged outward a bit from the branches of the pine, careful to stay hidden, but close enough to hear and partially see the action. To my knowledge, no one knew I'd escaped the throes of Kelvin and Leon. I was counting on them to be reluctant tellers of their mishandling of me. I recognized Cromwell! "Everything is late tonight," he said in his flippant way. I listened.

"Come on now, sweet thing, you got a long journey ahead of you, and struggling will only make it worse." The voice was Kelvin's. He was dragging something onto the ramp. A girl yelled out, but as quickly went quiet. Cromwell and the sheriff continued talking. A fourth man, likely, the train engineer, walked up to the group. Where was Leon?

I weighed my options. I was out of sight of Cromwell and the crew on the depot. The boxcar directly in front of me had a solid-looking black lock on its sliding door. Trying to open it would definitely make too much noise. Toward the back end of the boxcar was a two-foot-wide ladder leading up to the roof. I rolled several times toward it. My only option was up.

Cromwell called something to Kelvin. I could see foot action under the train and a second victim being dragged down the ramp. I slowly climbed the ladder, one step, two, three, four, and onto the roof. I felt the carpet cutter slip from my belt. I heard it hit the steps behind me and fall to the ground.

On the other side of the boxcar, the talking stopped. I lay still, trying to mesh myself with the roof. I heard footsteps coming my way. Do I get down and grab the carpet cutter or stay atop the car? "Who's there?" Cromwell yelled. I breathed deeply.

Scattered about the car roof about were small pebbles, blowback from wind gusts. I heaved a handful away from my position toward the woods where the sheriff had parked.

A flashlight beamed in the direction of the gravel. "Who's there?" the sheriff yelled. As feet hoofed down the walkway toward the sound, I crawled to the middle of the car.

"Forget about it, Donald," the sheriff said. "We got cats around here."

Below me in the boxcar I heard a thump and a cry.

How many did they have? Christina and the two who were already at Kelvin's. Three?

"I need to get going, men," the engineer said, his voice unaffected by what was happening before him. "I am already late."

"No wetbacks this trip, Jed?" Cromwell asked the engineer.

"Already dropped them off down the line," the engineer said. "But I do got something for you boys."

I rolled slowly over to the edge of roof.

The engineer handed a manila envelope to Cromwell, who peeked inside. Like vultures at roadkill, the other two vermin gathered around, apparently for their payoff.

I rolled over to the center of the roof and stared at the full moon.

90

HE DIDN'T WANT THE OLD GUY TO KNOW

O ne thing was curious about the brand of cigarette butt that Detective Wellsley and his partner, Tad Cheney, had dropped off as evidence; it was the brand Detective Cromwell smoked. A popular brand today. But, nevertheless, a brand that one of their own smoked. Detective Wellsley didn't want to bring up the coincidence. Making any kind of accusation about another cop was risky business. He told Cheney to call it a day. He needed time to think.

He drove past the small subdivision where Cromwell had purchased a condo after his most recent divorce. He hoped the cop's Buick would be in the driveway. It wasn't. No lights at the old cop's house. He turned off the ignition, gently closed the door to his car, and walked up the man's driveway.

The doors to the two-car garage were closed. Cromwell had vented in a precinct meeting that his automatic opener was misfiring and he had to park in his driveway. Wellsley doubted the overweight cop would have had the energy to lift the door without the gizmo. He tested the garage door handle. Locked.

He slowly moved to the front porch and tested the front door.

Locked also. He peered through the front window. A solitary lamp was left on. The living room looked more like a motel room after a maid's visit than a lived-in bachelor pad. Cromwell was a slob and slobs who smoked were notorious for leaving their butts in the ashtray. He could call the cop on his cell phone. What would be wrong with that? But at this point he didn't want to let the old guy know he was suspicious.

91

TRAIN HEADING OUT

Yolanda Morales had never imagined she'd find herself in a situation like this. But she was with her son, her nephew, and two neighborhood boys and felt fairly safe. John Wee lit another smoke as Roberto pushed the accelerator down, moving the Chevy up the hill toward the depot.

"Easy. Slow this old trap down," DeCarlos told Roberto. "And kill the lights!" Roberto dashed the headlights.

"Something going on up there," John Wee said, throwing out the smoke he'd just lit. "A train."

Both John Wee and DeCarlos pulled their small pistols from underneath their shirts. DeCarlos rested his weapon in his lap. Ms. Morales, sitting between her son and nephew, upon seeing the weapon, screamed out something in Spanish about having guns. Roberto quieted her in Spanish, saying it was okay.

"Stop," DeCarlos said, directing Roberto to pull into a wooded area and entryway between two budding maples.

Around a bend was a train heading out of the station. DeCarlos hopped out of the car first, followed by John Wee and Jesus on the other side. Roberto exited last. He told Ms. Morales to stay put. The boys gathered at the hood of the car. DeCarlos and Roberto went up the hillside toward the depot, John Wee and Jesus headed into the trees, away from the station.

I DROPPED INSIDE

The train jerked several times. I clung to the metal girder. Stay on or jump down? I peeked a look at Cromwell and the other two, the sheriff and Kelvin, gathered at the depot ramp. No sign of Leon. I'd cut him badly.

The train slowly began its chug away toward the river with me lying on top, tree branches hanging down onto the cars. A latched door lay up several yards in front of me and if not locked would lead me into the car. But I needed to get there before the train picked up speed.

My car jerked again, ramming the car in front of it. I crawled to the door. Hoping that I wouldn't be seen, I sat up and with both hands pulled back on the handle. The door slid back. I smelled hay below. If my calculations were right, the women, including Christina, were in there. I took one last look back at the train station. No one looking in my direction. I dropped inside.

A Couple of Jimmies

Wellsley stood at the front window of Cromwell's condo. *Clean living room*. He'd learned to trust his instincts, and right now they were telling him that something stank. Cromwell the slob had done a good job at disinfecting his place. What was that about? Had he turned over some new leaf? The man was a pig and left a trail of ashes wherever he went, tabletops, on his clothes, on the carpet.

Wellsley wiggled the door handle. Locked. He looked for any video cameras. None. Cops were notorious for being the last to install safety devices, believing the old-fashioned way to stop crime was the best—a .45. He took out his Visa card and slid it into the door crevice above the knob. A couple jimmies and the door opened.

Inside, Wellsley took a whiff of the cleaning fluid. He listened for snoring. Nothing. Why had the cop taken such great pains to clean up his place? Wellsley searched the room, eyeballing the couch and kitchen, which jutted out into the living room. Dishes put away, tabletops spartan and clean.

He walked down the hallway, which led to the master bedroom, hugging the wall, holding his .45, thumb on the safety, half expecting the cop to storm out with his pistol. The bedroom door was open. He stepped inside. The curtains were open. The bed made, no trace of the ol' man.

He opened the closet. No reason. Just instinct told him to take a peek. Clothes hung in uncharacteristic order. Lining the shelf above the hangers were boxes, most labeled "Pictures." In the corner was an empty holster. Next to it was an emerald ring. Wellsley picked it up. A woman's. An ex-wife's? He laid it down. He took the boxes down, sat, and began perusing the publications.

Coeds in Bondage, Volume One, Two, and Three. No storyline, articles, or even advertisements, just pictures of girls in compromising positions. In Volume Three, in the section named "New Features," there were pictures of several girls who appeared genuinely distraught.

Immediately, Wellsley's investigator mind tried to connect a face in the magazine with one he remembered from the pictures of missing women. He was new to the investigation of the town's missing women, and the names of the victims escaped him, but the faces were vivid.

On one page, a brunette was shackled and looked especially familiar. He studied the photograph. then set the magazine down. Was it abnormal for Cromwell to have the porno magazines? Most cops knew porn magazines left no trace of one's prurient taste, like Internet sites. He knew that cops often fell prey to the deviant lifestyles they were exposed to.

Wellsley put the magazines back on the shelf just as he had found them and began to close the closet. He stood for a moment then decided to retrieve the third volume, and tore out the page with the brunette. He could have taken a picture, but didn't want any trace of it in his cell phone's photo gallery. He tucked the picture in his pocket and slowly moved back to the living room. At the front doorway he took a last look around then eased himself back into the night.

94

It is Mr. Riordan

T he train jerked and chugged some more as I landed in a haystack to the smell of manure and to three figures tied and covered in gunnysacks. I lay for a moment, expecting someone to lurch out. The figures were motionless. My only weapon, the carpet cutter, was gone. I felt the lighter I'd found in the caboose on my rode into town, whatever use it might have.

"Christina," I called out. The train picked up speed.

I heard a gurgle from one of the girls. Then some muffled noises from the other two. I crawled over to the three. "Christina?"

I heard a muffled voice, "Mr. Riordan?" I untied the ropes securing the sack and a figure inside tried to sit up. I pulled off the rest of the covering. "Christina!"

She gasped for air and tried to talk, but began hyperventilating, then came a flood of tears. She hugged me then moved to help her fellow captives as we undid their ropes. When the sacks were off, all three women burst out in tears together. Between crying and hyperventilating, no words were spoken for several minutes.

I had hoped one of the captives would have been Penny, but both were brunettes and much younger, early twenties. Both were gaunt and looked like they hadn't been fed for days. Christina was the newest arrival and still had her color about her. "What are we going to do, Mr. R.?" she asked.

"I don't know, ladies, exactly what we are going to do. Allow me to introduce myself. I am Pat Riordan. Christina and I know each other. But what about you guys?"

"I am Tara Simon," the first girl said.

"Carrie Lindsey," the other said over sniffles.

I asked the who, whats, and wheres of their struggle, which told the story of kidnappings by men, who had dragged each of them into a van. Christina kept silent when Tara said the men who pulled her into a van were Hispanic. The girls continued slowly, saying they believed that the Hispanic men were not behind the ordeal, but that the older white men had instigated the whole thing. Both women could only say it was horrible what had happened after they were taken to a cellar.

Now wasn't the time to make the women relive their ordeal. "How is your strength?" I asked Tara and Carrie.

"We haven't eaten for several days," Carrie said. They were coming down off of something, likely small dosages of cheap heroin. Both women started to shiver. Best I could tell, Christina was sober.

"Ladies, we are going to have to figure out how to get off this thing. Unfortunately, the train engineer is in on it. And I don't know whether anyone else is on board."

Carrie and Tara were too weak to be much help. I knew that if we got too far down the line we'd be in trouble. I thought about Laddie, my Jeep, and Aunt Alice.

The gaunt-faced women stared blankly at me. "Either one of you own a dog?"

95

DeCarlos Screamed

C romwell pulled out his pearl-handled weapon he'd had specially made for his bigger-than-life-sized ego at the sound of rustling down the roadway. "You got rid of the faggot teacher, didn't you?" he asked Kelvin. Kelvin nodded. In the bushes beyond the track, two heads poked through.

DeCarlos crept up the hillside within feet of the train track. Roberto was yards behind, but more hidden in the bushes. Their mission was to find Christina, and that was all. Jesus and John Wee had disappeared somewhere to the south of the depot and out of sight. Ms. Morales was still slumped down in the car. There had been no clear strategy about what to do when they arrived at the depot, or, for that matter, any thought given as to what might await them.

DeCarlos raised his weapon, crouching closer to the ramp.

"Hold it right there, boy," a voice ordered from the darkness.

DeCarlos balanced himself on his knees and shot toward the sound. As soon as he did, he knew he'd made a mistake. Within seconds a sharp, pin-like prick buried itself in his shoulder then a gunshot. He fell back. His head hit the railroad track. Roberto yelled out "Ese" and stood up, yards down off the track. Then another gunshot. Roberto fell near his partner. He tried to reach over to grab Roberto's shoulder. Warmness, then pain.

Two men approached and stared down at DeCarlos. White men; one had on a cop's uniform. Another, with a pearl-handled weapon, bent down. "Nigger boy, why did you come looking for trouble this way?" He pressed his foot down onto DeCarlos' wound. DeCarlos screamed.

"We were looking for my man's family," he said, nodding as best he could toward a lifeless Roberto.

Cromwell stood up and said something to the sheriff. Both looked out into the bushes. Another man joined the two. "Go look behind the depot," the sheriff said to Kelvin. He stepped on the wound one more time. "Who sent you?"

DeCarlos wailed, "No one! We was just trying to find my partner's family."

"The Mexican chick," Cromwell said.

Both men lifted DeCarlos and dragged him up the ramp. Blood covered his T-shirt. On the tracks lay Roberto. The men threw DeCarlos into the wall. He fell, cracking something, ribs.

"Who knows you guys are here?" Cromwell asked.

DeCarlos groaned out, "No one."

"How'd you get here?"

DeCarlos breathed deep. "We, uh, hitched a ride, man."

The two men looked in disbelief at one another. "How many are with you?"

"Just us two, man. That's it, I swear."

"Hey, that one out there on the track looks like the beaner who snatched the grocery store girl for us," Kelvin said, walking over to the lifeless figure. He bent down next to Roberto and sniffed the man, like a bird dog at a kill. "I think this wetback is a goner."

DeCarlos moaned from the ramp. Cromwell nodded to the sheriff, as if giving a go-ahead, and walked toward Kelvin. The sheriff stepped back from DeCarlos. He pointed his weapon to the back of the boy's head and fired, one shot, then two. The boy's skull cracked like a melon. Blood spattered onto the sheriff's pant legs. Rooks cawed. The sheriff coughed then placed his weapon back in its holster. The gun squeaked against the holster.

"Let's get these bodies to the back of the depot," Cromwell ordered.

"And check the two for cell phones." He turned back onto the track, and attempted to lift the boy's body, but stopped when Kelvin volunteered, "I'll do it, boss."

"Get the plastic drop cloths from under the ramp," Cromwell said, pointing at the depot. "Wrap the bodies up and take them away from here. You know where to bury them." Kelvin nodded following the man's order.

Cromwell grunted as he bent to pick up the shiny blade of a carpet cutter lying to the side of the track. From the corner of his eye, Kelvin watched the man examine the small item.

Downhill from the tracks, tucked in behind some ferns, were John Wee and Jesus. Wedged between them was Ms. Morales. "Did you get it, ese?" Jesus asked John Wee.

Wee nodded, taking a last look on his phone at the video he'd taken of the shooting.

96

He'd Swing by Cromwell's

Wellsley had hidden the magazine picture he had taken from the cop's condo under a stack of sports magazines in his study. He had only been asleep for three hours, by his calculation, when he got up; too much nervous energy. He made coffee then showered and dressed, making certain that his weapon's safety was clicked on. He put a cup of the morning brew on the small table next to his wife's side of the bed. He kissed her as she slept, and left for the day.

He'd swing by Cromwell's. If the cop was home he'd feel better about breaking into his condo, from the standpoint that he could rationalize that the cop was just out late, and likely at one of the three strip clubs he frequented. But if the cop was still gone and not at work, then what?

∼

TWENTY MINUTES LATER, WELLSLEY PULLED UP TO THE COP'S CONDO just as a neighbor was backing out of the adjoining driveway. The white-haired senior gave a wave.

Wellsley had every right to be knocking on the cop's door. He would assess the cop's overall grief or concern if he were home. After all, Cromwell's young partner had been murdered, no less. A knock, then another. He brought out his packet of lock picks just as Cromwell drove up. Wellsley casually slipped the tools back into his pocket.

Cromwell sauntered up. Tired eyes. "Little early to be making house calls, Wellsley," he said. "What's going on?"

The younger cop wanted to be straight with the man and say he was suspicious about a lot of things related to Stephens-Christian's death. But he opted to just say that he was concerned about the man's welfare.

"Damn shame about the kid," Cromwell replied with a less-than-convincing tone. "Don't know how he let something like that happen. Come in. Or were you going to anyway?" Cromwell said.

"No, Detective, just concerned about how you are getting along. That's all. I'll check back with you later."

Wellsley hurriedly backed out of the driveway. His stomach knotted up, not so much because he'd broken into the man's home the night before, but for fear that there'd be reprisals cast on his family.

Inside his condo, Cromwell made a pot of coffee and thought about what needed to happen next. Things had gotten out of hand. Where had the two dead kids come from? One was the Mexican girl's family member. But how did they know to investigate the depot? No mind, they had been disposed of.

Something was bothering him though. No vehicle had been found in the woods. How did the two boys get to the depot? One said they'd hitched to the place. Had someone else been with them?

The three girls were long gone and, by now, were somewhere close to Texas, he guessed. How many people had he had to put down since this last transport? Stephens-Christian, the two minority kids. Who else needed to go? The faggot teacher had been taken care of by the two hillbillies.

He took out the bills from his part of the business venture. Five thousand. Not enough for this.

He rationalized this new line of work was justified because the city's pitiful pittance of retirement drove him to this life. The reality of the matter was that he'd always been a fiend. His sexual perversions drove his former wives away. He'd come to know about the trafficking end of things through a convict he'd busted.

For this new line of work, he'd solicited the help of his old high school buddy, now sheriff of Chapwell Falls. Mostly because he was in charge of a town with a railroad link, which was needed to carry the whole thing off. Both he and his buddy had been involved in activities of a sordid nature since they were teenagers.

Cromwell got up, went out to his car, retrieved the carpet cutter he'd found on the railroad track the night before, then returned to his easy chair. He stretched out, rubbing his fingers over the blade. This was the stupid hillbilly's toy, which he'd seen the moron use more than once on one of the catches. But how did the knife get on the track, and why hadn't the hillbilly Kelvin made a big deal about it when he picked it up? He hadn't probed Kelvin about the whereabouts of his missing partner, Leon.

He undressed in the living room and slogged off to the bedroom. He needed some shut-eye. So far, no one could pin anything on him. He hadn't left any physical evidence that he knew of, unless it was a butt in Stephens-Christian's alleyway. But then again, his smokes were a popular brand. He dozed off to the sound of the commuters on the expressway.

97

I Had Fallen Asleep
in the Middle of Three Women

Getting three women off a moving train would prove much harder than I had anticipated. But what I hadn't expected was my own overwhelming need for sleep. There was something euphoric about being up and having an elevated degree of testosterone. But sooner or later you need to crash. I had fallen asleep in the middle of all three women. Under different circumstances, one could have claimed I'd found a heaven on earth.

Sometime in the early a.m. hours, the sunlight poked through the car slats and brought me out of what had been an unusually sound slumber. The train was chugging along at a decent clip. I peeked a look at the countryside. By my guess we were somewhere in Oklahoma or Texas, heading for the Mexican border.

Christina was up and joined me. Groans and moans from the two other girls.

"Do you know where we are, Mr. R.?" she asked.

"South," I said, peeking another look out the crack.

"How will we get off of here?"

"We need to get this door open. I was too tired last night to try. If we can pry this open, then we have the option to jump when the train comes into another town."

"Why do people do things like this?"

I shook my head at the fact that evil existed and had gone unchecked. "No simple reason, girl," I said.

"I mean, the detective is supposed to protect us, not do all these things," Christina said, looking at the two women still wrapped in their burlap bags, huddled together and shivering in the morning cold, half asleep. "They need a doctor I think." For some moments we both sat, staring outside, trying to collect ourselves for our next move. We were brought out of our trance by the train whistle then a jolt, like it was coming to a bend. I pulled at the door again with Christina's help. Nothing.

We were nearing some small water-hole town with some grain silos and dilapidated stores and homes. The whistle blew out another signal. I told Christina to watch the outside, and searched the car for some type of weapon. Strewn in one corner were remnants of earlier travelers, bottles, milk cartons, and, oddly, two chairs and scattered newspapers. Under some horse tacking was a walking stick, with names carved into it. Not much of a weapon, but the best I could find.

"We's stopping, Mr. R.," Christina said. One of the girls started weeping.

"Why don't you help her out, Christina," I said. "Let me take care of the door."

I guessed it was early Monday morning. Some clangs, and then the train came to a complete stop. Our car banged the car in front, and the car behind us gave us a nudge. I poked my eye up next to a crack then my ear. No human sounds. Then, "The load is in car eighteen."

Car eighteen? When we'd left the depot, there had been no more than six to eight cars making up the train. We must have slept through the change at the switching station somewhere north. If that was true, this was a bigger criminal enterprise than just Cromwell and his country-bumpkin boys.

98

Pretty Women

C romwell had been asleep for two hours when his cell phone gave its relentless ring. He had one cell issued by the department, tied to a tracer, and another burner phone he'd gotten so he and the sheriff could communicate. He grabbed the city issue. "Yeah," he said, as indignantly as he knew how. *What day was it, anyway?*

"Detective, sorry to bother you. This is Wellsley. We are trying to piece together Stephens-Christian's last hours and are wondering if you could make it down this morning to help us out."

Cromwell collected himself. *This young jackal was up to something. At his door this morning when he arrived back, now he wanted a sit-down.*

"Yeah, I'll be down later." He didn't wait to get a response from the other cop, just closed the cell and rolled back over. The killing had made him numb to the niceties of daily conversation. He had little empathy and had no reason to be anything other than what he was. A burned-out cop who hated women and life. He threw his pillow at the wall and got up.

"Fucking idiot cop. Stephens-Christian should have minded his own business. And that young wife. I can deal with her the same way I've dealt with the other snatches."

He dressed in jeans, the same scuffed loafers, and a sport shirt, a size too small. He'd been on duty all weekend, not to mention the action at the depot and at Leon's house. He threw on a blue rain jacket to cover his gut and holstered up his Smith and Wesson.

He stopped by a Shop and Go on the way downtown. He somehow had to act sad over the death of his young partner. For a brief moment he got paranoid he was driving into a setup at work and that someone had made him. But if that had happened, surely Wellsley would have been all too happy to lead a posse to his place and cuff him in his own home.

At the precinct, Cromwell parked in the space reserved for detectives and went in. All was quiet. He keyed in his code and walked up the two flights of stairs to his office, panting. He went over his alibi. Hadn't seen Stephens-Christian since early in the evening of...was it yesterday or Saturday night, when the kid said he was going home? *Was that right? So much had happened since then. No big deal. Less said the better.* His office was empty. Hanging on Stephens-Christian's chair was a wreath. Some sentimental woman officer probably had hung it there.

"Glad you could make it, Sergeant," Wellsley said, entering from the door that led from the commander's office. The younger cop walked over. In his hand he carried a cellophane bag. He plopped the bag down in front of Cromwell.

Cromwell crushed out his cigarette and opened up the bag.

"Same brand as yours, isn't it? Evidence bag from the crime scene."

Dumb move. Cromwell picked out the butt. "Let me see," he said, picking up the butt. He looked up at Wellsley, who knew instantly what the cop had done.

"My brand. Bad for your health, you know," he said.

"Besides I think I did smoke at Stephens-Christian's when I swung by to talk to the wife." *He lied.*

Wellsley grabbed the butt out of Cromwell's hand and stuck it back into the baggy. The young cop's face turned beet-red. "Just checking, Sarge," he said, trying his best to collect himself from the blunder. "This is all we found at Stephens-Christian's place, plus a nylon rope found in some weeds in the alley, apparently used to do the job. And there was an antique clock stolen, the wife said."

Cromwell did a quick rewind of his actions. He'd stuffed a nylon rope in the teacher's apartment, which, while not the murder weapon, would link the faggot teacher to Stephens-Christian's death. Now all that was needed was a warrant to search his place.

Both men were quiet for a moment. "Damn shame about the kid," Cromwell finally said, as caringly as he could, but knowing it sounded fake.

"Pretty women," Wellsley said staring at the pictures of the missing women. "Damn shame."

"What else do we have on the kid's murder?" Cromwell asked. "This it?"

Wellsley studied the bulletin board and the girls' pictures. He stared at the photo of Carrie Lindsey. *Was it the same girl in the porn magazine? Brunette, hair shorter than in the bondage picture, but same oval-shaped face.*

Cromwell piped up. "What are you looking at? Think glaring at them is going to find our missing snatches?"

Inside the younger cop's hip pocket was the magazine page from Cromwell's condo. He wanted to throw it out on Cromwell's desk and get the man's reaction. *But it was too early for that.*

"Damn shame we can't find those girls. They have to be somewhere."

Cromwell took a gulp of his coffee. "Damn shame," he said.

99

THAT WAS LAST YEAR

T he sun had come up by the time Kelvin called Leon to help him bury the bodies in makeshift graves. Like concentration-camp guards they dumped the bodies, wrapped in plastic, several hundred yards off the grave they had made for Kelvin's wife, off of County Road 225.

Kelvin played back in his mind the recent events. There had been two burial spots, the first at the depot, where they'd buried the first woman's clothes, the one with the dog. What was done with her body? The killing of the woman with the dog had been all Cromwell's doing. That had been last year. The second burial was here, where they'd put Deidre.

As Kelvin let Leon throw the last clumps of dirt on the two boys, he wondered about the dog from last year's kidnapping. His wife's cousin had a similar-looking dog. He hadn't put two and two together until he'd seen the dog in the teacher's Jeep. The dog had been hanging around the neighborhood for some reason.

. . .

HE AND LEON HAD FOLLOWED THE WOMAN WITH THE DOG LAST YEAR, just as Cromwell and the sheriff had directed them to. They had engineered an accident in a parking lot, with the cops doing backup. The woman had her car towed and Cromwell had escorted the woman to her condo, where he'd knocked her out, then, he'd said, transported her to the depot, miles away. Cromwell had taken the dog too, for some reason.

But the woman awoke before she was supposed to, and instead of being cooperative she had become enraged and began screaming and kicking in the backseat. Cromwell said he hit her with the butt of his gun, which was just supposed to knock her out, but had done her in instead. Cromwell said he took care of her. He didn't say what he did with the body, only that the dog took off.

Anyway, that was last year. And the sheriff and Cromwell had said not to worry, because the woman had no family to speak of, except for a dead aunt and an estranged uncle. That taking had prompted the law boys to get the wetbacks to do it.

Leon spit again on the makeshift graves. *Idiot,* Kelvin thought.

Messy business. He checked his pocket for the cash he had made this go-round. With his wife gone, he had the house, and no one was the wiser, unless it was that cousin of hers. The cousin? Somewhere the man would turn up. Dare he tell the sheriff and Cromwell about their bungling that job?

If the teacher man was smart, he'd taken off. But the blade on the track? Coincidence. There are many carpet cutters lying around. But how did it get there? Cromwell had picked it up. Which meant what? Would Leon spill his guts that the teacher had gotten away? The retard hadn't said anything so far. If Cromwell had connected the dots, Leon would admit to the fact the teacher got away. And who could know what Cromwell would do.

What to do? Cromwell had gone back to the city and the sheriff had returned to his office to alert the city that there was no longer a threat from hazardous waste from the transport train. What a sham. The sun was up. And the train was somewhere down the track, in another state by now.

If he let the whole matter take care of itself, who would know the difference. Leon chattered on as Kelvin picked up the shovel and patted down the earth where the boys lay.

MISSION FOILED

J uanita Morales, her son, Jesus, and John Wee sat nearly catatonic in the bushes for what seemed like hours after the shootings at the depot. Ms. Morales knew if she and the boys were blessed and allowed to live, she would need to tell the authorities. After the bad men vacated the scene, Jesus let the car roll back down the hillside, lights off. The whole mission to find Christina had been foiled.

ACROSS THE FIELD, VOICES

T he voice outside neared. The girls huddled together. Christina was trying to do her part to quiet the whimperings of the other two, as another voice farther away from the nearest boxcar called out. A key-like click unhitched the boxcar door from the outside. I meshed myself against the inside wall, walking stick poised to clobber.

"Your radio is buzzing back here, Buford," a voice from down the track called out. Wasn't the guy at the depot in Chapwell Falls called Jed? Now a Buford.

Buford. What was it with these names? Kelvin, Leon, Jed, Buford. Straight out of *Deliverance*. I listened to Buford shuffle back toward the front of the train.

Saved for the moment. "Christina, help me."

She jumped up, and with two heaves we were able to slide the door halfway open. The other girls had quieted. I peeked out at the morning and saw two cattle yards, and ramps leading up to a loading platform in the direction where Buford had disappeared. Back down the track was prairie and desolation. In front of me were half a dozen huts some one hundred yards away; beyond, sagebrush and a dirt road, which seemed to lead to a town.

Within seconds, we were all outside. The earth was cold. I looked beyond the cars toward the engine for signs of our captors. We were easy targets if we made a run for it in the field. We tucked ourselves under the car. The girls followed me, rolling over to the other side and a new view. Christina brought up the rear.

I pointed toward what I hoped was an abandoned silo fifty yards from the track. "Run!" I ordered. It would be no time before Buford and his boys deduced that the girls had escaped. I hoped I was still an unknown quantity. Christina pushed the bedraggled girls ahead of her. I raced toward the silo, stopped, and waited for the three to catch up. Tara Simon fell. I ran back. I scouted a look at the train. So far, so good.

"Come on, girl. This will be easier," I said to Tara Simon, picking her up piggyback. She was a featherweight and ice cold.

Christina kept herself yoked to Carrie Lindsey as the girl fell then picked herself up, hoisted by Christina. Carrie fell again. At the silo entrance I dropped Tara and went back and picked up Carrie. Christina ran ahead and opened the door. Once inside, I shut the door with one last look to make certain we hadn't been discovered.

The silo had small slats, just wide enough to let in light for a check of the surroundings. I knew that it would only be minutes until Buford got wise and would decide to cross under the train to our side. And it wouldn't be too hard to figure out where the only hiding place was.

Across the field, voices yelled. Buford and his boys had discovered the open boxcar door. There were three of them, the best I could tell. I had left the walking stick behind. The silo was barren, except for a shovel, lying atop some cornstalks. A narrow ladder ran upward, then a catwalk, then the ladder continued upward, another catwalk, and the roof. Up was our only option.

102

Burned into Her Memory

After escaping sure death from two fiends who'd kidnapped her at the shopping mall, she had dragged herself to the road, broken leg and cuts—and had luckily been picked up by a family on their way home from a late-night revival meeting. They had driven her to the hospital, where doctors had examined her for assault, and a woman police officer had gotten a description of her kidnappers.

An artist had drawn likenesses of her attackers. The lady cop told her an all-points bulletin had been issued with descriptions of the two attackers. Renderings were being sent to all area and regional agencies.

SHE HOBBLED TO THE WINDOW OF HER APARTMENT AND PULLED OPEN THE drapes, the first time since she had been sent home from the hospital. She was bruised for life by the ordeal. Had she not had the strength to climb out the window of the shack that night and jumped off the cliff, she'd surely have been killed. Their faces and smell were burned into her memory.

103

He'd Catch Them Off Guard

T he sheriff answered his burner phone, knowing the call back was from Cromwell. He'd gone through a dozen or more burner phones since this taking business had started. He and Cromwell had taken precaution to buy each phone from a different venue, always mindful not to disclose their true identity.

The sheriff told the man about the fax he'd just gotten from Cromwell's station house. Sent by a Detective Wellsley. "They got an artist drawing of my two boys here. Stupid fucks. I told them not to do anything without my okay. But they took a woman last week on their own."

Cromwell told his old friend "the two nitwits" needed to be done away with. "Take care of it and I will help you clean up the mess. I'll drive up and be there within two hours. You know what to do."

The sheriff gave Cromwell directions to Leon's house, where he said the two would be. "I'll see you there, then. But don't make any calls to me until I look it over," Cromwell said, realizing that the two boobs were not the only extra baggage he had to contend with.

The sheriff studied the drawings of Leon and Kelvin. He'd taken the fax before the department secretary had time to look at the pictures. And he'd taken precautions to send his young deputy on a wild-goose chase out of town.

Everyone in Chapwell Falls knew one another. And while the renderings were crude, the drawings did depict Kelvin and Leon. And someone would have surely IDed them; especially since there had been rumblings from the school that something sinister had likely happened to Kelvin's wife.

There was more of a likeness to Kelvin than Leon. But then, Leon could pass for any hillbilly with a gut. He unlocked the bottom drawer of his desk and pulled out two plastic evidence bags. Carefully he lifted out one pistol, a nine millimeter, with the eraser end of a pencil, examined it, and placed it back in the sack. He did the same thing with the other bag and weapon. He lit a smoke and stared at the bags.

He stuffed the evidence bags in his brown jacket, checked his gun clip, and stepped outside. It was early morning. By now the two nitwits had buried the kids from the depot and gone to Leon's place to unwind with a beer. He'd catch them off guard. As long as Leon's nephew or sister weren't there, all would go well.

The sheriff drove the Crown Victoria out of the small city lot. It was still too early for the paperboy who delivered the big city edition. He parked several houses down from Leon's, got out, and undid his holster.

He could hear country music playing inside Leon's house. He walked around to the back of the house and up the steps. No need for words. He carried plastic bags, with two nine millimeters zipped inside.

"I see you got your fridge stocked with brewskies. You want another one, fat shit?" Kelvin called from the refrigerator.

"Yeah," Leon said from the living room.

The back door opened. Kelvin turned at the sound. For a second he smiled at the figure, but then flinched at the sight of the gun. Instantly he knew the sheriff wasn't there for a social call. He heaved the bottle at him. The sheriff quickly unloaded a shot to the skull. Kelvin fell back against the refrigerator. For a moment the sheriff stood over him, but quickly turned his attention to Leon.

From the living room, Leon yelled out his friend's name. The sheriff moved quickly, aiming square center above the brow. Within seconds Leon was sprawled on the sofa. Eyes open. The music still blared. The sheriff didn't know if the music was loud enough to cover the shots. But then again, he was there on official business.

He flicked off the power to the CD player and took a look out the front window. No curious onlookers. From his jacket he pulled out one of the bags, removed the gun, and placed it in Leon's hand, index finger on the trigger. He fired a shot in the direction of the kitchen and let the gun drop to the floor by Leon's now-lifeless body. *He should have done that before turning the music off. No mind.*

He stepped back to the kitchen. He removed the other weapon from the evidence bag and fitted it into Kelvin's hand. He then discharged it into the wall toward the back door. His story would be that he had showed up to ask the two derelicts where they were the night of the kidnapping. Both men fired at him. He returned fire, instantly killing both men. All nice and tidy for now.

104

FAKE BEARD

Cromwell drove to Chapwell Falls and parked the Jeep he'd "borrowed" from the impound lot between two service trucks of the water softener company. He put on the fake white beard purchased at Lil's Fun Shop and let the adhesive settle into his pores then pulled the baseball cap over his bald pate. He took out a pair of size twelve-D sneakers from the box, stuffed Kleenex in the toes, and slid his feet into them.

He moved quickly through the small parking lot, across the street, and into the connector alley that split this neighborhood in two. The sheriff said Leon had a large wood engraving that read "Party Down" over the back porch, which could be read from the alley. The sheriff would be there waiting. There were no other cops in town, other than a young deputy, whom he hoped the sheriff had sent on some errand.

He started to grab for a smoke, but stopped, remembering his previous mistake. Slowly he walked, keeping to one side of the alley. He peeked over one fence. Not Leon's. He walked on. The neighborhood was quiet. Several more houses. A dog barked. He peeked over the fence. The sign! Leon's. Had the sheriff left the back gate open liked he'd asked? He slid up the latch and walked into the small backyard.

There was a light on in the back of the house. No shades pulled. If the sheriff had done the job already, he should have pulled the drapes. He slowly pulled off the beard and stuffed it in his windbreaker pocket. He checked his weapon. He stepped up to the porch and listened. There was some commotion in the room. He fitted on the latex gloves and undid the safety on his weapon. He stepped into a pantry.

The sheriff was just standing in the middle of the kitchen in an apparent daze, looking down at what appeared to be a dead Kelvin. Cromwell walked in and softly said, "Bobby."

The sheriff turned around. He gasped out a sigh at seeing his friend. He looked at Cromwell and said, "I didn't think I'd have a conniption over this thing. But I did."

Cromwell said, "Where's the other fool?"

The sheriff pointed to the living room. "Take a good look at the guy again and make sure that it all makes sense," Cromwell said. "You will have to play back what happened to someone, I'm sure." The sheriff obeyed his longtime friend's order and retraced his steps back to the living room.

Cromwell quickly assessed the kitchen situation. Kelvin lay dead on the floor, on his back, feet facing the back porch, eyes wide open in horror. The sheriff returned from the living room. "All good. Looks just like Leon shot at me and I returned fire. Bullet can be found lodged in the living room wall."

"Good," Cromwell said. "I heard something outside. Make sure no one is out there."

"Hope it's not Leon's sister and her kid. Don't know what happened to that kid." The sheriff headed out the back door and listened to the early-morning sounds. Incessant barking of a dog. He walked to the fence and peered over. Nothing. He opened the latch to the front gate and walked to the driveway to look around. Nothing. Across the street in the garage of the house for sale, more barks. He crossed the street. He approached the garage, unclipping the safety on his gun. More barking in the garage. Inside a parked Jeep, frantic to get out, a dog pelted out more barks. He'd seen the vehicle before. He'd run a check on it later. He undid the car door. A young golden retriever barreled out and ran, first toward Leon's, then it stopped, sniffed, and took off toward the town center.

He watched the ordeal, breathed a deep sigh, and then walked toward Leon's.

Inside, he said, "Nothing out there, Cromy. We are..." Then something troubled him. Cromwell had moved Kelvin's body 180 degrees so his feet pointed toward the living room. Cromwell motioned the sheriff around the body toward the living room.

"Just trying to lay this thing out so there won't be any questions. Help me, buddy. Stand back about six feet."

The sheriff puzzled, but again obeyed, moving his girth toward Kelvin's feet. "Good," Cromwell said. Then Cromwell raised the cocked gun in Kelvin's hand, slightly pointing it in the sheriff's direction. The sheriff reacted by pulling out his weapon.

"Step back. Now forward," Cromwell said. Again the sheriff followed orders. As he stepped toward Cromwell and Kelvin's body, he felt a sharpness, followed quickly by blackness.

105

Body Resting Positions

T he sheriff fell to his knees, face smashing into the wood floor a foot away from Kelvin's boots. His weapon dislodged from his grip and bounced a few inches from his right hand. Cromwell stayed motionless for a moment, letting gurgles seep out of the sheriff. He let the last breath leave the sheriff then checked for a pulse. Made more sense for Kelvin to shoot toward the body cavity than the head.

He examined the scene and recapped how he hoped it would appear to anyone investigating. In this hillbilly county, he doubted whether forensics would be applied with any level of sophistication. The bodies' resting positions would speak to what happened.

Whoever did the follow-up would conclude the sheriff entered the house from the front, probably not knocking, to follow up on an APB for two men who looked like the artist's sketches. The sheriff surprised the derelicts; shots were fired, resulting in three dead bodies. Nice and tight. Possibly too tight, but by the time anyone wanted to make sense of it, he'd be long gone.

Leon would have stood up and shot at the sheriff when he entered the house. The bullet missing the sheriff lodged in the doorway leading into the kitchen. The sheriff returned fire, killing Leon with a square shot to head. Kelvin turned from the refrigerator to assess the commotion.

When the sheriff entered the kitchen, Kelvin shot the sheriff in the chest area, which prompted the sheriff to kill him, again with a shot to the head.

There were inconsistencies, but they might not be noticed for days. Should he have left the figures lying as the sheriff had situated them? No mind now. A forensics team would have to be called in from another county. That would allow him time for the planned getaway. He surveyed the scene one last time. The sheriff's cell phone and burner phone? He rummaged through the dead man's pocket. There! He checked the surroundings for the cells of the two hillbillies. Once he had collected all the cells, he dropped them into a grocery bag he found in the kitchen.

He left as he had entered, through the back door. He put on his disguise. As he took the alley back to his car, he had to stop himself from lighting up a smoke. He needed to dump the gloves somewhere. The Salvation Army bin at the mall was as good a place as any.

It was dawn. Again he was amused; the sheriff had done a good job of keeping this little town in fear. *Bio waste transport. Keep doors shut at all announced times!* Cops could tell the public anything and they'd believe it.

He had carefully planned his getaway, even down to taking early retirement and the pension, which right now was being deposited in an offshore account in his dead mother's name. All the cash he made from the takings, he'd kept and would use that money for the trip, first to Canada, then, who knows where?

Back at the Jeep, he put the sheriff's cell phones, the burner, and a standard issue he had under one of the front tires, and his own burner cell under the other. Some connection could be made with GPS. But then again, he'd be gone. He got in and slowly drove the car over the phones several times, listening to the crunches. As he headed out, he lit up a long-overdue smoke. He'd ditch his own phone. There could be no digital trace of his whereabouts.

106

REPORT A MURDER

Juanita Morales, John Wee, and Jesus had driven home in silence. Her daughter had been abducted and her nephew had been killed in front of her. It was time to go to the police. She rousted her son, Jesus, who'd fallen asleep despite all that had gone on. She waited while he dressed.

She would have to speak English to the authorities. It was the right thing to do. Tell all. Even though her boy had come into the country illegally, he was a good boy. So was his cousin. Neither deserved to be treated the way they had, especially her nephew.

"Can I help you?" the lady police officer asked. John Wee stood slightly behind Juanita and Jesus.

When Juanita said slowly, "I want to report a murder," the woman held up her hand, signaling Juanita to stop. Several minutes passed, and when a young, clean-cut officer arrived by the name of Wellsley, Juanita and Jesus were escorted to a nearby room. There they sat and were offered coffee.

Juanita began to recount to the police officer the story from the night before. She wished there had been an interpreter for her to tell her story to. She nodded for John Wee to share his camera video with the officer. Afterward, she heard the officer tell another policeman to call the Feds about the train. "And get some bearing on all trains bound west and south. We'll need to get some air support from somewhere."

Wellsley dialed up Cromwell's cell number. Miles away, a Samsung reverberated. Cromwell looked down at the number. He recognized it as a city-issue number given to all detectives. He let the phone ring several more times. While the screen didn't identify the name of the calling party, he figured it was likely the new kid, Wellsley. He sped up toward the interstate and north. He threw the phone out into a field.

107

GET UP THE LADDER

I let each girl catch her breath. All three, exhausted, fell onto the cornstalks. I cracked open the door, enough to check the action outside. Coming toward us was the man called Buford, I guessed. He had a snub-nosed pistol and seemed to know what to do with it. "Christina, get the girls up the ladder!" I ordered.

Christina began pulling up the other two women. As she did, a black snake slithered out from the underbrush. Christina screamed first then the other two. The snake disappeared into the pile of stalks.

"Fuck!" I said.

Buford stopped at the screams then yelled out, "Over here!" to his partners.

"Get up the ladder!" I shouted. "Now!"

Christina first pulled up Tara, the smaller of the two. Carrie followed close behind. Buford slowed his gait, waiting. If the girls got up the ladder to the catwalks they'd be safe for a moment. But the ladders weren't pull-ups, so after Buford disposed of me, he'd have no trouble getting the girls. But then again, I was hoping Buford and the boys didn't know about me yet. I needed a miracle.

108

Oh, Girlies

The shovel lay in the cornstalks, new and little-used. Perfect. All the girls were now up the ladder and were secure for the moment. I heard Buford nearing. I grabbed the shovel, stepped back from the silo door, and waited. My hope was the others hadn't caught up to him, which would give me enough time to whack him, take his gun, and then do what?

"The bitches are in here. Hurry, you two! We ain't got time to fuck around! We got a schedule to keep!"

"Hold on, boss, we're coming!"

I guessed the other two were at least several hundred feet away. My heart raced. The girls were curled together on the first catwalk. Buford slowly cracked opened the door.

"Oh, girlies. You is holding up the train. And you know it's not good to keep the engineer waiting." He laughed sadistically.

I took a deep breath. The man stepped into the darkness of the silo. The door closed partway behind him. "Oh, girlies."

I swung the shovel square across his face, which knocked him against the door, slamming it shut. For a moment he stood, dazed, then blood trickled out his nose. I swung again. He fell forward. His head hit the floor, splitting open like a watermelon. Blood trickled out of his mouth. I took the small weapon out of his hand and backed against the silo wall.

I was no weapons expert, but guessed the gun had no more than six shots. I couldn't see whether the safety was on or off. Outside I heard Buford's two partners. Somewhere, in the distance, but nearing, was a *whooshda, whooshda* sound.

The *whooshda, whooshda* neared. "The Feds!" one of Buford's men called out. There was silence for a moment as the sound neared, then, "Let's get the fuck out of here! Buford! It's a military chopper! Let's go!"

I cracked open the door. The *whooshda, whooshda* intensified as the military craft approached and slowly set down like a big dragonfly. Seconds later, several helmeted soldiers, each carrying an automatic weapon, filed out of the craft. The lead soldier pointed to the train engine then signaled three of his men toward the caboose.

"What is it, Mr. R.?" Christina asked.

One of the other girls moaned out, "Are they coming?"

"I don't know. I'm going to check it out. You guys stay put."

Slowly I walked out toward the copter and waved at the soldier in charge, forgetting that I had Buford's gun in my hand.

A lead soldier yelled out, "Drop the weapon!" I did. "On the ground!" I kneeled down. The commander type ran up and kicked Buford's pistol away. "Where are the women, you scum bucket?"

I tried to point back toward the silo. Then Christina called out from the door,

"No! Mr. R. is with us!"

"Cuff this piece of shit," the commander ordered one of his men, who ran up huffing, automatic weapon ready for action. The commander ran toward Christina; two other soldiers followed. Within seconds, Buford was dragged out, groaning, followed by Tara and Carrie. Each woman had her arms draped over a rescuer.

Christina ran over to me to ward off the commander, who had returned to my side, ready to begin his interrogation of me. She knelt down. "He is my teacher. He saved us!" she said.

I rolled over and looked at the rest of the scene unfolding. Two soldiers were walking the other girls toward the copter. The *whooshda, whooshda* of the blades had slowed.

The commander brought Buford over and began questioning us as if we were partners in this whole thing, but Christina quickly broke in. In reasonably well-spoken English, between sniffles, she told the commander about my deeds. But that didn't persuade him to uncuff me.

All three girls were escorted to the copter. Buford and I were taken aboard also, and cuffed to a hitch in the back of the craft. As the helicopter lifted, three state trooper vehicles arrived on the scene. The cuts I'd gotten escaping from Leon and Kelvin had been reopened. The least of my worries.

109

Beautiful Fort Sill

E xhaustion took hold of me and I drifted off to the sound of
copter blades. Minutes later, possibly longer, I was awoken by
a shake. The commander was peering down at me. He'd
removed his helmet. "Okay, partner, we're down and back at base. The
little miss up front," he said, motioning toward the cockpit, "claims you
are as much a victim in this whole thing as she and the others. That
right?"

I just nodded, knowing that when being interrogated by the police
or any authority, the less a suspect said, the better.

"Okay, let's go," he said. As I was escorted to the front of the
aircraft, I looked for Buford and the girls but saw no trace of them.

I turned. "Where are we?"

"Beautiful Fort Sill, for as far as the eye can see. Right smack in the
middle of Tornado Alley."

I stepped down onto the ground and took a quick look toward the
western sky. The commander hopped down behind me and pointed
toward a Jeep. He jumped in front of me. I followed.

Feet away, he said, "Take our man here to the MPs, Corporal Lopez.
He also needs a run over to Reynolds." I got in the vehicle and gave a

short smile to the soldier, who just looked at me dryly. With a salute to the commander, Lopez crunched the gears and sped off. I let the wind wake me up.

At a brick wall, which had "U.S. Army Field Artillery School" inscribed on it, we were waved through by a sentry. Lopez took a hard right and pulled up to a building. The sign on the front read "Temporary Headquarters, Investigations—Fort Sill Military Police." He left the Jeep running. "This is your stop," he said. "When you're done, tell the duty officer you need to go to Reynolds, the hospital. Just go in," he nodded toward the small front door. "They're expecting you."

I breathed deep and walked inside to a small lobby and the stares of two suits. They introduced themselves as being from the Oklahoma City FBI office. A soldier with captain's bars joined the three of us. "Mr. Riordan," the captain said, "this way."

I smelled of sweat and likely manure from what had been a day, more or less, in the boxcar. At a room labeled "Interrogation," one of the FBI men directed me inside and toward a small table and chair.

"Have a seat." I did.

The captain, like the commander at the helicopter, looked like an image from a recruiting ad—rugged-warrior good looks. He leaned against the wall behind me.

"So now, Mr. Riordan," the lead Fed said, taking a seat. "Tell us how you wound up on a train with three young women, headed toward the Mexican border."

I told the story the best I could, starting with how I knew Christina and how I came to Chapwell Falls, which related to my missing cousin, Deidre. With each turn of my story the G-man narrowed his eyes with disbelief.

"Now, Riordan...Mr. Riordan," he said, taking off his spectacles, rubbing his nose, then putting them back on again. "You expect us to believe you hopped on a speeding train and then climbed down into a boxcar to save the day for these unsuspecting young women?"

"Come on, sport, we aren't stupid, " the captain said from several feet behind me.

I was tired and wasn't up to being humiliated. But somewhere from inside me, I mustered up calmness. I remembered Sensei's antidote for fear: don't react with an angry tone.

"First of all, the train wasn't speeding," I said. "It had slowed down coming into Chapwell Falls."

They waited for more.

Just as I began to continue, a soldier came in and put a note down in front of the fed and whispered in his ear. He read the note, frowning as he did so, then handed it to the captain. The cop read it, also frowned, and said, "Well, Mr. Riordan, while your story seems fishy at best, you got corroboration from your young friend and the other women, as well as from the police back home. It looks like you are free to go."

I was directed to the front of the building where I'd entered and told to wait there. I sat. A stern-looking corporal sat behind a computer monitor, typing. She didn't bother to make eye contact until she finished what she was doing. Then she got up and walked over to me. She stopped, broke a half smile, and handed me the slip. "Your bus ticket. We will transport you to the station. Questions?"

"That was quick. Too late to ask for a plane ride back home?" I said, not expecting anything other than a brush-off.

She smiled, almost warmly this time. "I'll get you a ride to the depot," she said. "Oh, you'll need to be cleared by the base doctor first. Orders."

Within minutes, a Jeep took me out of the gated area and to the hospital. After a very brief exam by a female captain, I was given a medical clearance to leave the base. I was given a duffel bag with Walmart-issue pants, shirt, shoes, and undergarments, and was pointed to a place to shower, shave, and generally clean up. Once done, I was taken to the town bus depot.

110

Was the Ordeal Over?

The Lawton bus station was a remodeled building just off the town's central mall. I got a cup of coffee and a donut with traveling dollars courtesy of Uncle Sam. My ticket had a transfer at Springfield then home. I nearly dozed off on the wooden bench. Was the ordeal over?

I had been exonerated of wrongdoing, according to my recent interrogators. What one had said was, "The girls corroborated my story. And the police back home had also." I was certain the police back home did not include Cromwell.

Christina could pin him for the kidnappings, assaults, and who knew what else, as could the other two girls, I guessed. Buford, who was captured at the silo, would surely cry like a baby about who was running the trafficking side of things. Probably Cromwell, or maybe the sheriff.

What about Deidre and Penny? Was Deidre dead? According to Professor Sarah Augustine, my Trail friend, Penny, was. She thought it was a good possibility that Penny's spirit had cajoled me to get involved in this whole thing.

The blue dress! Was it still in my closet? If the cops found that, I would have some explaining to do. And Laddie. I'd left him at Leon's. Had someone picked him up? And Pig?

The PA system announced my ride. I'd have a several-hours trip to Springfield then home—and whatever awaited me there.

111

One of Their Own

C hristina, Tara Ann Simon, and Carrie Lindsey had been flown home by military transport after preliminary physicals at the Lawton base proved they had not been assaulted. The two older women suffered from exhaustion, and presented PTSD symptoms from captivity. Christina was in the best condition and related what had transpired in her kidnapping at the hands of Cromwell, whom the FBI had put out an APB on.

When the military transport landed at the airfield, south of town, swarms of reporters, broadcast and print, charged the plane. Missing was reporter Cynthia Crystal.

The women were shuffled off to town via a police motorcade, followed by the troop of media vehicles. The five p.m. news, local and national, aired broadcasts from the city law enforcement center claiming a human-trafficking ring had been cracked.

Wellsley and his partner, Cheney, had arranged for Christina's mother to pick her up through a personnel exit, and found housing for the other two girls, who had no one locally. Once that was arranged, both men went to brief the chief of police on what they knew about one of their own, who was nowhere to be found.

112

What Can You Help Us with?

I made the trip from Lawton to Springfield in one piece. While waiting for my transfer home, I watched the whole news story on TV. My name, so far, had been left out of it. I called Sensei, the old-fashioned way, pay phone, collect, just as my bus departure was announced. He answered with a concerned, "Hello, so glad you call, Pat. Much talk about the story you talk about. Where are you?" I filled him in.

"So glad you safe. When news say 'teacher,' I know it you. I know you not involved in this." I asked Sensei to call my aunt Alice and let her know I'd call later. Just as I was about to hang up, Sensei said, "Dog here. Came last night scratching on front door of your apartment building. Your neighbor girl coming in there, drop him by here. He ask where you are. Ha ha."

Sensei said he would keep Laddie until my return. Right now, I didn't want to explore any notions about how Laddie found his way to Sensei's from where I'd left him in Chapwell Falls.

The ride home would put me in town in the early a.m. hours. I tucked myself into a backseat and set my Army-issue duffel next to me, hoping no one would join me on the four-hour ride up Forty-Four. I fell asleep to the hum of the bus tires on the road.

I WAS AWAKENED BY THE DRIVER ANNOUNCING I WAS HOME. I TOOK A DEEP breath, gathered my duffel bag, and dropped down to the pavement and into a slight mist. Momentarily, I had images of reporters gathering, calling out my name, asking me to impart the real story. But the parking lot was empty, except for a lone taxi.

Now what? I was a good five miles from my apartment. It was two a.m. I was about to hail the cab when a sedan pulled up in front of me, flashing its lights. A plainclothes cop got out, leaving the car running. The cabby drove off.

"Mr. Riordan?" I nodded. "Detective Wellsley. Can I give you a lift?"

We shook hands. Immediately I sensed that he was cut from a different cloth than Cromwell. Mid-forties, he had a trace of gray in a full head of hair, neatly cut just over his ears. He was dressed more like a professor, sport coat and turtleneck, than a cop. I got into the sedan and he explained how he came to know my whereabouts.

"We have a lot of unanswered questions about this whole ordeal, Mr. Riordan. The young women are safe and have asked about you. Seems you are their dragon slayer."

Wellsley steered the police issue slowly as the mist turned to rain. He told me about the apparent ambush of the Chapwell Falls county sheriff by two ne'er-do-well types, and that all three were found dead in a house in town.

"According to the young ladies, those three, as well as Cromwell, were all in on this thing. Did I mention that Cromwell's partner, Stephens-Christian, was murdered prior to the killings in Chapwell Falls? We have completely ruled out his involvement in the crime. In fact, Stephens-Christian's notes are one of the few things I trust to shed some light on this whole thing."

Wellsley turned on the wipers to intermittent speed.

"His notes mentioned Penny or Margaret Theriault, the woman you somehow became acquainted with."

He waited for me to respond. I didn't.

~

AT MY ABODE, THE ALLEGRO APARTMENTS, HE PULLED OVER. "WE searched your place and found this." He handed me two plastic evidence bags. In one was the blue sundress. In the other was a nylon rope. "Do you know who these belong to?"

"I'm not sure I do. Look, Detective, I'm not going anywhere. In fact, I don't even have a key to my place." I inadvertently checked my pocket for my keys and felt the lighter I'd picked up on the train caboose. I'd put it there when I changed my clothes to my army issue. "Can this wait until tomorrow?"

Wellsley dug down in his pocket. "I forgot to return this to that old lady. Couldn't find the manager. Had a hell of a time getting her to hand over your key, even with my badge and all. Tell her I'm sorry. She certainly loves your ass. Must be a relative of yours."

"I just bring her paper up so she doesn't have to get out."

"Get some sleep, Mr. Riordan." He looked at his watch. "Two thirty in the a.m. Sometime this afternoon, drop by and see me."

113

D.A.S.

I turned my key and immediately heard meows from my room-mate. Pig serpentined around my legs.

"Boy, I forgot all about you." I picked him up and felt for lumps. He was surviving feline leukemia. No lumps. I checked his dish and found it full of dry morsels.

Left beside the bowl was a note: "I fed him to keep him quiet. Ms. S. let me in. Your mail is by your recliner. M." The "M" stood for Mara, my gothic-garb grad student neighbor, whom I had been at odds with over the three years I had been at the Allegro.

She had played her music into the a.m. hours. I hadn't complained, except for the first week she'd moved in, which was enough to get on her bad side. She'd let me know on more than one occasion that she thought I was an old man trying to relive my college days by living on campus. This day, I was glad to have her on my side.

I sat in my La-Z-Boy and pulled back the recliner. How many days had I been away? Three? Seemed like a century. Pig finished the dry morsels and hopped up for some cuddling. We both fell asleep to the hum of the AC.

My landline awakened me. Six fifteen. Where was my cell, my jeep? Chapwell Falls.

"Mr. Riordan?"

"Yes."

"Wellsley here."

I waited.

"After I dropped you off, I was informed that a body had been found in the Chapwell Falls area. Your cousin Deidre was reported missing from there, right?"

"Uh...that's right." A sick feeling churned in my stomach.

"I'm sorry to tell you, but it may well be her. Would you be willing to come to the morgue to take a look?"

"When?" I said.

"As soon as you can. Say twenty minutes. The morgue is on Calmer Street, just off Broadwell. I'll come by and get you."

I had fallen asleep in the recliner, too tired for a shower and change of clothes. Pig meowed for some more morsels. I fed him and hopped in the shower. Images of Deidre ran over me.

Wellsley was waiting for me outside the Allegro. I scooted into the sedan. "Have you been to the morgue?" he asked, with a solemn look.

"Not in this city. I did visit one out West when I was working investigations for the court. But I've never had to ID anyone."

Wellsley described how hikers had come to find the body. "Pretty eaten up by the coyotes. Damn shame. Been dead at least several weeks. M.E. said apparent cause of death was blunt force to the skull. Does your cousin have any identifying marks?"

I remembered three moles Deidre had on her lower abdomen. Her sister, Maureen, used to tease her about her "triangle" when we kids went swimming.

At the morgue, we parked. I took a deep breath and got out. A morgue tech in a white lab coat greeted us at the door. He knew why we were there. As he led us down the hallway, the smell of formaldehyde permeated the air. My chest tightened. The tech looked to Wellsley for the next move. "Masks?" the tech asked us.

"No," Wellsley said. I declined also.

Wellsley stopped me before the kid pushed open a door. "Our usual procedure for this type of thing is to have a viewing from outside the room. But we can go inside if you're sure you are okay with that."

"I'll be okay."

I followed Wellsley in. The room was cold, quiet, and eerie. The florescent fixtures hummed. Standing next to a covered figure on a gurney was the M.E., I guessed.

"Dr. Lee, this is Mr. Riordan," Wellsley said, introducing us. Dr. Lee nodded.

"You ready?" Wellsley asked. I nodded. Wellsley motioned for the M.E. to pull down the sheet draped over the body. The face had been chewed beyond any recognition, but mid-torso there were three moles in the shape of a triangle. I stepped back. My eyes welled up. I nodded.

Wellsley took a blouse with the monogram D.A.S. from another gurney and asked if I could ID it. "Deidre's married name was Deidre Ann Simpson," I said.

Wellsley said that dental records would be used to confirm the ID. He apologized to me for my loss then asked if I'd accompany him to his office for some follow-up.

114

AND DON'T LEAVE TOWN

A media van was parked in front of the law enforcement center when we arrived there. Inside, Wellsley swiped his security card at the entryway. I followed him to a familiar office. "Have a seat."

Wellsley took the photos of Carrie Lindsey and Tara Simon down from a board and placed them on an adjoining shelf. From under his desk, he pulled out the plastic evidence bags with the blue dress in one and the nylon rope in the other.

"I was going to grill you on how you came by the dress and the nylon rope we found in your apartment, but I reviewed Stephens-Christian's notes and saw an entry he made saying Cromwell had entered your place when you weren't there. No mention of him planting evidence, but I have to conclude he did. So no need to get into any more follow-up."

Wellsley gave me the look-over. "You OK with that?"

I said I was.

"But the big piece to this puzzle I can't quite figure out is your connection to this Penny woman, Margaret Theriault... She has been missing for a year. No body found. If we can somehow get a DNA sample from the dress and figure out how we can match it to her, then even though it was found in your place, we have to connect the dots to Cromwell. I'll not get into asking you what you know about the dress. But Stephens-Christian's notes say you had been in contact with this Penny woman recently, and were even at her aunt's condo. Doesn't make sense." He smiled and raised his brow, scooting Cynthia Crystal's recent news story in front of me. "For the record," he said.

No Miranda. Good.

He turned on a small microphone, then quickly shook his head, reckoning with the futility of it all. "Fuck, or not," he said, turning off the device. "Just educate me."

There was a lot I could explain. But nothing, according to Wellsley, that was pressing, other than his curiosity about Penny and whether she really had something to do with how everything unfolded. She had everything to do with why I found myself in this predicament, but that was between me and Penny.

I was about to elaborate, although briefly, when he continued. "And this Cynthia is missing, or at least no one at the paper has seen her."

"Wow!"

"But that's for another discussion, and not your concern."

I didn't tell him I'd talked to her.

"Well, hopefully she will turn up... But, just to clarify, Detective Wellsley, I wound up in Chapwell Falls looking for my cousin Deidre. And all that followed was related to my search for her." *Half-truth.*

"And again, I am sorry about her. And I know if you haven't called her mom, that will be tough.

"So as to Margaret Theriault, I wish I could explain how I wound up at her place. Stephens-Christian's notes indicated, did you say, that I just had contact with her, before Cromwell pinned her disappearance on me, even though she's supposedly been gone for a year. As I told Cromwell and Stephens-Christian, I first met her walking on the trail here in town. Later I saw her at the grocery store, and that final time, I gave her a ride to her aunt's after a car-bump altercation. After that I never saw her again. And this was all within weeks."

Wellsley shuffled his notes. "And as to the dog?"

I sighed. "Well, when I was at my cousin Deidre's house, the dog was there. He actually seemed frightened, so I took him with me. He had no collar. I checked around there. No one seemed to know who he belonged to. So..."

"And where is the dog now?"

I was about to relate what Sensei had told me about Laddie somehow finding his way back to my place, when there was a knock on the door.

A police corporal entered. "There is an all-hands-on-deck meeting, Detective. ASAP in the conference room," she said.

Wellsley nodded to the officer. He looked at me and half smiled. "So, the bottom line for you, Mr. Riordan, is that you have been exonerated of anything to do with the kidnappings. We have no body for Ms. Theriault. And whatever happened between you and her, well, that is something we can talk about later. Likely, Cromwell had something to do with Ms. Theriault, or Penny, as you call her, going missing. We can tie that up later. I'd give you a ride home, but..."

"Business calls."

"Right. I'll be in touch."

He opened the door. "But don't leave town."

115

Bring Your Questions

At home, I stretched out in my recliner. Pig hopped aboard. Sensei had Laddie. I needed to pick him up and piece together the rest of the puzzle. How did the dog get from Chapwell Falls to Sensei, an hour away?

My most pressing duty was to call Alice before the paper printed a story about Deidre. She likely had heard something, with all the news stories. Wellsley had said he'd leave the preliminaries about Deidre to me. I dialed up Alice, realizing she'd be awake.

After I related the news about Deidre, which Alice took first with a silence then with a cry and a half minute of muffled tears, she said, "Other than that other daughter, who never calls me, you are all I have left now. Are you okay?"

I said I was. Under different circumstances, I would have driven up to tell her the news. But I was too tired. We made an appointment for the weekend, when I was hoping matters would settle down.

I laid back in my recliner. Pig purred. The ceiling fan whirled. I picked up the mail that Mara had brought in. A schedule of summer school classes fell out and opened to the page of the Anthropology Department's courses.

I zeroed in on an instructor's name, Sarah Augustine, and the short description of her course. *"Ghosts and Spirits: Spirits and ghosts are commonplace across most cultures. The relationship between the living and the nonliving world varies. Bring your questions and experiences to the class. Dogs allowed."*

I felt a draft. I pulled up my tattered blanket and closed my eyes. Far off, a whisper. "Take care of Norris," a slight brush of my hair, then sleep.

EPILOGUE

He scooted up in the deck chair for a better view of the two women leaning against the ship's railing. Each woman threw out small breadcrumbs from a paper sack toward the seagulls. Both giggled as the gulls did a kind of hanging dance in the wind, waiting for toss-outs.

He took out his passport from an inside pocket. Raul Albert Nettermeyer. He chuckled about the acronym, RAN. That's what he did. And so far, so good. He sipped at his stein of lager then slid down in the deck chair.

The breeze felt good. He watched the women some more then pulled the fedora down over his bald pate and closed his eyes. In his finger he twirled an emerald ring. A new beginning. He smiled.

REVIEWS ARE ESPECIALLY IMPORTANT FOR AUTHORS BECAUSE THEY provide a point of reference for new readers. Please help by leaving a line or two of what you thought about the book on your favorite book retailer site.

I would most appreciate it.

Coming Soon by J. Michael McGee

Book Three of the Pat Riordan Series *The Cues*

Pat Riordan has settled into a teaching post at the college when his colleague, Joe, mysteriously dies in the hospital.

Left without an administrator to head up the school's new Investigative Cold Case Project, which Joe started, Riordan and another colleague, Phil Rister, are called upon to take up where Joe left off.

As the weeks unwind, Riordan and Rister, with the help of former homicide detective, Mike Finn, begin to see connections between Joe's death, a decades-old murder and eerie series of unsolved cases of missing women.

These connections called Cues, take the trio into the underbelly world of the college town and ultimately to some influential town players.

Eyewitnesses and confessions are non-existent, but clues, once understood, bring the evil out of hiding.

This is the third novel in the Pat Riordan series, but the second book with Riordan as a sleuth.

ALSO BY J. MICHAEL MCGEE
BRICKED

Book 1 of the Pat Riordan Series

Jobless and divorced, Pat Riordan takes a little-sought-after teaching job at the District's school for the hard-to-handle, Wolfcreek.

His sense of loss makes him a good fit for the boys of the school who call their banishment from the mainstream "bricked."

Doug Donovan, the school's principal, agrees with Riordan that gentle, but firm teaching strategies are the best way for their kids to learn. But ego-driven administrators, who want the school location for more promising students, feel otherwise and start a campaign to discredit the school staff and curriculum.

As the school year unwinds, Riordan finds his way into the personal life of one of his students, Bobby, and gets thrust into the role of rescuer when Bobby's mother is abused by her live-in boyfriend.

Bricked follows Riordan, the students, and staff, in what might be the school's final year.

ABOUT THE AUTHOR

Mike McGee is a licensed professional counselor and former teacher, newspaper reporter, and superior court investigator. He currently lives in Columbia, Missouri. *The Slip Swing* is his second novel.

~

For more information, visit me at
www.jmichaelmcgee.com

www.ingramcontent.com/pod-product-compliance
Lightning Source LLC
Chambersburg PA
CBHW031621100726
47898CB00006B/1892